The Sundial

by

Fred M. White

Double9 BOOKS

The Sundial
by Fred M. White

ISBN: 978-93-70810-12-9

Published by

DOUBLE 9 BOOKS
2/13-B, Ansari Road
Daryaganj, New Delhi – 110002
info@double9books.com
www.double9books.com
Tel. 011-40042856

ABOUT THE AUTHOR

Fred Merrick White, better known by his pen name Fred M. White, was born in 1859 in West Bromwich, United Kingdom, and died in 1935 in Barnstaple, United Kingdom. He was an English writer who became well-known for his novels and short stories, particularly in the genres of mystery, crime, and science fiction. White wrote prolifically during the late 19th and early 20th centuries, with one of his most notable contributions being the "Doom of London" series. This collection of six science-fiction stories imagines a series of catastrophic events that devastate London, a theme that resonated with the growing anxieties of the time about industrialization and modern life.

Throughout his career, Fred M. White also wrote detective stories, with works like The Mystery of the Four Fingers becoming significant examples of early mystery fiction. His storytelling style was marked by complex plots, twists, and the exploration of human nature under pressure. Although he did not achieve the widespread fame of some of his contemporaries, his work had a lasting impact on the genres he explored. His parents, whose names are not widely documented, supported his literary pursuits, allowing him to focus on his writing.

CONTENTS

CHAPTER I
A BLIGHTED LIFE

The bitterness of it tasted dry and insipid in John Charlock's mouth, like Dead Sea fruit. It was only lately that he had found out that all he had longed and hoped for since the early days was nothing more than vexation of spirit.

This process had been gradual, but it was none the less painful for that. It mattered nothing now that fame and fortune had come to him through the medium of his brush and pencil. For Charlock had fought his way up from the bottom. He had known what it was to starve. He had often slept in the open parks. And now everything was changed, and he stood almost unrivalled as a portrait-painter. And at the same time he appeared to have found the one woman who could make his happiness complete.

It was only five years ago, yet it seemed to Charlock like a lifetime. Perhaps he had been to blame; perhaps he had been harsh and hard, but the gulf between his wife and himself seemed to have been bridged over since the boy came.

And the child was slipping away, as an evening primrose blooms and dies within the compass of a night.... It had been a weary vigil and cruel withal, since there was only one end. The doctor held out no hope. He had told him that the boy could not last till morning, and that was why Charlock had sent the nurse away, so that he might be with his child till the end. Very quietly he crept back to the bed again and stood looking down at the small, white face. The features were so colourless that death might have come already, save that the lips were parting and the eyelids twitched. The child had spoken his last words. Charlock would never hear that voice again.

The end was very, very near. The tiny life was drifting out to sea with the tide. As Charlock stood there his eye noted the sudden change, his quick ear caught a fluttering sigh. There was no need to tell him that the boy had gone.

Well, that was over, at any rate. Charlock felt quite calm and collected. There was no great grief in his heart. He supposed it was all for the best. Perhaps it would have been a pity if little Jack had grown up to the knowledge of a divided household. But it would be a divided household no longer. And the sooner Kate Charlock realised that the better. Of course, she would have all the sympathy and he would have all the blame. Not that he cared much about that. A great artist like John Charlock was beyond the measure of ordinary criticism. No doubt his was a sour, saturnine nature. No doubt Kate Charlock was pitied by all who knew her. It seemed almost a tragedy that a woman so pure and beautiful should be allied to so uncouth a being as Charlock. These strange thoughts ran through the painter's mind like a thread of scarlet intermingled with a warp of black.

Well, the boy was dead. Charlock repeated the words over and over again, as if forcing himself to realise it. He had sat there for hours watching the small light burn lower and lower in its socket, while his wife slept in her own room. She had persistently refused to believe that there was anything radically wrong with the boy, though she had asked Charlock to call her in case a crisis might arise. Perhaps Charlock had forgotten about his wife. But the boy was dead, and Kate Charlock lay asleep, happily oblivious to the toy tragedy.

But she would have to be told. She must be aroused at once. Quietly Charlock crossed the corridor and entered his wife's room. He gave a quick, contemptuous glance at all the signs of extravagance and luxury which was the dominant note of the place. Here was a Duchesse dressing-table, littered with silver toilet appliances. The air was heavy with perfume. A pair of wax candles gleamed on either side of the dressing-table. In an armchair close by a figure in black lay fast asleep. The hangings from the bed were thrown back, and on the bed itself lay a heap of discarded clothing. With a sudden outburst of anger Charlock shook the figure in the armchair. The woman opened her eyes.

"What has become of your mistress?" Charlock asked hoarsely. "Now, don't tell any of your lies to me! Where has she gone?"

The maid began to whimper, but it was no use to wriggle and prevaricate under those stern eyes. There was something in the square, grim face of John Charlock that caused most people to fear him. He looked positively cruel.

"She has gone out, sir," the maid stammered.

"Oh, she has gone out, and she left you to wait up for her? She went early? It was a few minutes past ten when your mistress came to bed, and I was to wake her if anything—happened."

An insolent look came over the maid's face.

"If you want to know, she's gone to Mrs. Bromley-Martin's," she said. "It's no business of mine, and, though I am a servant, I am not used to being spoken to like this. If you looked after your wife a bit better there wouldn't be so much talk."

"Talk!" Charlock echoed. "What do you mean?"

"Ask the other servants. Ask your neighbours. Ask them what Mrs. Charlock does in the garden by night. It is all very well to be fond of solitude. If it could only speak, that old sundial could tell a story or two. Once they used to hide love-letters in trees. Nowadays they have got a better idea than that. If I were you——"

But Charlock was not listening. It was doubtful, even, if he had noticed the studied insolence of the French maid. He strode back to the chamber of death and locked the door behind him. He was thinking of men who had killed their wives for less than this. He was filled with the heartless cruelty of it, the cold-blooded cruelty and deceit. How could a mother have slipped away in this fashion, knowing that her child was so ill? It was no excuse that she had been sanguine of his recovery. From the very first she had refused to believe that there was anything wrong with the boy. And doubtless that was why she had gone off, thinking that her husband would be none the wiser. And once he had regarded her as one of the best of women and the sweetest. He had not been much of a squire of dames, except from a business point of view. But Kate Chantrey had been different from the rest. Her beauty was so *spirituelle*. Those great brown eyes of hers were clear and pure and soulful as those of a Madonna.

Bare-headed, Charlock walked through the garden and out into the road. The dawn was breaking in the east and pearly mists were rolling up the valleys. But Charlock saw none of these things. In a vague kind of way he noticed the old sundial at the bottom of the garden, with the fountain round it—that marvellous piece of carving which had been one of his extravagances on his last trip to Venice. It looked fair and chaste in the light of the early morn. There was nothing about it to suggest a vulgar *liaison* such as that at which Hortense, the French maid, had hinted. Charlock would have dismissed the idea contemptuously, but somehow he could not get it out of his mind; and yet it must have been mere servants' gossip. Kate Charlock was too inordinately selfish, too fond of the luxuries that her husband's money provided, to compromise herself even for so fascinating a man as Arnold Rent. Charlock knew that Rent was a friend of his wife's, a man whom she professed to understand and sympathise with. But the matter had never troubled him before. He could trust Kate. Assuredly he had confidence in her so long as her interests were his.

He came at length to his destination. He walked across the lawn of Mrs. Bromley-Martin's house. He could see two figures on the balcony. With a bitter smile he recognised his wife.

"The woman pays," he muttered to himself. "Oh, yes, the woman pays right enough, but it is generally the man who finds the money. Presumably God in His wisdom has some use for women like that, but it is hard to see where that fool of a fellow comes in. I dare say he fancies her ill-used and ill-treated, and tied to a brute unworthy of a mate at all. And yet as I stand here, knowing everything, I am not surprised that Rent should be deceived. Well, he shall have his chance to learn his lesson as I learnt mine. It seems almost a pity to intrude upon a scene of high emotion like that, but it must be done."

Charlock bent to listen again. There was no word of the conversation that escaped him. Then he saw the hostess emerge and claim his wife's attention. A wild desire to rush into the drawing-room, to overturn chairs and card-tables and drive those puppets into the open air seized him. They longed for a new sensation. They were very near having one at that moment. Checking the insane impulse, Charlock passed through the open window and entered the drawing-room. The close, highly spiced atmosphere seemed to choke him. His mind went back, now, to the great trouble which he had just gone through. There sat the woman who should have shared his vigil, smiling and sorting her cards as if she had not a care in the world.

It was hard to restrain the reproaches that rose to his lips. It was a tense task to approach the card-table quietly and lay his hand upon his wife's arm. It was small wonder, too, that the grip should have been close as that of a vise.

CHAPTER II
"THE DESIRE OF THE MOTH"

"It would be quite safe," Kate Charlock had said to herself. John was so foolish about the boy. He always took the gloomiest view of everything. She would retire to her bedroom and would pretend to be asleep. She could dress herself and slip across to Mrs. Bromley-Martin's and pass the night in the fascinating pursuit of bridge. Nobody would know. She would be back by daylight. And then she could take her husband's place by the boy's bedside.

She had forgotten everything in the excitement of the moment. She leant forward as the game finished.

"Mrs. Charlock cuts out," the dealer murmured.

She rose reluctantly and another gambler eagerly took her place. The subdued lights of the shaded candles touched drawn faces. Now and again came a cry of annoyance from some plunger whose luck was past bearing. Outside, the silence of the night was coming to an end. The trees murmured with the first touch of the morning breeze. As Kate Charlock crossed the room towards one of the French windows a man followed her. One of the card-players elevated his eyebrows and smiled significantly at his partner, who happened also to be his hostess. Her eyes twinkled in reply.

"Who is the man?" he asked.

"Arnold Rent," was the reply. "They say he is going to be President of the Royal Society. He is a man of various attainments. He is writing a series of essays on the follies of Society. I believe electricity is his specialty. But he says he came here to-night to gain experience."

"That was ingenious of him," the questioner said sarcastically. "He couldn't have come to a better house. All the follies and frivolities worth seeing can be found here."

"That is right enough," Mrs. Bromley-Martin said placidly. "I thought it was awfully sweet of him to choose me out of so many others. I am living in hopes that perhaps he will mention my name in one of his essays, and then how furiously jealous all the rest will be! Still, I like Arnold Rent. He is so terribly cynical. In the old days he would have made an ideal libertine."

The man under discussion crossed the room and stood by Kate Charlock's side. She turned her beautiful face to him, her eyes smiled a welcome. It was by no means the first time the two had met under Mrs. Bromley-Martin's roof.

"There is a seat on the balcony," Rent said. "Shall we sit there and chat for five minutes? The atmosphere of that room is positively poison to me. It seems incredible that civilised men and women, endowed with all the blessings of life, can sit down and deliberately pass their nights like this."

A gentle sigh escaped Kate Charlock's lips. Her face glowed with sympathy; there was a sad expression on the lovely features.

"Is it as bad as you expected, then?" she asked.

"Oh, worse, infinitely worse. In their way these people are just as heathenish as the Romans of the Empire were. What a strange thing fashion is! Your friends come down here ostensibly from the Cowes Regatta, but they have played nothing but bridge all day since Monday. It disgusts me to see young girls given over to the vice of gambling, heedless of aught else. Forgive me if I wonder why you come here. It cannot be out of sympathy with women like Mrs. Bromley-Martin and her class."

"Perhaps not," Kate Charlock murmured. She sighed again in the same gentle fashion. Her eyes had a far-away look in them. "Perhaps I am like the man who is on the verge of a breakdown from overwork, or the man who falls back upon brandy to drown some overwhelming sorrow."

The words came slowly and sadly. In the first flush of the dawn Rent did not fail to see the look of patient unhappiness on the face of his companion. Many fair women Arnold Rent had seen in his time, but never one who appealed to him as Kate Charlock did then. He had been too seriously engaged in study to think of women in the abstract. This tall, fair creature in silver grey appeared to be asking mutely for his sympathy. It was such a perfect face, too, a face that seemed to be out of place here. There was a suggestion of sadness in the glorious eyes, as if the woman nursed some secret sorrow and hid it bravely from the world. Nine men out of ten would have picked out Kate Charlock as a perfect confidante in the hour of trouble or affliction. And Arnold Rent had heard whispers of the story of her life. He turned to her quickly, forgetting his cynicism.

"Do you speak from experience?" he asked.

A wave of colour swept over her face.

"You have no right to ask that question," she said.

"That is true, but I am not speaking out of vulgar curiosity. It was yourself who hinted that you came here to escape your own thoughts."

"Did I say as much as that?" Kate Charlock asked absently. "You must make allowance for us poor women who have seen enough of the world to know that it is the woman who always pays."

"So you are one of the women who pay, are you? Do you know, I guessed that the first time I saw you. There is something sad and pathetic about you. And yet I am sure you are brave and strong. But, tell me, is the trouble likely to last?"

"I am afraid so," Kate Charlock murmured. "It is such a terrible thing for a woman to be tied to a man who has no sympathy with her. But I am speaking disloyally of my husband."

Arnold Rent pursued the subject no further. He had heard something of the kind of man that John Charlock, the famous artist, was. Despite his brilliant genius, despite the position which he had attained from the ranks of the people, he was spoken of as a boor and a savage brute where his beautiful wife was concerned. Strange, Rent thought cynically, how frequently men like these win the pearls among womanhood. He was about to say something of this kind when the hostess darted suddenly out and pounced upon Kate Charlock. With a sigh of protest the latter rose.

"You must come and take my hand," Mrs. Bromley-Martin shrieked. "I am called away for the moment."

With a self-sacrificing smile Kate Charlock returned to the drawing-room, followed by Rent. After the sweetness of the morning air, the atmosphere of the room was close and repellent. The gamblers sat jaded and weary, their faces ghastly where the light fell upon them, but the greedy light in their eyes was still as keen as ever. Rent could hear the swish of the cards as they slid over the green baize tables. He could hear the click of gold and the rustle of bank paper. His heart beat faster as he stood watching. What chance could there be for the common people, he asked himself, when the rich amused themselves like this? It was so demoralising, too. It seemed almost impossible to believe that the keen-eyed, eager woman sorting her cards dexterously could be the same sweet creature who had been seated by his side a few moments ago. If ever woman was in need of spiritual support, that woman was Kate Charlock. What a glorious thing it would be to play the game of platonic friend, to show her how to suffer her misfortunes calmly. She was the sort of woman, too, who in happier auspices might be a maker of history. Rent could understand men going mad for the sake of a face like that, or travelling to the end of the world to obey her lightest wish. He wondered what manner of man it was that treated so beautiful a creature with cruel indifference.

He was still wondering when the open French window was flung back and an intruder entered. The intruder was not in evening dress. He was attired in a shabby flannel suit, his hair was dishevelled, his short brown beard in disorder. The man's face was a strong one, and there was an almost sinister suggestion of power about the short, blunt nose and deep-set, gleaming eyes. There was anger as well as bitter contempt written on the features as he strode across the room towards the table where Kate Charlock was seated. By instinct Arnold Rent knew that he was face to face with Mrs. Charlock's husband.

The stranger strode up to her and laid his hand on her arm. Her features turned a shade paler as she glanced up.

"John," she faltered. Just for a moment it occurred to Rent that the woman's face had a guilty air. "What are you doing here like this? Is anything wrong?"

"Oh, I know I am out of place," the stranger said grimly. "Mrs. Bromley-Martin has asked me more than once to call, and now I am here. I have come for *you*."

The speaker's stern, clear tones rang through the room, and cards were dropped for the moment. The hostess laughed.

"Oh, don't mention it," she said. "I love originality. You can't think how tired one gets sometimes of bridge in a drawing-room."

All eyes were turned upon Charlock, and he seemed to have become master of the situation. He walked to the windows and jerked up the blinds. The clear glow of the morning fell on tired eyes and painted faces that looked ghastly white and drawn. There was no sign of a smile on Charlock's face.

"Take the tables and play outside," he said. "That will be something new, something for the papers to chatter about. But I am intruding here, and I want my wife. You will come at once. I beg your pardon, I am sure I did not mean to hurt you, but I am a little beside myself to-night. You will know why presently. I will go outside and wait for you."

CHAPTER III
"HOME, SWEET HOME!"

Unconsciously, Charlock had tightened his grip on his wife's bare arm. A cry of pain escaped her, a murmuring, uncomplaining cry which drew a hum of sympathy from the onlookers. The red band on the white flesh was plainly visible. Rent, standing by the table, ventured a word of expostulation. Charlock saw that he was a handsome man, with a clean-shaven, sensitive face, though the eyes were resolute, and the firm lines about the mouth denoted strength of character. So much the better. As to the rest, he wore the dress coat of modern civilisation. This was Kate's sympathetic friend. There was something like a sneer on Charlock's face as he turned to Rent.

"I am extremely sorry," he said. "You will forgive me, but I am quite out of place here. And in that respect I ought to have your sympathy and support, my dear sir."

The other man's face flushed, and he bit his lip. The retort was so obvious, so keen and pungent, that many of the onlookers made no efforts to restrain their amusement. Kate Charlock rose from the table and turned to the stranger.

"Would you mind getting my wrap for me, Mr. Rent?" she said. "I am sure, John, that Mrs. Bromley-Martin will excuse you, and I know you would prefer to wait outside for me."

Charlock muttered something, and turned upon his heel. It was no time now for nice conventionalities. After the close and stuffy atmosphere the outer air was cool and refreshing. Charlock passed his hand across his eyes. He was trying to realise what had happened during the last few minutes. He could remember nothing of what he had said and done. There was but one picture uppermost in his mind—the picture of a tiny figure lying white and motionless upon a bed. That was all Charlock's world to-night.

While he stood waiting, Kate Charlock lingered in the hall for a moment with Arnold Rent. There was an angry gleam in the man's eyes as he folded the wrap round his companion's shoulders.

"You poor, dear child," he burst out. "So that is your husband? You will forgive me for daring to speak like this——"

"One forgives everything when it is dictated by kindness such as yours," Kate Charlock murmured. "But I assure you it is nothing. It is only his manner. If you think I am in danger you are mistaken."

"But his face," Rent protested. "The look in his eyes. I was watching him when he caught sight of you. I saw murder written there. I could not rest if I stayed here. You will not mind if I follow you as far as your house? I will take care not to be seen. You may think this is an extraordinary suggestion, but we have been friends for a considerable time, and you know that I would do anything for you."

There was passion as well as sincerity in the speaker's tones, and a tinge of colour crept into Kate Charlock's cheeks. She raised a pair of dewy eyes to her companion's face.

"You are more than kind," she murmured, "but I know your life is one long self-sacrifice. I know what penance it must be to you to spend a long evening among shallow, heartless people such as these, but your mission lies with people like us——"

"But you do not identify yourself with them, surely?" Rent cried. "No, no, you are a broken-hearted, disappointed woman, striving to forget your unhappiness. I confess I am sorry to see you here to-night, but your future is in no danger. If we had only met before——"

"Hush, hush," Kate Charlock said hastily. "You must not talk like that. I—I dare not listen to you. As you would not be faithless to your own vows, you would not have me faithless to mine. And so long as I can come here, and forget my miseries, so long as I can meet you, I feel that I am safe."

Arnold Rent thrilled with a curious feeling as he listened to those impassioned words. It was impossible to doubt the sincerity of them, impossible to be anything but sorry for the beautiful, unhappy speaker. Her voice was dangerously low. There was an appeal in her eyes that set Rent fairly trembling.

"I must come and see you," he said. "You will tell me the whole of your sad story. And now I must not detain you longer, seeing that your husband is waiting for you. But I am going to follow you home, all the same."

Again came the look of gratitude in Kate Charlock's dark eyes. Then she turned away, as if afraid to trust herself further, and joined John Charlock in the garden. The pearly mists had rolled away. There was a deep, roseate flush in the eastern sky, but as yet the sun had not risen. A distant church clock struck the hour of three.

John Charlock strode along with his hands in his pockets, his sombre eyes fixed upon the ground. The silence was growing intolerable. It seemed to Kate that she must speak, that she could not endure it longer.

"How did you find out?" she asked.

"I went to your room," Charlock explained. "I found your maid fast asleep, and I compelled her to tell me where you had gone. Did I make a fool of myself to-night?"

"You were not polite," the woman murmured, "and——"

"And all your friends are profoundly sorry for you. It must be a terrible thing for a woman of your temperament to be allied to a brute like myself. And to think that I should humiliate you by dragging you home like this! Your lot is indeed a hard one. Think how happy we might have been had I only been blessed with a more amiable temperament! Think how you have helped me in my work, and how unflinchingly you have spent my money!"

Kate Charlock shivered and trembled, the tears gathered in her eyes, and the scarlet mouth was quivering.

"What have I done?" she protested. "Why shouldn't I go out? If I had told you I was going, you would have been annoyed with me, you might even have forbidden me. And all this because you fancy that the boy's life is in danger. It seems singular that a hard, unfeeling man like you should make such a ridiculous fuss over a child. It was kinder on my part to slip away without saying anything. It isn't as if the poor little fellow is any worse than he was yesterday."

Charlock clenched his hands behind his back. He was trembling from head to foot with an overmastering passion. A red mist floated before his eyes, and something seemed to oppress his breathing. It was only for a moment; then he was his grim self again.

"The boy is better," he said, "far better. In fact, there is no cause for anxiety any more. I will never trouble you about him again. Why, you will know presently. Now you will oblige me by coming this way.... There, fond mother! Look at that!"

The woman stood just for a moment, beginning dimly to comprehend. She placed her hand to her head. A moaning cry escaped her lips. With faltering steps she crossed the room and laid a long, slim hand on the child's face. For a while she neither spoke nor moved. No cry escaped her lips. Then, at length, she turned to face her husband. But he was gone.

He had shown her enough, and more than enough. In the face of the tragedy any word of his would be superfluous. If she did not benefit by such a lesson as this, assuredly he could teach her nothing. She had nothing to learn.

His heart was very sore and heavy within him as he walked out of the house and down the garden. Here was the garden of his dreams—the place he had planned in his mind when fame should come to him. It was here in this perfect spot that he and Kate were going to dwell for ever in their floral paradise.

What a fool he had been! Yet that fair face and those pensive eyes would have deceived a more polished man of the world than John Charlock. He knew now for a certainty that he had given up everything for beauty devoid of heart. And one of the worst features was that the woman who cared nothing for him was wasting his money with a lavish hand. He ought to be happy and comfortable, instead of which he was up to his neck in debt and difficulty. He almost smiled as he looked at the ancient sundial which he had given so much for, merely to please his wife, but he regretted his folly now. The price of a portrait had gone to purchase that white marble. Charlock walked towards it in a sour frame of mind. He could have found it in his heart to destroy the whole thing. And yet, even in the moment of his trouble, he saw that the fountain was no longer playing in the carved basin round the base of the dial. Some dark object lay there. He fancied he could see a dress fluttering in the wind.

He moved forward more quickly. At the same moment one of the gardeners came down the path. The man came in response to Charlock's call. Together they bent over the object in the basin. Charlock's face grew pale. The gardener shouted in open-mouthed dismay. They had the object out on the grass now—a black, wet, horrible thing, with pale, sodden face.

"Hortense, my wife's maid!" Charlock whispered. "How did she get here? How could she have fallen in?"

"Excuse me, sir," the gardener said huskily, "but it looks to me like foul play. A grown person would hardly drown in so little water. And look at that ugly bruise on her forehead. You may depend upon it, there has been mischief here."

CHAPTER IV
SACKCLOTH AND ASHES

There was trouble and enough to spare in the house of John Charlock. A day or two had passed. The child was buried, and the blinds were drawn up once more. It was characteristic of Charlock that he held his grief sternly in hand and devoted his energy and attention in striving to get to the bottom of the mystery which surrounded the death of his wife's maid. The affair had created a sensation in the district. It was held to be so important that it had passed out of the hands of the local police into those of Scotland Yard. As to the girl's past, nothing could be discovered. No trace of her relatives could be found. And it could not be proved that she had been entangled in any love affair. Robbery was not the motive, either, for she had a well-filled purse in her pocket and wore a handsome gold watch.

Yet, in some way, Charlock felt that the woman had been more or less of a dangerous character. He had never liked her. He distrusted her manner, which had always been a mixture of humility and veiled insolence. She was just the sort of creature who would have stooped to blackmail, and from this point of view Charlock was working. But a week had passed, and nothing had happened to throw light on the mystery.

And, besides, Charlock had other things to occupy him. He had made up his mind to end the present intolerable state of things. He was waiting now in his studio for his wife. The paint brush hung idly in his hand and his thoughts were far away. This was John Charlock in one of his most dangerous moods. He turned upon his wife a pair of sullen, brooding eyes.

"Well, what do you want?" he demanded.

"I am sorry to intrude," Mrs. Charlock said coldly, "but we cannot go on like this."

"That is true," Charlock said, a grim smile playing about the corners of his mouth. "If it is any consolation to you to know it, some change must be made. I have sat opposite to you for three days now, with hardly a word, but your thoughts have been to me like an open book. You have made up your mind what to do. Your programme is clear. Now that the child has gone, and there is no tie to bind us, you think it would be far better not to remain under this roof. Grossly extravagant though you are, you are shrewd enough, when it comes to a question of money to spend. You calculate, I suppose, that my income is about four thousand a year."

"Really, you fill me with pain," Mrs. Charlock murmured.

"Our Lady of Pain!" Charlock sneered. "Good heavens, do you want to pose after we have been married five years? Why, there is not a cranny in your soul that holds a dark place for me. I say you have reckoned it all out, and you are going to propose that I should share my income with you and give you a free hand to do as you like. This opportunity of martyrdom is not to be lost. Think how you would look wearing a crown! What a picturesque figure of a long-suffering woman you would make! And all your friends would pity the dear saint and condemn the malignant husband. But we need not go into that. Do you know that I am over six thousand pounds in debt? I have not a single commission on hand and hardly know where to turn for the money to pay the servants' wages. This is one of the tricks that fortune plays a man who gets his living as I do. Two of my commissions are in abeyance, and two other pictures may never be paid for, because the men who ordered them are dead. It sounds like a romance, but it is literally true. And of this load of debt that hangs about my neck like a millstone, less than two hundred of it belongs to me! Putting aside the expenses of the household, which have not been heavy, in the last two years you have pledged my credit for more than four thousand pounds. You said nothing to me. You ordered what you wanted. I have one bill here for five hundred pounds from a Bond Street milliner. You may call this only thoughtlessness, if you like, but I call it mean and dishonourable. And with all your beauty and sweetness and sympathy, you are little better than a criminal. And the joke of it is, it is I who have to pay the penalty, I who will incur the contempt of honest men, while you get off scot free. But there is going to be an end of all this. Before the week is out everything shall be disposed of."

Kate Charlock looked up swiftly. There was something like a challenge in her eyes. The mantle of sweetness and resignation had fallen from her shoulders.

"Do you mean to say you will give up this house?" she demanded. "Do you mean to tell me that you will sell the furniture? Surely there is no necessity."

"I owe all that money," Charlock said doggedly, "and I am going to pay it off. I could easily whitewash myself as other men do, but that is not my way. To be candid with you, there is a bill of sale on the things here which covers their value, and, at any time, my creditors could come in and remove everything. Now, make the best of it. Revel in your extravagance while it lasts, for the time is getting short. And you shall have your opportunity to prove to your friends that you are the saint they take you to be. Everything I can lay my hands upon I shall realise for the benefit of my creditors. I will not rest till the last farthing is paid. It will be a question of rigid economy for a couple of years, and then I shall be able to look the world in the face once more. But in future there is going to be no London or Paris for you. We shall move into a three-roomed cottage, where we shall not even keep a servant. I will take the rough work off your hands, and in return you will do the housework and cooking. I intend to keep back no more than three pounds a week from my earnings until my debts are paid. That is all I am entitled to. This you can share with me, or, if you prefer it, you can have thirty shillings a week to live upon. If you take legal proceedings to obtain more, you will find that no Court will ask a man to give his wife more than half his income."

Kate Charlock stood white and rigid, striving in vain to force a smile.

"You are mad," she said hoarsely. "You could not do it. Think of your position! Think of what the world would say!"

"Did I ever care what the world said?" Charlock cried. "What does it matter, so long as one's good name remains unsmirched? I have no more to say. I have no desire to argue the thing farther. I have already taken the cottage and furnished it. You have till the end of the week to make up your mind. You will please yourself whether you come with me or not, and I care little or nothing what your decision may be. Now, as I am busy, I shall be glad to be alone."

Mrs. Charlock crept from the studio to her own room. There were real tears in her eyes. She was trembling from head to foot with a sense of humiliation and disappointment. She no longer doubted what her husband had said. She knew that when John Charlock had made up his mind to a thing it was as good as done. And he was doing this deliberately, in order to spite her, to wound her most susceptible feelings, because she had made such a terrible mistake the night of the boy's death. He would not understand her point of view. She could not induce him to believe that she had never dreamt the end was so near. No mother would have gone away had she known what was likely to happen. And as to Charlock's debts, it would have been easy to retrench and wipe them off by degrees.

Kate Charlock wept as she looked about her. It was a beautiful house, luxuriously and artistically furnished. All Kate Charlock's friends envied her such a place.

To give it up was an act of mean and cowardly vengeance. The thing would never have been thought of had the boy lived. It never occurred to the passionate, weeping woman that John Charlock valued his honour beyond his comfort, for there were scores of people in the smart set to which she belonged who never paid their debts at all. There were members of that charmed circle who boasted of this and were thought none the worse of.

Here were the beautiful pictures, the magnificent furniture, the marvellous old silver which Kate Charlock had bought from time to time. Here was everything that made life sweet and enjoyable, and she was commanded to resign it all, and live alone in a draughty cottage with the man whom she regarded less as her husband than as her jailer. Two years' penal servitude at least! The thing was impossible, insupportable!

She must tell somebody. She must confide in someone. But in whom? Among her frivolous friends, who would give her a measure of broad and genuine sympathy? She could only think of one person, and the colour crept into her cheeks as she recalled Arnold Rent. Then she became conscious that a servant had come into the room and stood watching her curiously.

"Well?" she demanded. "What do you want? Don't you see that I want to be alone?"

"It is Mr. Rent, madam," the servant said. "He is waiting in the drawing-room, and would like to see you."

CHAPTER V
"BUT YET A WOMAN"

The thing was opportune, almost providential, or so Kate Charlock thought. She came down to the drawing-room, a subdued smile on her face. She seemed to fit into the room, to be part and parcel of it, like a pure jewel in a beautiful setting. And yet what a pity it was that no happiness went with all this. The thought flashed through Arnold Rent's mind as he shook hands with her. She had looked fair the last time they met, but now, clad in deepest black, she appeared even more attractive. Rent was not often at a loss for words, but he felt strangely awkward at the moment.

"I hope I am not intruding," he murmured, "but I am going away to-morrow, and I could not leave without telling you how grieved I am at your loss. It must have been a great shock."

The ready tears rose to Kate Charlock's eyes. Although she had troubled little about the boy when he was alive, she had persuaded herself that she had sustained a loss which no lapse of time would heal.

"It was a terrible shock," she murmured, "so unexpected. What must you think of me when you remember how I was spending the evening at the very moment——"

"But, of course, you did not know. How could you know?" Rent protested. "I have a much higher opinion of you than that. You must try to bear up. Remember that life has its compensations, even for the most miserable. You have a beautiful home. I never saw a more charming place."

Mrs. Charlock hesitated a moment.

"I think I had better tell you," she said slowly. "Even this home is not likely to last long. Whatever his faults may be, my husband is a genius, and everybody knows that geniuses are bad men of business. I am afraid I am not altogether blameless myself. I took it for granted that we had plenty of money. When my husband told me last night that he was hopelessly in debt I was positively staggered. He says he owes six thousand pounds, and he upbraided me bitterly for what he was pleased to call my extravagance. He accused me of being the author of all the mischief. But I am too much accustomed to his bitter tongue to take much heed of that. He always likes to see me well dressed. He has never complained like that before. I suppose he wanted to humiliate me. Indeed, he has been far worse since the child died. It is a wicked way to treat a mother. It is refined cruelty to taunt me with being away on pleasure when the boy was dying.... Oh, I don't see how I can endure the life which lies before me. So long as we are here, where there is plenty of room and we need not see much of one another, I might manage to rub along. But to go away to a tiny cottage——"

"A cottage?" Rent echoed. "Is your husband mad?"

"Sometimes I almost fear he is," Mrs. Charlock said in a whisper. "Since our loss he has been terrible. And now he has it in his mind to remove to a labourer's cottage and live on a few shillings a week until his debts are paid. Surely no sane man could behave in that way! I am ready to retrench, but when I think of the life that John has mapped out——"

The speaker's voice broke with a pathetic catch. She pressed her handkerchief to her eyes. There was something in the speech that tickled Rent. His assumed sympathy was not so keen and clear as it had been. Charlock was a fool, a passionate believer in self-sacrifice. And, moreover, he was playing into his hands. But probably he was not moved by any nice considerations of honour and had adopted this course to humiliate the beautiful creature who sat opposite.

"You are going to leave him?" he asked hopefully.

"I am afraid so," Kate Charlock said. "Surely, I can make a living, though I have been brought up in a very useless fashion. If you would only see my husband, you might persuade him——"

"Presently," Rent said. "Just now I am more concerned with yourself. Whatever happens, you will always have a friend in me. And you must not hesitate in the hour of need. Fortunately, I have the command of a considerable amount of money——"

"Oh, I couldn't do that," Kate Charlock cried. "How good and kind you are! If I had only met you before I threw in my lot with John Charlock.... But what am I saying!"

The woman rose to her feet and threw out her hands towards Rent. Her soft, pleading eyes were turned upon him. They were not wholly devoid of passion, and impulsively Rent stepped forward and took her hands in his. For the moment he had forgotten everything—his characteristic prudence, even. A sudden recklessness possessed him. What he was doing he hardly knew. Then, a moment later, he awoke to the fact that Kate Charlock was in his arms and his lips were pressed passionately to hers.

Yet there was no sense of shame in Rent's mind, only a feeling of exultation and the knowledge that this woman cared for him. It was impossible to believe otherwise as he looked long and ardently into her eyes. Then, very slowly, he put her from him and walked towards the door. The game was his if he did not lose his head.

"This must not happen again," he said. "I am shocked to find that I am as human and weak as the rest. And I have no blame for you, nothing but the deepest and sincerest pity. Oh, what a false and treacherous world! It is hateful to think that you must go on living your life here— —"

"Not here," Kate Charlock said quietly. "A lonely cottage, where I shall have to do my own work, and sit day by day opposite— — Oh, I cannot bear to think of it! I will go mad. I shall do him some mischief—of that I am certain."

"No, no," Rent said sternly, "not if I can prevent it. I will see your husband now and try to argue with him. If you will show me the way— —"

Charlock looked up from his easel with a frown on his face as Rent entered. Then the frown changed to a bitter smile as he bade his visitor be seated. He waited for the latter to speak.

"I have been talking to your wife," Rent began lamely. "She tells me that you are thinking of leaving."

"Oh, did she? Perhaps she told you that I was up to my eyes in debt, and that I am not going to rest until every penny has been paid. That is why I am leaving and have furnished a small cottage in the neighbourhood. After all, I am not asking my wife very much. For the last three or four years she has had everything that the heart of woman could desire, and now I am asking her to pay the penalty. You can't eat your cake and have it, you know. Really, my good sir, as a man of the world, you ought to applaud my resolution."

"So I do," Rent murmured. "But you will pardon me if I ask you a plain question. People say you are a hard man. They say that your wife's lot is not a happy one. I do hope and trust that in the step you are taking you have no desire to humiliate the lady— —"

"Stop!" Charlock cried. "You are going too far. I hear you are fearless and outspoken. I know you are a man of sense. And seeing you are candid, let me be candid in return. If I had married a plain, commonplace woman, would you take as much interest in her as you do in the lady whom I have the honour to call my wife? Ah, you are silent. I thought so. Yes, those are very pleading eyes. That is a very sad, sweet countenance. And doubtless I am a brute, because I can watch the tears fall from those eyes with a smile on my lips. Did it ever strike you that there may be another side to the question? Oh, I am not going to speak of it. You are quite free to form your own conclusions. And now you have come to persuade me to modify my scheme. Is not that so?"

"I must confess that I had some such idea in my mind," Rent admitted. "It seems so hard upon your wife."

"Oh, I know," Charlock said, the bitter sneer still on his face. "It is always the woman who pays. But I am busy now and have no time to discuss this matter. Come and see me again, say to-morrow evening, about eight o'clock. Then you shall have an answer to your question. You are a well-meaning man, but, like most of your class, you have no knowledge of the world and you fail to see the grim humour of the situation. It is rather amusing, don't you think, for a married man to be lectured by a bachelor? Some day, when your time comes——"

Charlock turned to his easel and refused to say another word. With a feeling that he had been baffled, Rent left the house. He walked slowly across the fields, the vision of Kate Charlock's beautiful, pathetic face occupying his mind to the exclusion of everything else. He tingled as he thought of that passionate caress. The feeling of hope was drowned in an unreasoning exultation. And yet he ought not to see her again. He had his future to consider. That chapter must be closed for ever. But as he walked along, for the first time in his life, Arnold Rent regretted his aims and the career which he had mapped out for himself since his schooldays.

CHAPTER VI
A SCIENTIFIC DISCUSSION

Much at the same moment two men were sitting on the deck of a yacht, drifting idly before a light breeze in the Solent. One was a young, keen-faced fellow, with quick, alert eyes and a restless expression, who was known as Malcolm Grey. He was regarded as a coming man in science, more especially in electricity. Already one or two discoveries of his bade fair to revolutionise hitherto accepted theories, and he was engaged upon a series of investigations which had for their end the promulgation of life and the alleviation of human suffering. Scientific folk were looking forward with interest to the next pronouncement of Malcolm Grey.

His companion was a very different-looking man. He was short and inclined to be stout. The outline of his figure denoted great personal strength. His piercing black eyes had a humorous twinkle. A heavy dark moustache concealed the lines of his mouth. Dr. Tanza was a scientist, also, but his researches were more concerned with humanity, and particularly with the cause and prevention of crime. Tanza had devoted most of his life to this important subject, and, though some of his theories had been laughed at once, some of the best men in Europe were coming round to his way of thinking. Certainly he had been marvellously successful on two or three occasions and had operated upon the brains of criminals with the most amazing effect. As to the rest, he used his yacht and his great wealth for the sole purpose of developing his hobby. It was a small matter to him to travel half-way round the world to interview a wretched creature who had invented something atrocious in the way of fresh and startling crime. For the moment he appeared to be taking his leisure, though his friend knew that he had something on his mind.

"And now," said Grey, "tell me why you brought me down here. You know how busy I am and how precious my moments are. What have you in view?"

Tanza lighted a fresh cigarette and sipped his after-luncheon coffee with a ruminating air.

"I want your assistance," he said. "I think it will be worth your while. It isn't every day that I come across a criminal problem that interests me, but I think I have found one in the case of the mysterious death of Mrs.

Charlock's French maid. Charlock is a man difficult to approach and resents interference of any kind. As it happens, you are acquainted with him, which makes our task easier. Between ourselves, I mean to get to the bottom of that affair, because I feel certain that here is a new phase of crime."

"Why do you think so?" Grey asked. "I read the account of the inquest and I didn't notice anything out of the common. I don't see how a woman of her class could have enemies in her household. She was a self-contained foreigner, mainly interested in saving money, and she seems to have kept apart from the rest of the domestics. The rest of the servants are English and appear to be of a humdrum, respectable type. As far as I can see, her death happened naturally. The woman was fooling about by the fountain, slipped on the marble and stunned herself against the sundial. That would account for the bruise on her forehead. She was unconscious when she fell into the water and consequently was drowned. The thing is simple."

"That is because you haven't studied the subject," Tanza said placidly. "I flatter myself that I have an unerring instinct for this class of thing, and that is why I feel sure that we have dropped upon something new in the way of crime. You have forgotten that the doctor who made the *post-mortem* testified that there was little or no water in the lungs, which is rather against your drowning theory. Besides, one of the witnesses said that the woman's clothing was slightly singed. And, in addition to this, what could the Frenchwoman want in the garden at that early hour in the morning? Charlock swore that she was in the house just before daybreak, and soon after it was light he himself found her lying in the fountain. Depend upon it, she went to keep an assignation and met her death that way."

"What, in broad daylight?" Grey asked.

"That," Tanza said, with the air of a connoisseur, "is just where I am puzzled. It must have been nearly broad daylight, at any rate, when the woman left the house, and the sundial was in full view of the front windows. We've a precious clever rascal to deal with, I know. I have gone into all the records of new and ingenious crimes, and in all my experience I can find nothing to fit this case. That is why I called you in. The murderer is up-to-date and uses all the modern appliances which are not as yet known to the police. A good many of them may still be outside the ken of the average scientist. And the more my mind dwells upon the matter the more sure I am that science has been invoked by our miscreant. As you are well versed in all the latest discoveries, I asked you to spend a few days with me and make an examination of the scene of the trouble."

"Shouldn't we be rather intruding?" Grey protested. "Charlock is a very queer sort of man."

"I know that. In writing to him for his permission to test certain of my theories I mentioned that I was a friend of yours and that I should bring you along. I received a characteristic reply to the effect that I had best mind my own business, but that so long as you answered for my *bona fides* no objection would be made. So we are going off this afternoon, and here is the boat coming to fetch us. I don't expect a very warm reception."

John Charlock was walking about the grounds when his visitors arrived. Despite his sternness he looked miserable. For the time being he could not work. He felt that he would be able to do little or nothing until he had disposed of his expensive household. He had another plan, too, in his mind, but for the moment it was not ripe for execution. He extended a more or less cordial welcome to Grey, but his manner to Tanza was chilly. If the latter noticed it, he did not disclose the fact.

"This is very good of you, my dear sir," he said. "I hope you will not think I am here out of mere curiosity, for I am quite convinced that the death of your wife's maid was no ordinary occurrence. Having devoted most of my life to the study of crime, my experience tells me——"

"I have heard of you, of course," Charlock said civilly enough. "And, if such is your opinion, it is entitled to every respect. If I can do anything to help you I will. But I am certain that you are mistaken."

"We shall see," Tanza said drily. "In the first place, will you be good enough to show us the famous sundial where the accident took place, and perhaps you can tell me whether the poor woman's dress was singed? Was it round the skirt, for instance?"

"Personally, I could see no trace of it," Charlock said. "There was a certain fraying of the cloth round one of the wrists, and a swelling of the hand, as if the fingers had been recently charred. But, then, my wife tells me that Hortense inadvertently put her right hand on a pair of almost red-hot curling tongs a day or two ago, which gives the incident a very prosaic complexion. I think you can dismiss the singeing idea altogether."

For the moment the doctor looked disconcerted. But he had no intention of discarding his theory. He dropped behind, discussing the matter with Charlock, while Grey went forward to the part of the garden where the sundial was situated. He stood there admiring the beautiful carving of the marble and thinking how appropriate were the surroundings. The fountain was playing again. The sundial was like a gleaming statue in the sun. The Latin inscription on the top glistened in brass letters. There appeared to be nothing to connect the sundial with the cruel and cold-blooded murder. And, though Tanza talked scientifically about his theories, he did not appear to be making much progress.

"You are wrong," Charlock said. "I am sure the whole thing was no more than an unfortunate accident. I don't care what the doctor says. However, I sha'n't be here after to-morrow, but you are at liberty to come whenever you please and make what investigations you like. And now, if you will excuse me, I will get back to the house. You will pardon me if I don't ask you to come in."

Charlock turned away none too graciously, and the Italian doctor shrugged his shoulders.

"It is as well we are alone," he said. "I shall yet convince our friend that I am right. All the same, I am bound to confess that we look like having our trouble for our pains. Now, I suppose you don't see anything suspicious, anything which is hidden from unscientific eyes?"

"As a matter of fact, I can," Grey said quietly. "Only I waited till our friend was gone. Look here!"

He stooped and picked up a small object, which he slipped upon his thumb. Tanza lifted his brows interrogatively.

"Oh, it's a clue," Grey smiled. "What is it? Why, it is a finger torn from an india-rubber glove!"

CHAPTER VII
THE PHOTOGRAPH

Malcolm Grey handled the piece of dirty india-rubber almost tenderly. There was a smile on his face which somewhat irritated Tanza. The little Italian, usually so quick at picking up a clue, was quite baffled now. His instinct told him that Grey had made an important discovery. He stretched out his hand eagerly.

"Let me look at it," he said.

"Certainly," Grey said good-naturedly. "Look at it, by all means, but you won't make much out of the thing. It is simply a finger of a glove made of india-rubber, which might mean anything. But to me it conveys a good deal."

"And to me it conveys nothing," Tanza replied. "Now, let me see. Who are the sort of men who wear india-rubber gloves? I suppose they are manufactured for a certain class of sportsmen. I know they are used by electricians, and latterly by up-to-date burglars. You know these gentry have adopted india-rubber gloves to obliterate finger-marks. No doubt one of the fraternity has been here, though I am bound to confess that we are not getting much farther. What do you make of it?"

"If you don't mind, I won't tell you yet," Grey said. "Of course, you have already invented a theory of your own, which may be right and which may be wrong. You may not agree with me, but it is possible that if I tell you my theory you will modify yours, to the destruction of, perhaps, a really logical sequence of ideas. Now, if you keep your notion to yourself and I keep mine to myself we may get a definite conclusion all the sooner. Don't you think I am right?"

"Well, perhaps you are," Tanza said thoughtfully. "As for me, I have already got a notion, so we will both preserve our ideas and see which leads to the goal first."

"I am glad you said that," Grey remarked gravely. "I must confess that when I picked up that finger-stall I was startled. It indicated a fresh train of thought to me. It suggested one of the most startling and most original crimes of modern times. The idea came to me like a flash. But it is one thing to discover the source of a crime, and quite another to put your hand upon the criminal. And now, if you don't mind, I think I should like to be alone.

There are one or two things I want to do before I can put my theory into practice, and it would be much more prudent if I exercised this discretion by myself."

"Right you are," Tanza said gaily. "I will return to the yacht. I suppose you will be back to dinner?"

Grey made no reply. Already he seemed to be immersed in his own thoughts. He was more or less oblivious of the presence of his companion. When he was alone he walked round the marble basin of the fountain, scrutinising every inch of the ground with minutest attention. Round and round he went, with his eyes bent upon the earth, his body doubled. But though he spent some considerable time there, nothing seemed to reward his search. He shook his head as he turned away from the fountain, and proceeded to walk backwards and forwards across the lawn, like a man searching for some object which he has dropped. It was not till he got to the edge of the grass that his face lighted and a grim smile trembled on his thin lips. From the gravel path he took up a mass of silk thread all ravelled up together, and a little farther on was a piece of wire about the length of a pin, and also a small square of india-rubber not larger than a postage stamp. These trivial objects Grey placed in an envelope which he put in his pocket. As he looked up he saw Charlock watching him curiously out of one of the windows of the house. He was about to move away, when the artist beckoned to him. He lingered a moment, and Charlock appeared at the front door and asked him curtly if he would come in.

"I want to ask you a question or two," Charlock said. "You seem to have built up a pretty good reputation since we used to meet at the Old Bohemian Club in Craven Street. I believe you have studied medicine, among other things?"

"Quite right," Grey smiled. "All the same, you don't look as if you want a doctor. You are the picture of health."

Charlock smiled in his grimmest fashion.

"Am I?" he said. "In that case my looks belie me. I am not a crank or a faddist, but certain signs which I have had lately are not to be disregarded. I am strong enough physically, but those early days of poverty have left their mark. It isn't good for a young man to starve for weeks at a time, as I used to do. And of late I have been working far too hard. You see, the trouble that worries me is here."

Charlock laid his hand upon his heart. He seemed to have some difficulty in speaking. The smile died from Grey's lips and he became serious. He had seen too many men of perfect *physique* with that fatal heart weakness to make light of Charlock's fears. He motioned him to a chair.

"Take off your coat and waistcoat," he said, "and let me listen. It is as well to be on the safe side."

The speaker laid his ear to Charlock's heart for a moment or two, and when he rose there was a certain gravity in his eyes, which Charlock noticed with a cynical smile.

"Well," he said, "is it very bad?"

"No," Grey said gravely. "I don't think so. Of course, I can't be absolutely certain without a stethoscope, but I think there is nothing organically wrong. You have been overstraining yourself and there is a weakness which is more or less pronounced. A month's holiday, with plenty of open air and exercise, will put you right again. Still, there is another test which ought to settle the matter. Do you happen to have such a thing in the house as a bottle of sal volatile? Or a little brandy would do."

"No brandy for me," Charlock said. "I never touch the stuff. I shouldn't wonder if there was a bottle of sal volatile in that unfortunate maid's room. I understand that Hortense was hysterical and used to doctor herself with the remedy you speak of. I'll ring the bell and see."

A servant came in answer to the summons, but she stood hesitating as Charlock told her what he needed. She was a domestic of the country type, with vacant face and staring eyes. She shook her head stubbornly.

"I couldn't do it, sir," she said. "I wouldn't go into Hortense's room—no, not if you was to double my wages. It isn't safe, my mother always said, to go into the room of a suicide. It makes you feel that way yourself."

Charlock appeared to be on the verge of an explosion of temper, when Grey cut in. Expostulation was useless.

"Oh, never mind," he said. "Show me the room and I'll look for myself. Now come along. I won't even ask you to come inside. If you will point out the room to me——"

The round-eyed domestic accepted the compromise cheerfully. She piloted Grey up the stairs and indicated a room at the far end of the corridor. Then she retired precipitately, to Grey's great amusement. He knew that it was useless to argue with rustics of that sort. He entered the room and glanced around him.

The bedroom was comfortably furnished. There was a variety of pictures and knickknacks on the walls, and a book-shelf was laden with French novels. The maid had furnished her bedroom in imitation of a lady's boudoir. She was of luxurious habits, too, for a fire was laid in the grate and an attempt had been made to light it. Paper and sticks were charred away, but the coal had been obstinate and had refused to burn. A few letters had been torn up and thrown in the back of the fire, and these, for the most part, were charred and smoked until only a few words could be read. In a spirit of idle curiosity, Grey knelt down and examined these. He smiled to himself at his own weakness. Clearly he had caught this fever of investigation from his Italian friend. After a moment or two, however, his amused smile vanished, he grew deeply interested. A fragment of one of the letters was in his hand. He could make out a few words thereon, among which stood out prominently the expression "be cautious," and then, lower down, the still more significant words "the sundial."

There was nothing on the back of the paper, nothing more to indicate the writer's meaning. But, whoever the writer was, he had conveyed a warning to Hortense by means of his letter, and in some strange, inscrutable way that warning was mixed up with the old Roman sundial. No doubt the maid had torn up the letter and thrown it on the fire while the sticks were still burning, taking it for granted, of course, that the letter was destroyed.

"A lucky find," Grey murmured to himself. "There is more here than meets the eye. I shall have a fine story for Tanza. Still, it is one thing to know how a crime is committed and another to discover the perpetrator. I wonder if I can find a further clue—hallo!"

Grey almost started as he pulled from the grate a photograph which had been torn across the middle. He placed the two pieces together and examined them by the light of the window. There was a puzzled expression on his face as he looked at the photograph, which was that of two men dressed for some outdoor sport. One face was strange to him, but he recognised the other.

"Arnold Rent," he muttered. "Rent, to a certainty."

CHAPTER VIII
THE RUBICON

John Charlock had finished his breakfast and was busy with his correspondence. He looked up presently as his wife came in. The tall, slender figure looked graceful and attractive in the thin black dress she was wearing, and Charlock's artistic eye was pleased with the picture. He knew that Kate's gown was an expensive one, and that there was about it a marked, if subdued, suggestion of festivity. His brows contracted. Surely that dress must have been ordered since he had spoken of the need of economy.

"Your grief is chastened," he said. "It is good to see how you are bearing up under your crushing sorrow. You have come to the conclusion that it is your duty not to repine. Well, what is it? Going off somewhere for the day? A little innocent enjoyment will do you no harm."

"I was thinking of it," Kate Charlock said coldly. "I am going to Southampton to spend the day with some friends. But I shall be back in time for dinner."

Charlock rubbed his hands together slowly. There was a peculiar smile upon his rugged face.

"Oh, I am glad to hear that," he said. "Whatever you do, don't forget to come back to dinner, because I have a pleasant surprise awaiting you. I was not sure until I got my letter this morning, but now all doubt is removed. Good-bye and a pleasant day to you. Make the most of your chances."

Kate Charlock asked no questions. She had no curiosity concerning her husband's meaning. She came back in the cool of the evening. She passed through the lodge gates and noted the untidy state of the drive. The place was littered here and there with straw and shavings. The marks of the wheels of a heavy waggon were to be plainly seen on the side of the lawn. Kate was vexed, for she had always prided herself upon the symmetry and tidiness of her garden. She looked towards the gardener's lodge, and, to her surprise, observed that it was empty.

Her heart sank with a foreboding of coming evil as she quickened her pace towards the house. Here the litter increased. Shavings and scraps of paper had blown across the velvet lawn, a broken packing-case or two stood by the front door. With feelings of alarm and agitation, Kate Charlock looked up at the long rows of blank windows, which seemed to be staring her out of countenance. The window-boxes with their brilliant flowers had gone and the fine lace curtains and the rose-tinted silk blinds had vanished. Where a few hours before had been the picture of a refined English home was now mere chaos and desolation. With faltering footsteps and trembling limbs, Kate Charlock passed through the front door, which stood wide open for all the world to enter.

Her footsteps echoed on the bare boards. More by instinct than anything else, she called her husband by name. She could hear her voice echoing from room to room. She knew now that the place was absolutely and entirely bare. Then there was the sound of an answering footfall and John Charlock stood by the side of his wife in the dismantled drawing-room.

"Well," he said, "and what do you think of it? I promised you a surprise, and here it is. For days I have been expecting the creditor who holds the bill of sale to carry out his threat and remove everything. This morning he informed me what he was going to do, and he has done it. Save your own belongings, which are packed away in your dressing-room, the house is empty. I didn't tell you this before, because I did not wish to spoil your holiday. But you will see that it is impossible to remain. Fortunately, the cottage is ready. Now, if you will dry your eyes and try to play the woman, we will go off together where we can have a roof over our heads and no more of this sickening anxiety for the future. Come."

Charlock held out his hand, but the woman shrank from him. There was terror as well as grief in her eyes. She shuddered with loathing from head to foot. She could not do it. Come what might, she could not do it. In her heart of hearts she had never expected such a crushing blow. It was so like John Charlock to spring it on her in this cruel fashion.

"No," she said, as she wiped the tears angrily from her cheeks. "Between you and me there is an end of all things. I am not coming with you. If I were starving at this moment I would decline to cross the threshold of your cottage. Oh, you need not worry. I shall make a living somehow. To-night I shall stay with Mrs. Bromley-Martin and ask her advice and assistance. Henceforward our lives shall be spent apart."

"And that is your last word?" Charlock asked.

"I have no more to say, except good-bye."

Charlock turned and strode resolutely from the house. There was a queer smile on his face, though his heart was hot and angry. He passed out through the gates in the direction of his cottage. He gave no heed to his wife standing in the deserted home. And he had gone out of her mind directly.

What was she to do? How would the next chapter in the story read? She had spoken bravely enough about her friend Mrs. Bromley-Martin, but she knew in her heart of hearts how shallow and insincere all the so-called friendships in her own set were. Still, she was not penniless. Her husband had told her where she would find all her belongings, and her jewels were worth some hundreds of pounds. She would gather those together and go and stay at a hotel for the night. She was still debating the matter in her mind when she heard footsteps in the hall, and her courage deserted her for the moment. She drew a breath of something more than relief as Arnold Rent came forward.

"This is almost providential," she sighed. "How did you come to know that I was in such sore need of you?"

"That was prosaic enough," Rent said, with a strange thrill in his voice. "I came to see your husband by appointment. He promised me an answer to my arguments, but I did not expect to get it in such a dramatic way as this. Still, I was prepared for what I have found, because I met Mrs. Bromley-Martin just now and she seems to know everything. She is very sorry for you, but when I suggested that she should place her house at your disposal for a few days, she flatly refused, saying that her house was already too full. My dear Mrs. Charlock, what do you propose to do? How can I help you?"

Kate Charlock threw up her hands in despair.

"I am stunned," she said. "I am overwhelmed by this cruel stroke. Now you see what manner of man my husband is. Now you see the creature that I have had to put up with. A few minutes since he taunted me with my extravagance and, with a sneer on his lips, offered me the shelter of his cottage. I don't profess to have more courage than most women, but the worm will turn at last, and I refused to go. He has left me nothing but my belongings, nothing but this desolate house. Ah, it is a true saying that it is always the woman who pays."

A simulated indignation swept over Arnold Rent. Then his heart softened to tenderness and love and pity. Why should this beautiful woman be left alone in the world? Why should he not help her? Good heavens, how blind John Charlock must be! Thousands of good men would give all they possessed to have the affection of a creature like this. She stood there in a supplicating attitude, her large, pathetic eyes turned on Rent. She was asking him as plainly as words could speak for counsel. Passionate sobs were breaking from her. She held out her hands to Rent, murmuring piteously that he was the only friend she had in all the wide world. He caught those hands in a firm grip. He forgot everything in the delirious excitement of the moment. Once more the woman was in his arms, his lips were pressed to hers, and she was sobbing on his shoulder.

"Oh, I know this is terribly wrong," she murmured. "But I am so miserable and so helpless. What can I do? What am I good for, except to be the faithful wife and companion of some good man who can understand me and whose heart is entirely mine? But that is a dream. Tell me, Arnold, that you are not ashamed of my impulsive action."

Rent made no reply for the moment. His mind was moving quickly. He looked eagerly and vividly into the future. He could see his airy castles vanishing before the fragrant breath of the woman who had abandoned herself to his embrace. In an instant all was gone to the winds, and a mere man, palpitating and trembling with sheer humanity, was holding in his arms that for which he was going to forfeit the world.

"Not another word," he whispered hoarsely. "I am glad I came here to-night, both for your sake and mine. You shall have no more anxiety for the future. We will live for that future, you and me. Dearest, I could not let you go. Say you will let me act for you. Your honour is safe in my hands."

CHAPTER IX
BEYOND THE BRIDGE

Kate Charlock regarded the speaker with startled eyes. The crimson wave stained her face and she stood as if the mere suggestion petrified her. It was as if she had suddenly stepped into a world of sin and trouble from some Arcadia where such things were only heard of or discussed in whispers.

It was magnificently done, so spontaneous. Arnold Rent was moved to a real, deep admiration. It seemed strange to him that any man could be cruel to so beautiful a saint. He waited in a kind of rapture for Kate to speak.

"Oh, no, no," she murmured. "You cannot mean it! Do not think that I am angry with you. Do not think that I am blind to the enormous sacrifice that you are making. You are speaking on the impulse of the moment. Think of your future!"

"I am not," Rent cried. "If anybody had told me this yesterday I should have repudiated the idea with scorn and amusement. But yesterday and to-day are far apart, and I do not recognise myself as the same man. And I mean every word that I say. Otherwise, what would become of you? You could not go back to that man now. It is out of the question."

Kate Charlock pressed her hands to her eyes and shivered. The gesture was more eloquent than any words could be.

"Precisely," Rent went on rapidly. "Though I understand what is uppermost in your mind, you stand at the parting of the ways, both of which end in what the world calls folly. But is it folly for you to strike a blow for your just rights? And, really, you couldn't go back to the man whom you hate and despise."

"But there is a middle course," Kate Charlock murmured. "I can go out into the world alone. I can get my own living, as other unhappy women have done before me. And you will help me."

"That I will," Rent said. "Ah, I am afraid you do not realise what a terrible task it is. And, mind you, nobody cares for your future but me. You have no friends among the people with whom your life has been cast lately. Not one of them would stretch out a hand to save you."

Kate Charlock shook her head sadly. There was no occasion for Rent to tell her that, for she knew it far better than he did. In worldly matters this man was a mere child by the side of her. She glanced at her hands—those long, slim hands which had not done a day's work for the last six years. And Kate Charlock knew her limits. She knew perfectly well that she was not clever, that her mental equipment was slender. She read no literature, beyond the last thing in neurotic fiction. Her education had been quite perfunctory. Save in the direction of the stage, there was no opening for her. And, with all her great talents, a stage career was precarious, if not problematical.

She had nothing except her beauty and the sweet, alluring sadness of her smile. On one point she was resolved: she was never going to share an humble cottage with John Charlock. As she stood there, meek and resigned, with the slow dawning of a smile upon her face, she was reckoning up her chances as avidly as any Cheap Jack at a country fair. She saw the risks. She had a luminous grasp of the situation. Her mental vision was clear and cold as crystal.

She had done with John Charlock—of that there was no question whatever. She would be no slave of his any more, even if she had to live on the dry bread of adversity. There was an end of that. Possibly she might live upon the sale of her fine jewels till she could get a footing on the stage, but that was a slow process even to the cleverest. And here was this chivalrous fool holding the gate open for her to pass, ready to sacrifice his future for the mere shadow of one of her sweet, sad smiles.

Was the game worth the candle? she asked herself. She was regarding the crisis from her point of view alone. She was not giving Arnold Rent as much as a single thought.

It would be slow enough, she knew that perfectly well. Audacious as she was, in her heart of hearts she knew that she would have to bend before the storm and the stress of the chatter which was sure to follow. Even the most liberal members of her own smart set would turn a cold face on her for the time being, though they might wink at her as they passed by.

For the time being! Ah, that was the crucial point of the problem. It would be impossible to stay in England. She would have to go abroad for a time—her means were too limited for England. Rent would be rich—and her husband's heart was weak! Then she would take care that her story was told. She would see that among her friends the sympathy was all for her. Still, that meant there was a long time to wait. In the meanwhile, could she live in fond hope? Once more, was the game worth the candle?

On the other hand, as far as Kate Charlock could see, there was no other game to play. Fate had thrown this chance into her hands and she was not disposed to release it. Besides, Arnold Rent was rich. At any rate, if he were not rich himself, he had a very wealthy mother who idolised him. That mother was going to be a bit of a stumbling-block later, but that was Arnold Rent's affair and did not concern the woman. On the whole, Kate Charlock had made up her mind. But it would never do to throw herself into the arms of this man merely at his bidding.

"I ought to have time to think," she said. "It is cruel to press me in this way, and there is your own future to consider. Do you know that I shall be a millstone round your neck, and that, as soon as the world knows that we have thrown in our lot together, your ambitions will die a natural death?"

"That is how I expected you to speak," Arnold Rent replied. "Always so unselfish and considerate for the feelings of others, always putting yourself in the background! My dear, sweet saint, what are those paltry ambitions of mine compared with my love for you? Who am I that I should set out to reform the world single-handed? Why should not the world know your story, for that matter? I may be obscured for the moment, but when people come to understand I shall rank as high as ever. With you by my side I could do anything. We could set up a creed and programme of our own, based on the broader doctrines of true charity. I little thought when your husband asked me to meet him here to-night— —"

"To meet you here to-night?" Kate Charlock cried. "Do you mean to say that you came here by appointment? Oh, now I begin to see. Now I begin to understand."

She checked herself suddenly. She pressed her handkerchief to her eyes as if overcome with the excess of her emotions. The action filled Rent with deepest and sincerest pity. It was not for him to guess how near the woman had come to betraying herself.

So this had been part of John Charlock's revenge. He had thrown these two deliberately together at the very moment when defenceless beauty must most need champion and defender. A less wise and more honest woman than Kate Charlock would have told this to Rent, heedless of the fact that his own suspicions might have been aroused. But not Kate Charlock.

"I don't quite understand," she murmured. "Why should you have been asked to come here to-night at all?"

"Well, you see, I ventured to expostulate with your husband. I pointed out to him how cruelly his new project would bear upon you. It was not a pleasant interview, I assure you. Finally, he asked me to come here this evening at eight o'clock, when he would give me a practical idea of his decision. I little dreamt then what he meant, but I see it plainly now. The man is a monster in human form, Kate, a cunning scoundrel, who is not worthy to associate with honest men. Do you think he really intended that you and I—— Oh, you know what I mean. I cannot put it into words."

"He gave me the choice of going with him," Mrs. Charlock said bitterly. "That much is in his favour. And I suppose he could not help the fact that his creditor was determined to avail himself of his powers to take everything away. I am trying to think as fairly of my husband as I can. It is probable that he has forgotten about you."

Kate Charlock spoke eagerly. Indeed, she appeared to be sincere in her defence of her husband. If any suspicion rankled in Rent's mind, it had to be laid to sleep at once. But there was no suspicion in the man's mind, nothing but admiration for this woman's spurious single-mindedness and love and truth.

"We will say no more about it," he cried. "Meanwhile, we are wasting time. There is nothing in this desolate place to attract you, no memories to keep you lingering here. And, in any case, it is too late to draw back. Get what things you want and I will go down to the village and procure a conveyance. You are not afraid to be left here alone?"

Kate Charlock smiled reassuringly. There was nothing she desired better than to be left alone for a moment or two. She went almost gaily up to the room where her belongings had been stored. Her heart was light within her as that of a child. The sweet, innocent smile was still upon her face. But the smile was faint and wan when she came down again.

"My jewels are gone," she moaned. "The safe has been forced. No, my husband would not have done that. It was Hortense. The wicked woman! Oh, the wicked woman! But perhaps I had better keep this from Arnold Rent."

CHAPTER X
THE FIRST OF THE FRUIT

The darkness was gathering by the time that Rent came back and Kate Charlock had her property gathered together. She had not packed up many things—just the necessaries for an extravagant woman like herself. The rest could follow later. She trusted to her tact and discretion to make the future smooth. Rent would have been dismayed if he had known how clearly she could read his mind. She had no intention of compromising herself. She was merely going to make use of him. But he need not know that yet. He need not know how perfectly she was able to take care of herself. A deep plot lay at the back of her mind, a means by which she could bring her husband to his knees. This was no senseless, confiding creature putting her future in the hands of a man she had known only for a few months. That she had seen more of him than her husband was aware mattered nothing. She did not fail to note that Rent looked greatly annoyed.

"I have been detained," he explained. "A business matter. I may have to come back to-morrow. But I can take you in the car I have borrowed as far as Portsmouth. Then we can get on to Devonshire as soon as possible, where I want you to stay with my mother. I know she will be glad to help you. That will be the means of stopping all idle gossip."

"How thoughtful you are," Kate Charlock murmured, as the chauffeur disappeared. "I have not burdened myself very much, because I thought that later—but I hardly dare to think of that. If you knew how frightened and terrified I am— —"

The speaker broke off and a little sob came from her throat. It was dark now, and Rent took her in his arms and soothed her with loving words. It was too dark to see the outline of the figure standing by a belt of shrubs facing the door. But on the still air every word and sound carried, so that John Charlock, from his hiding-place, missed nothing. He would have been hard put to say why he had returned. Perhaps his conscience had smitten him. Perhaps it had occurred to him that he was treating his wife with undue severity. But the fact remained that he was back there again, prepared with a new proposition.

For the moment he had forgotten Arnold Rent. The man had never come into his mind again, though, at the time, he had meant to give Rent a sharp lesson on the prudence of minding his own business. He had come back through the shrubbery in time to witness a tender little scene in the porch. A wave of sudden anger passed over him. Then he grew calm and collected. After all, why should he interfere? Why should he come between this heartless woman and her platonic flirtation with this besotted fool—this business man gone mad?

For, man of the world as he was, Charlock had not yet grasped the true inwardness of the situation. That his wife was an actress to her fingertips he had learnt by bitter experience. Doubtless Rent had arrived to keep the appointment and thus these two had come together. Charlock smiled bitterly to himself as his mind dwelt upon the dramatic story which his wife must have had to tell. He could imagine how the woman would play upon the feelings of the man as a master plays upon an instrument. And the setting to the play was worthy of the great actress herself. No doubt Rent had been so moved by the whispered wrongs of this outraged wife that he had placed all he possessed at her disposal. Doubtless he was removing her to the loving custody of some relation who would take care of her for the present. But how far things had gone Charlock did not know. If he had, he might have interfered—and again he might not. It all depended upon his sardonic mood for the moment. He stood there now, erect and motionless, and disposed to watch the thing to the end. Presently the great car jumped forward, and a few moments later the tail lights had vanished down the drive.

"Well, why not?" Charlock murmured. "Unless I am greatly mistaken, Arnold Rent is a long way from being a fool. A little more knowledge of the world, and he is likely to be a force to cope with. Let him find out for himself. Let him learn what I have had to put up with. It will be an education for him. Upon my word, though he little knows it, I am going to prove that young man's greatest benefactor."

Meanwhile, the great car sped on through the darkness, with Kate Charlock and Rent behind and the driver in front. They were very quiet and subdued, for, after the first moments of his mid-summer madness, Rent could not be blind to the seriousness of the step he had taken. And the woman by his side, following his every mood and phase of thought, played up to him like a past mistress in the art of emotions. She laid her head tenderly on his shoulder and sighed, as she nestled up to him.

"You do not regret already?" she whispered.

"Regret?" Rent murmured passionately. "I will never do that. But one does not burn one's boats and mock all the shibboleths without realising the responsibilities that one is casting aside. I do hope that you understand that much, Kate."

Under cover of the darkness, the woman yawned slightly. She was beginning to long now for the life and bustle of the hotel, and, besides, she had not dined as yet, and, like most people who have their feelings well in hand, she was possessed of a healthy appetite. She jumped down briskly from the car as it pulled up at the Royal Solent Hotel, and the hall porter, majestic in his uniform, threw back the heavy plate-glass doors. To Rent's annoyance, the lounge was thronged with people in evening dress. He had forgotten the presence of Royalty in Portsmouth. He had expected to have the hotel pretty much to Kate and himself. It was no far cry to Southampton, and there was the chance of being recognized by somebody who knew one or another of them. Still, sooner or later, the ordeal would have to be encountered and dealt with. The thought had hardly flashed through Rent's mind before a strikingly handsome woman in evening dress rose from the lounge and came towards Kate Charlock. Then, as she caught sight of the man by her side, she appeared to hesitate, and something like a scornful smile swept across her dark features, and she slowly went back to her seat. But, all the same, she continued to stare at Kate Charlock and her companion. Kate grasped Rent's arm.

"Lady Strathmore," she whispered. "I am certain that she recognised us. Did you see how she came down the hall and then turned back? I wish we hadn't come here."

It was the first blow, and the woman staggered under it. She stood there, perplexed and uneasy. In a dim kind of way she comprehended the fact that Arnold Rent was ordering rooms for himself and Mrs. Charlock. It all came to her in a kind of dream. But she roused herself presently as Rent laid his hand upon her arm.

"This way," he said. "Come along."

They passed up the whole length of the lounge, so near to Lady Strathmore that Kate Charlock could have touched her. For the life of her she could not restrain one glance in the direction of the woman in black, and just for a brief moment their eyes met. Lady Strathmore's face was rigid as a mask, and her features had just a tinge of scornful amusement upon them. But there was not the slightest trace of recognition. Then, as the couple passed by, Lady Strathmore turned and whispered something to her companion, and both broke into a rippling laugh. With a feeling of thankfulness, Kate Charlock opened the sitting-room door.

"That is done," Arnold Rent said. He placed his hands on the woman's shoulders and looked down into her eyes. "Never mind, Kate. Always be kind to me, because, for your sake, I have given up my life's ambition to-night."

In a kind of fever, Rent went down the stairs in the direction of the lounge. He was furiously angry now and inclined to be quarrelsome. He would have liked to have it out with the woman who had slighted Kate Charlock. A month ago he would have laughed at his own folly and been scornfully amused at the idea that he should so far forget himself, though he had long had a passionate admiration for Kate. Even now, he was not quite clear what he was going to do. Up to the present he was inclined to play the honourable part. Even now he had only the woman's true interests at heart. Strange that he should have been so foolish. Strange that he should have imagined that his mother would take the same view of the matter as himself. But, then, she had always spoilt him in the past, and, though she was a rigid Puritan, doubtless she would continue to do so in the future.

Rent was shaken out of these thoughts by a hotel servant who approached him with a telegram. The man held out the envelope.

"You are Mr. Rent, sir?" he said. "Pardon me, but I think this must be for you. It is so strange a name."

Rent looked at the envelope in wonderment. No doubt the message was for him, though he was at a loss to know how any friend could have found him out. He opened the message and read:

"Danger here. Come back at once."

"How did they find me?" he murmured. "How did they get on my track? It was thoughtful, at any rate. Still, danger or no danger, I cannot go back."

CHAPTER XI
THE DOCTRINE OF PLATO

Across the breakfast-table Kate Charlock was smiling sweetly, but it was doubtful whether she heard a single word that Rent was saying. She was busy with her own thoughts, which were none of the sweetest. In the first instance she thought that she had counted the cost of her action, but on second thoughts she was not so sure. Still, she was satisfied she could not have complied with John Charlock's order, for it was nothing else. She would have to make the best of it now. She was eager to get away from England until the scandal had blown over. Kate Charlock was by no means devoid of vanity, and Lady Strathmore's studied insolence of the evening before had cut her to the quick. There was the danger of a repetition of this kind of thing so long as she and Rent remained at the Royal Solent Hotel.

But she was not blind to the material side of things. It had been the height of folly to go further without having first made overtures to Arnold's mother. If she should display anything like hostility, then, indeed, Kate might be said to have stepped out of the frying-pan into the fire.

"Oh, you needn't feel worried about that," Rent said, looking up from his paper. "No one ever yet was afraid of my mother. She is gentle and kind-hearted, but if she takes up the cudgels on anybody's behalf she can be amazingly firm. I don't think you need have any anxiety as to my mother."

The shadow of a contemptuous smile flickered across Kate Charlock's face. From her point of view, Rent's description of his mother was not reassuring. It was an outbreak of firmness of this kind that Kate Charlock had most reason to dread. It never occurred to Rent that his mother's firmness might take a wrong direction. Despite his handsome face and intellectual strength, it seemed to Kate that in many respects he was little better than a boy compared with her. The saint-like woman by his side could have acted as school-mistress to him. In her mind's eye she already pictured Mrs. Rent, heart-broken and humiliated at the prospect of the ruin of her son's prospects, and never yet was there mother who regarded her son's wife as in any way worthy of him. While Rent was babbling praises of his mother, Kate sat pondering the magnitude of the task which lay before her. So far she had hesitated to discuss the plan of campaign, but it would have to be done now. The proper thing was to strike while the iron was hot, to go straight to Devonshire and confront Mrs. Rent with the cataclysm before she had time to hear of it from good-natured friends outside.

"Of course, your mother will have to know," she said sweetly and thoughtfully. "I am looking forward to seeing her, and yet I dread the thought of meeting her. You will have to be prepared for a disappointment, Arnold. Your mother is certain to be shocked. She would be less than human if she does not lay all the blame upon my shoulders."

"Never," Rent cried. "I will make it quite clear that the blame is entirely mine. I wrote a long letter to my mother before breakfast, fully explaining everything— —"

"You have not posted it, I hope. No? Well, I am glad of that, because I would prefer that letter not to go. There is only one thing for it—we must travel to Devonshire at once and your mother must receive the first intimation of what has happened from your own lips. Of course, I shall come with you. I am looking forward to the interview with the greatest possible dread, but my duty is clear. Besides, we must get away from here. Can't we go this very afternoon?"

Rent reproached himself for his thoughtless selfishness. He was prepared to do anything that his companion desired. But nothing could be settled before lunch. Most of the people had finished their luncheon, so that the two had the room to themselves. From the long balcony outside came the sound of voices, and Kate Charlock flushed uncomfortably as she recognised Lady Strathmore's tones. She had an uneasy feeling that she was the subject of discussion. A moment or two later Lady Strathmore herself came into the dining-room. She flashed a brilliant smile in Rent's direction, but she seemed to be unaware that he was not alone. A sudden anger possessed Kate Charlock. With audacious passion she came forward and held out her hand.

"You seem to have forgotten me," she said sweetly.

"Absolutely," the other woman murmured. "I am afraid you have a distinct advantage over me, though when I come to look at you again I see you bear a strong likeness to Mrs. John Charlock. But, of course, a dear saint like that would never so far compromise herself as to be lunching here with any man but her husband. Mr. Rent, can I have a few moments' conversation with you?"

The stroke was so swift and merciless, so utterly unexpected, that Kate Charlock had no reply. Overwhelmed and uncomfortable, with the tears smarting in her eyes, she sank into a chair, without the slightest attempt to detain Rent. His face was crimson, too. The corners of his sensitive mouth trembled, but he followed Lady Strathmore politely to the balcony.

"I am going to be candid with you," she said. "Oh, I quite understand how things are. I am a woman of the world and can judge for myself. It is a pity you are not a man of the world, also, or this would never have happened. Can't you see for yourself that you ought not to stay here? Surely you recognised me last night. I am speaking for your own good, because you are a young man whose education in some respects has been sadly neglected. Take my advice——"

"You are mistaken," Rent exclaimed. "And as regards Mrs. Charlock, she is as good and pure as any woman——"

"Oh, I have heard all that before," Lady Strathmore said, with a pitying smile. "You see, I happen to belong to the same set as Mrs. Bromley-Martin, and we are not so shallow-minded and frivolous as you appear to imagine. One side of a story always holds good till the other is told. Don't you think John Charlock has a side to the story as well?"

Rent muttered something incoherent. Recalling to mind now his strange interview with John Charlock, he could not see that the latter had a single claim to consideration. It was useless to discuss that matter with this hard, worldly woman.

"I see that I am wasting your time," Lady Strathmore went on. "Still, I might as well tell you that Mrs. Bromley-Martin and some of her friends are coming to have tea with me this afternoon at four o'clock, and if in the meanwhile you discover that you have important business elsewhere, why—well, good-bye. Wonderfully fresh and bracing atmosphere this morning, don't you think?"

The shrewd woman of the world smiled and went her way. Arnold Rent's thoughts were not pleasing as he returned to the dining-room. Already he was beginning dimly to comprehend the far-reaching effects of his impulsive action, but his heart smote him as he noted the pathetic droop of Kate Charlock's shoulders as she sat toying with her lunch. Lady Strathmore was right. It was necessary to go away at once. It might be possible to reach Devonshire before night, and, on the whole, it would be better to say nothing to Kate about the impending visit of Mrs. Bromley-Martin and her frivolous friends.

"What did she want?" Kate asked wearily.

"Really, I can hardly tell you," Rent stammered. "I don't think she meant to be unkind, though she is a bit hard. The gist of our conversation was that I should get away at once."

Kate Charlock smiled in her sweet, melancholy way, though her heart was hot within her and passionate words trembled on her lips.

"We must try to forgive her," she said gently, "though she was very cruel to me. But she is right about leaving, and the sooner we set out for Devonshire the better. If you will pay the bill, I will go up—what is the matter?"

"Upon my word, I am very sorry," Rent stammered, "but I have only a few shillings in my pocket. In the excitement of yesterday I forgot all about money. Of course, I could telegraph to my solicitors, but even then I could not hear till the morning. Still, I know one or two people here, and I will go out at once and see if I can borrow a few pounds. I sha'n't be long."

She sat there till a waiter came into the room with an envelope in his hand. With some agitation she noticed that the handwriting was that of Rent. She waved the waiter from the room and, in a frenzy of eagerness, tore open the envelope. There were only a few words hurriedly scrawled on the back of a visiting card.

"There is no help for it," the missive ran, "but I must go back to Cowes at once. The business is urgent and admits of no delay. Stay where you are until I return. At the very most I cannot be longer than two hours."

There was passion as well as hate in Kate Charlock's eyes as she tore the card into fragments.

"What does this mean?" she asked. "Can he intend to leave me here? But, no, I cannot possibly believe anything of the kind. And yet, how very awkward!"

CHAPTER XII
A CRIME OR NOT?

It was the day following the dramatic disappearance of Kate Charlock, and once more Tanza and his companion were on board the yacht. The Italian had been away most of the morning, and had only arrived in time for lunch. He appeared to be on excellent terms with himself. There was a merry twinkle in his eye as he contentedly sucked his cigarette.

"You are not going to tell me anything, then?" he asked.

"My dear sir, there isn't anything to tell you," Malcolm Grey replied. "I won't say that I haven't made a discovery or two, because that wouldn't be true. At the same time, I stick to my original idea of keeping what I know to myself. We will both go our own way and see what we can make of it. But I am more or less convinced that your original suggestion is correct, and that there was foul play in the matter of the French maid."

Tanza's eyes sparkled brightly.

"I have never had the slightest doubt of it," he said. "I have an instinct for that kind of thing. I knew that we had to deal with a scoundrel above the common. The whole thing is most fascinating. I suppose you have heard the latest development?" "Indeed, I haven't," Grey said. "Tell me."

"Mrs. Charlock has left her husband. There are a good many versions as to the cause of the quarrel. But, at any rate, she has gone, apparently leaving no trace behind her. I dare say there are faults on both sides; he is a hard man, and she is an extravagant, thoughtless woman. One never knows what a man of the artistic temperament is going to do. It seems that Charlock has disposed of his household goods and has made up his mind to spend the next year or two in a cottage."

"Posing, I presume," Grey said cynically.

"No, I don't think so," Tanza went on. "He is too great a genius to indulge in childish follies. He can afford to leave that kind of thing to the log-rollers. I understand that he has outrun the constable, and that he has every desire to get on terms with the world again. Anyway, his wife wouldn't go with him, and I believe they have separated. As the man is a friend of yours, I thought you might have heard about this."

But Grey shook his head. The information was news to him. He was a little annoyed, too, because there were certain facts which he expected to gather from Charlock. He sat there debating the matter for a short time in his mind, then announced his intention of seeking out Charlock. It was possible the artist had not left the neighbourhood yet, and there was no time to be lost. Tanza raised no objection. He hinted that he had work to do himself and that he could dispense with Grey's company for the rest of the afternoon.

A little time afterwards Grey walked up the drive of Charlock's house. There was nothing in the condition of the grounds to indicate that the place was empty. The lawns had been freshly cut, the flower-beds were trim and neat as usual. It was only the blank, staring windows and the litter of straw on the front door which told the story. As Grey stood there the door opened, and Charlock himself came out. There was a grim, significant smile on his face.

"You are astonished to see this?" he asked.

"Not in the least," Grey said. "I should not be astonished at anything you did. But, if it isn't an impertinent question, why are you acting in this fashion? It seems almost a sacrilege to strip a beautiful place like this. And if you must leave it, why not have let it furnished?"

A cynical laugh broke from Charlock's lips.

"It takes time to let a furnished house," he said, "even a little paradise like this. And the lesson loses nothing of its force because it is administered promptly and speedily. When I bark, I bite. And I don't want to give warning. Ah, you don't know what it is to be mated to an extravagant wife who has no consideration for any one but herself. I should be, at the present moment, a rich man. I have no vices. My personal expenditure is nothing. But I do love to be surrounded by things that are good and beautiful. That is why I spent so much in furnishing this house. I thought I was one of the happiest of men. I thought I was going to lead an ideal existence. But I found I was tied to a woman whose one idea was fashion, who thought nothing of playing at gardening in a Paris frock that cost fifty or sixty pounds. And one day I awoke to the fact that I was on the verge of bankruptcy. Great Scott! how those bills came rolling in! There was only one thing to be done—to act at once. There are no half measures with me. I cut everything adrift. I have taken a labourer's cottage. I told my wife she would have to live there with me and do everything till every farthing was paid. And now she has gone."

Charlock spoke harshly and bitterly. It was rarely, indeed, that he mentioned his own feelings. But the wound was too recent. And there was something in Grey's manner that invited confidence.

"Your wife will think better of it," the latter murmured.

"Will she? Yes, perhaps, when the leopard changes his spots an Ethiopian his skin, but not till then. Oh, everybody will side with h course. Everybody knows that I am hard and harsh and difficult to with. She will pose as an injured woman, and the blame will be r indeed, she has begun to do so already. What do you think of her ma a convert of Arnold Rent? Fancy that cynical man of the world, who w stick at nothing to gratify his ambition, forfeiting his future for the sal my injured wife! That is the idea. He has become her champion. I pres he is going to look after her welfare till I am forced to make her a pr allowance. Probably you will hear of the thing again in the law courts well-known artist and his outraged wife, and all that kind of thing. Wel them take what steps they like; I sha'n't trouble to defend it. And yet bel it all there is a comedy so amusing that I feel inclined to laugh in spit myself. What do you think of my wife's going down to Devonshire to an asylum under the roof of Rent's mother? And what do you think of as an honoured guest in the same house? I am not joking. The thing is in own hands; indeed, it is more or less imperative, especially as I am not busy, and an early commission is essential. There is a situation in a play you! Think what Pinero would make out of it! But why should I bore with these sordid details? They cannot interest you."

Before Grey could make a suitable reply Charlock held out his h and bade his companion a blunt good-day. He turned back to the h and banged the door behind him, as if ashamed at this display of feeli was not often that the strong man cried aloud so that the world might of his hurt. He was furious with himself that he had done so now. seemed to Grey that it would be in bad taste to attempt to follow his and clear up the points which had been the object of his journey.

He walked out of the gates and down the road to the outskirts of t to the newly erected buildings where, until the past day or two, Arn had been conducting a series of experiments in wireless telegra office was close to the shore. One or two workmen were engaged w apparatus the like of which Grey had not seen before. It was onl that he should be interested in what was going on, that he should a moment or two, until the office door opened and a clerk emer some directness of manner, but civilly enough, he asked Grey' The scientist turned to face the man, abnormally thin and tall—a face like faded yellow parchment, lighted by a pair of sombre, s eyes.

"You seem to have forgotten me, Swift," Grey said. "Hav much during the last two years?"

The tall man gasped. His features twitched convulsively for a moment. Then the colour of his face changed. A sullen red tinged the parchment hue, leaving it still more pallid a minute afterwards.

"Mr. Grey," he stammered. "What do you want here?"

There was something embarrassed, almost guilty, in the speaker's manner. Grey smiled as he replied.

"I am interested in all these kinds of things," he said. "But don't think I come here to learn your secrets. As a matter of fact, I called to see Mr. Rent."

"He is away," the tall man explained. "But now a piece of business has turned up and I am telegraphing him in the course of the day. Is there anything I can tell him?"

"I don't think so," Grey said thoughtfully. "Anyway, there is no hurry. And how are you doing? Have you got over the old weakness? For, if so, you are likely to realise the old ambitions, after all. Don't think me impertinent."

"I don't," Swift said indifferently. "I am only human, and I begin to realise that I shall never be able to cope with that accursed thing. Still, I am better than I was, and I am fairly happy here doing congenial work. You see— —"

What Swift was going to say was cut short by the appearance of a third party. He was a slight, dapper man, with prominent features and sleek, glossy hair. His manner was heavily dashed with audacity. He was ludicrously overdressed, and he carried the fact that he was an unregenerate scamp written in every line of his face.

"You are wasting your time," Swift said coldly. "Mr. Rent desires me to say that he does not know you and has no desire to see you. I hope I make myself plain."

"Oh, very well," the stranger said. "In that case, I will wait till Mr. Rent comes back and see him personally. I shall find a way to refresh his memory, and don't you forget it. I don't allow anybody to play the fool with Ephraim Bark."

CHAPTER XIII
MODERN FRIENDSHIP

As Kate Charlock sat debating her position with anxiety, the door opened cautiously and a gaily dressed figure slipped into the room. The place seemed to be half-filled with billowing draperies and the air was heavy with subtle perfume. Kate Charlock turned in amazement upon the intruder.

"Jessica!" she gasped. "What are you doing here?"

"You may well ask that," Mrs. Bromley-Martin tittered. "But a little bird told me what was going on, and when I had a wire from Lady Strathmore this morning asking me to bring a mob over to tea this afternoon, I jumped at the opportunity. My word, what a time we have had all morning pulling your character to pieces! And just now, when Belle Langley bet me a dozen pairs of gloves I dare not come up and interview you, I closed like a shot. Well, what have you to say for yourself?"

From head to foot Kate Charlock quivered with indignation. She was not blind to her own folly, but, then, she had so hedged herself in with self-pity that she did not regard herself as the average woman who has fallen away from grace. Her case was quite different. But she merely smiled as she replied.

"I have nothing to say for myself," she responded. "I am content to leave my character in the hands of those who, like yourself, are acquainted with my unhappy domestic life. My husband chose to turn me out of house and home, and the punishment should be his more than mine. I know that socially my life is finished."

"Terribly sad," Mrs. Bromley-Martin laughed gaily. "I am not going to blame you. You are no worse than two-thirds of us, as you know very well. Besides, we ought to be grateful to you for giving us something fresh to talk about. Still, we shall miss our tall, white saint who was the connecting link between ourselves and absolute respectability. But I must not stay longer. One has to be careful, you know."

"Yes, with a reputation like yours, one has to be," Mrs. Charlock said sweetly. "You may tell your friends that they need not trouble to waste their sympathy upon me. I am quite happy."

Kate Charlock's looks belied her words as Mrs. Bromley-Martin flitted from the room like some great gauze butterfly. She had little enough to be happy about, she told herself; from the bottom of her heart she resented the patronage of her late visitor. At length she was roused from her reverie by the entrance of a servant with a telegram on a tray. It was addressed to Rent, but Kate opened it and glanced carelessly at the contents. Her face did not move a muscle as she turned to the waiter and told him that there was no reply.

Yet the few words were calculated to disturb. They were charged with meaning and called for immediate action. It was clear that the telegram came from Arnold Rent's mother.

"Have just received your letter," the message ran. "Am terribly surprised and shocked. On no account come here, as I am travelling to see you and will call to-morrow afternoon.

"HELEN RENT."

Kate crushed the flimsy paper into a ball and tossed it contemptuously into the fireplace. A moment later and she was reading the words again thoughtfully. Doubtless some enemy had done this thing, and the words brought the reader no sort of comfort. Kate Charlock recognised courage and stern determination of purpose on the part of the sender of the message. Her ready wit saw that it was necessary to strike a counter-blow without delay. It was evident that Mrs. Rent would adopt a firm attitude and could carry out her part far better in the Royal Solent Hotel than under her own roof. She must start for Devonshire instantly as the only possible way of saving the situation.

Would Arnold Rent really return? It was getting on towards five o'clock and he had been gone for two hours. With a sigh of mingled impatience and surprise, she heard him coming along the corridor. He looked uncomfortable.

"Upon my word, I am very sorry," he said, "but, as luck would have it, I have not been able to find a single friend. We must wait till I get money from my solicitors to-morrow morning. The delay is maddening!"

"Meanwhile, what are we to do about this?" Kate asked, as she held out the telegram. "This is from your mother."

"Perhaps it is a good thing," Rent said. "It will save us a journey, at any rate. You must not be annoyed with my mother. It is only natural that she should feel like that, till the case is explained to her. When she has seen us and heard everything she *must* be on our side. We can have dinner here and spend the evening together."

For a moment a gleam of anger came into Kate Charlock's eyes. She felt a wild desire to lay her hand upon Rent, to box his ears, to do anything as an outlet for her rage at his crass stupidity. She schooled herself, though as she stood there her finger nails were cutting into the white flesh of her palms.

"You don't understand," she said. "Your mother may forgive you, but she will never forgive me. If we meet here, there will be an end of everything. But under her own roof she will be bound by the dictates of hospitality to listen to what we have to say. I have been looking out the trains, and if we start within an hour we ought to reach our destination this evening."

"It shall be as you please," Rent said tenderly. "I will go with you now, if you choose. There is one little thing you have forgotten—I have no money, and the railway people won't give credit——"

"Oh, please don't raise these obstacles," Kate Charlock cried wearily. "I suppose you carry a watch?"

"Oh, no, my dear, I never carry one. And if I did, what use would it be to us just now?"

In spite of herself a laugh broke from Kate Charlock's lips. Would this man never improve? She crossed the room to her dressing-case and took out a diamond bangle.

"There!" she said. "You are going to have a new experience. I daresay you will have no difficulty in raising twenty pounds on that. You understand what I mean? I have nothing else to spare."

Arnold Rent inclined his head shamefully.

"Oh, I am speaking of a pawnbroker. There is no need to flush and look uncomfortable, because the thing has to be done, whether you like it or not. And, besides, there is no disgrace in the transaction. The pawnbroker keeps open his shop to do business and is as anxious for your patronage as the butcher or the grocer. Ask the first policeman you meet where you can find a respectable shop, and the rest will be easy."

"My dear girl," Rent said, with a hardening of his lips, "I couldn't do it. We must wait."

Kate Charlock shot one glance at him. Then she laid her head upon the table and burst into a flood of tears. The strategy was successful, for Rent jumped in agitation to his feet and slipped the bangle into his pocket.

"For Heaven's sake, don't cry," he said. "For your sake I will do anything. I had quite forgotten——"

His voice trailed away in an incoherent manner. He grabbed at his hat and left the room. The woman's eyes dried like magic. A smile trembled on her lips. But the anxious feeling did not leave her. Her heart would not lighten till the express train pulled out from the station on its long journey to the West. The fight was coming and Kate Charlock did not mean to fail.

Despite the extent of his infatuation, the pill was none the less a bitter one for Rent to swallow. He was back again at the hotel presently, with the sovereigns jingling as he came in.

"I am glad that is all right," she said. "And now tell me why you behaved so badly just now? Surely you could not have had business of so great importance as to take you away from me in a crisis like this! It is not as if you were engaged in trade. Now tell me what it was. You can trust me."

An ingenious prevarication trembled upon Rent's lips, when the waiter entered the room with a further telegram. Rent glanced at it more or less carelessly, but, though he was conscious his colour changed, he managed to drop the telegram coolly in the fire.

"The business was not my own," he said, "therefore I cannot tell it you. But I am afraid you will have to be patient. That telegram came from the same quarter and admits of no delay. You won't mind very much if I go back to Cowes now and return in the morning?"

Kate Charlock swallowed her passion. She saw that the time had come to act and struck accordingly.

"Very well," she said. "In that case I will go back to my husband. It is not yet too late and I am not ashamed to meet him. It must be one thing or the other."

Rent stifled what sounded like a groan.

"As you like," he said. "I shall not be the first fool beguiled by a woman!"

CHAPTER XIV
BARK IS CONFIDENTIAL

Malcolm Grey stood somewhat uncomfortably outside the little office on the seashore, hardly knowing what to do. In some vague way the features of the person who called himself Ephraim Bark were familiar, though he could not place the man. He would have stayed a little longer, only he seemed to be in the way; it looked, too, as if he were listening to a private conversation. He knew Arnold Rent by reputation and personally. He was aware that the latter had the character of a man about town, not too scrupulous where his passions and fancies were concerned. One or two strange tales had come to Grey's ears, though, at the time, he had paid small heed to them. And here was a man, whom no gentleman would touch without gloves, actually speaking as if he held some power over Rent. No man who did not feel positive of his ground would have spoken in that bullying way, especially as the fellow gave every indication of being a coward if he came to be tackled.

At any other time Grey would have dismissed the incident with a shrug of the shoulders, but he had his own reasons now for learning all he could concerning the past history of Arnold Rent. Therefore he lingered to see what was likely to be the upshot of the interview.

He saw Swift's hands clenched with passion. He saw the desire to strike down the intruder gleaming in his eyes. Then Swift restrained himself, as if suddenly remembering that this was an occasion when diplomacy was wiser than strength.

"It is useless for you to hang about here," Swift said. "Mr. Rent is not in the neighbourhood, and I don't suppose he will be back before morning. You can come and see him if you like, but I should not advise you to do so."

"That's all very well," the aggrieved Bark burst out. "But what am I to do in the meantime? And why should he have everything while I've got nothing? By the time I have had my dinner I sha'n't have a cent to pay my lodgings. Just hand over a sovereign or two to go on with. Do you hear?"

"I hear," Swift said coldly. "I regret that I have no money to spare. And I don't think I should let you have it if I had. Come, clear out, or I'll have to put you off the premises."

For the moment it looked as if the truculent Bark would show fight, but he contented himself with vague threats and innuendoes as he turned on his heel and sauntered away. Grey no longer doubted that the man had a powerful hold on Arnold Rent. He waited a few moments, discussing general matters with Swift; then he, too, strode into the road and followed Bark. There was no occasion to introduce himself to this individual, for, without a moment's hesitation, Bark raised his curly brimmed hat with what he believed to be refined and courtly politeness. Grey pulled up at once.

"You'll excuse me, Mr. Grey," Bark said effusively, "but I hope you won't mind doing me a little favour?"

"You know my name, then?" Grey said. "I ought to recognise you, but my memory plays me false."

A look of deep cunning came into Bark's eyes.

"You can't know me, sir," he said, "considering that most of my life has been passed in Paris. But I know you by sight and reputation, because I am by way of being a bit of a scientist myself. I came down to see Mr. Rent, and this is how they treat me! And to think of what I've done for that man, to think of what I know about him! Why, I have only to raise my little finger and say the word, and before a day passed our friend——"

A judicious fit of coughing put an end to further revelations on the part of Bark. He seemed to realise that he was going too far and instantly changed his tone. But this did not deceive Grey.

"Ah!" said Bark, "I am talking too fast, as usual. You might think by my tone that I was threatening Mr. Rent. As a matter of fact, I am only disappointed at his carelessness. But it is very awkward for me. Here am I with only a few shillings in my pocket, which would have been fifty pounds if I had seen Mr. Rent. Now, will you be offended if I ask you for the loan of a fiver for two or three days?"

Grey hesitated for a moment. Would the expenditure be justified? Then, by inspiration, it occurred to him that perhaps Tanza might know this plausible scamp. Certainly it might be worth while to temporise.

"I am sorry," he said, "but I have very little money in my pocket. I can let you have ten shillings, if you like."

Bark audibly expressed his disappointment.

"Well, perhaps I can do better than that," Grey, said, with a smile. "Let me give you the ten shillings to go on with, and if you will be on the landing-stage to-night at nine o'clock I will meet you and give you the balance of the five pounds. I suppose that will be convenient?"

Bark's eyes gleamed with a greedy light.

"Spoken like a man and a brother," he cried. "Now, there's a pal for you! There's a friend in need when a poor chap is down on his luck through no fault of his own! Mr. Grey, you're a gentleman. And it is evident you know another gentleman when you see him."

"I hope so," Grey said drily.

"That being so," said Bark, ignoring the sarcasm, "I will be on the landing-stage at nine o'clock. Thank you very much. In my hard-up state even the half-sovereign is acceptable. You will excuse me if I leave you, as I have an appointment to keep, a business matter involving thousands."

So saying, Bark, with another flourish of his hat, swaggered off down the street. Grey smiled to himself as he saw the flashy little adventurer turn into a public-house. Then, in a thoughtful frame of mind, he went back to the yacht in search of Tanza, whom he found sprawling in a deck chair, deeply engrossed in his eternal cigarettes and reading a French novel.

"What news?" the Italian asked gaily. "I see you have had an interesting morning by the expression of your face. At any rate, your conversation will be more engrossing than this book. Now unbosom yourself."

"There isn't much to tell you at present," said Grey. "I have been following up my investigations and have ascertained one or two important pieces of information. I rather wanted to see Rent, but he is away. I went down to his place, where I found an old friend of ours in the person of John Swift."

"Oh, indeed!" Tanza exclaimed, lifting his eyebrows. "Now that is a man who was made to adorn anything he touched. If he could only keep away from the infernal drink he might now have been one of our leading scientists. What is he doing in these parts?"

"Acting as assistant to Rent," Grey explained. "But that isn't what I wanted to talk to you about. I don't mind telling you I have got hold of a most important clue, and as all roads are said to lead to Rome, so everybody I am meeting at present seems to be more or less mixed up with the matter I have in hand. While I was talking to Swift a man turned up and demanded to see Arnold Rent. He was very disappointed to find that Rent wasn't at home and was at no pains to disguise his feelings. His manner had a suggestion of blackmail about it. Also he seemed to be pretty sure of his ground. I don't suppose I should have given the fellow another thought had I not felt sure I had seen him somewhere. And I thought perhaps that you, with your amazing acquaintance with all sorts and conditions of scoundrels, might know something about him."

"Have you managed to learn his name?" Tanza asked.

"Well, yes, I did, if he doesn't happen to be passing under some *alias*. He is called Ephraim Bark. Rather a curious sort of name, isn't it?"

"I know him quite well," he said. "That is his name. At any rate, I never heard him called anything else. He is a most plausible and ingenious rascal, and I should very much like to meet him again. I suppose you have his address; if so, we will seek him out and entertain him after dinner."

Grey explained exactly what course he had adopted, and Tanza was pleased to signify his approval. So it came about that shortly after nine o'clock the two proceeded to the landing-stage. There they found Bark arrayed in a somewhat resplendent evening dress, the effect of which, however, was slightly marred by the fact that the linen was exceedingly dingy. But he carried it all off with a truculent air. Obviously he had spent a good deal of the half-sovereign in liquid refreshment, and was in a condition which in a less seasoned drinker might have been called an advanced stage of intoxication.

"Well, Bark," Tanza said cheerfully. "So we have met again. No, you needn't trouble to express your gratification. You are coming on board my yacht with Mr. Grey to give us certain information we are in need of."

"Lumme, yes," Bark said, with some emotion. "I'll tell you anything. I couldn't refuse an old friend."

CHAPTER XV
ILL TIDINGS

In its modest way, Alton Lee, which stands upon the South Devonshire coast, was quite a show place. There the Rents had held their sway for the best part of three centuries, since the founder of the family first came West and built the old house, which his successors had altered out of all recognition. The history of the family had been fairly uneventful. They had married with their neighbours, and more than one heiress had come along to swell their fortunes. For the most part they had been people of moderate ideas, clean-living, healthy-minded men and women, not endowed with too much intellect, and perfectly contented with their lot. At present the Rents were represented by Arnold himself and his mother, an elderly lady, who was exceedingly popular with all who knew her.

Ever since Arnold Rent had left school his mother had been more or less afraid of him. That she was passionately devoted to her only son goes without saying; but she herself had been brought up in the simple, narrow way. She had an almost morbid horror of anything that was in the least unconventional and a mighty regard for her neighbours.

And her boy was totally different in every respect. The knowledge that he had an inclination for work had filled her with tranquil happiness and a sense of security, which, however, was not destined to last. There being several livings in the family gift, there had been no reason why Arnold Rent should not settle down to the career of a country parson. But from the first he had other plans which in Mrs. Rent's opinion were almost revolutionary. The limited field did not appeal to a man of his views and restless energy, and with many misgivings his mother had seen him start an entirely different career of his own choosing in London. That he was squandering money on this did not matter. The past three or four generations of Rents had not spent anything like half their income, so there was money enough and to spare. There was no anxiety on that score.

From time to time Mrs. Rent had reports of her son's progress. She was convinced that knighthood was within his grasp if he could only control some of his advanced ideas and bow to the voice of authority. At any rate he was strong and good and in earnest. On the whole, it seemed to Mrs. Rent that Providence had been more than kind to her.

She was in the garden now busy among her roses. The rose gardens at Alton Lee were famous. Even in that well-favoured spot there was nothing like them. And the lady of the house fitted well in with the picture. She walked with a slight stoop; one long, slender hand was closed upon an ebony crutch-stick; her delicate features were half hidden by a large, shady hat. For the rest, her hair was grey and abundant, and her blue eyes beamed with a kindly expression. She was the embodiment of an elderly lady of the old school, which is fast becoming extinct. With all beneath her she had the widest sympathy. No tale of distress found her unmoved, but she had undemonstrative pride, for all that. There were people in the neighbourhood who said that Mrs. Rent was haughty and distant, but most of these were newcomers whose money had been derived from trade. As to the wealthy financiers who play so prominent a part in Society to-day, not one of them would have been permitted to cross the threshold of Alton Lee, though Mrs. Rent was always pleased to see the little curate's wife to dinner.

She cut the last of a basketful of large, dark, red-hearted roses and dropped into a garden seat with a sigh of placid satisfaction. It was a perfect afternoon, with just the suspicion of a breeze rustling the great oaks in the park. Across the middle distance a herd of deer moved slowly and gracefully. Away to the west the blue sea lay placid in the sunshine. From one of the side paths a girl came along, carrying a huge mass of sprays of maidenhair fern in her hand. She was not particularly tall or strikingly beautiful, but there was a rare attraction about Ethel Margrave's face that grew upon one the more her features were studied. But the eyes of deep blue were the chief attraction. No one ever failed to notice these liquid azure lakes which drew to her every man and woman of her acquaintance. She came gaily along and dropped into the seat by Mrs. Rent's side.

"My dear auntie, how busy you have been!" she exclaimed. "I thought I should have been in time to cut at least half those roses for you; but I suppose I stayed too long in the greenhouses admiring the orchids. I won't get the drawing-room flowers done before tea-time, at this rate."

Mrs. Rent smiled indulgently at the speaker. Next to her son, there was nobody in the world whom she loved as deeply and sincerely as her niece, Ethel Hargrave. If she had one wish left ungratified, it was that Arnold and Ethel might some day be master and mistress of the old house. The dream had gradually deepened till it had become almost a passion, but it looked now as if the elderly lady was going to be disappointed. Perhaps the young people had been too much together to fall in love with one another. At any rate, Arnold Rent had always looked upon Ethel as a sister. And there was something in Mrs. Rent's disappointment that had a touch of pain in it. Those kindly blue eyes could look keenly enough at human nature sometimes, and

Mrs. Rent had more than a suspicion that Ethel cared deeply for her son. There were moments when this knowledge filled her with anxiety.

"Let us sit here and talk a little longer," she said. "There will be plenty of time for your drawing-room flowers. Did I tell you that I had a letter from your father this morning? He hopes that he will be able to get away from Australia for a long holiday at the beginning of next year. What a long time it is since you saw him! And what a pity it is that you photograph so badly! I have been thinking it over lately and I am going to give my brother a surprise. I have been in communication with one of the most famous artists of the day, and he is coming here to paint your portrait."

"What a distinguished honour!" the girl laughed. "My dear, you are making quite a Society woman of me. Will the picture be exhibited in next year's Academy and be reproduced in the ladies' papers? Really, I ought to be quite angry with you for such extravagance."

"Oh, I am glad to find you don't mind," Mrs. Rent replied. "Besides, I want a proper picture of you myself. We were only talking about it the last time Arnold was here. By the way, have you heard from him lately?"

The girl flushed at the mention of Rent's name.

"Oh, dear, no," she said. "Arnold is much too busy to trouble about a simple country girl like myself. The last time I heard from him his letter was one of tirade and abuse of the doings of Society. I understood he was moving in it himself, so that he would be able to speak from personal knowledge. Do you know, my dear aunt, I wish Arnold wouldn't be so dreadfully serious. One feels a poor creature by comparison. I should like to see him do something foolish. You know what I mean."

"Oh, I think I do," Mrs. Rent smiled. "It would be nice if he made a mistake or two and came down here for us to sympathise with him. But one never feels sure of Arnold. I expect to hear every day that he has gone over to the Rationalists, or taken monastic vows, or some equally dreadful thing. But you may be sure that Arnold would never do anything to make one blush for him."

The mother spoke with a serene pride that brought an answering smile to Ethel's face. Attached as she was to Arnold Rent, she would have preferred him to be a little more human. Like most girls who live a good deal alone, she had her imaginative moods, and was fond of picturing Arnold as wounded in a conflict and coming home for her support and sympathy. She dismissed the mental picture now with a sigh of impatience. There was not the least likelihood of Arnold stepping from the straight path. He would go to high honours in the world. He would marry some noble woman of great intellectual attainments to help him in his work.

"I think we spoil him," she said. "However, it is no use talking about it. But, surely, my eyes don't deceive me. That must be Mr. Westlake coming down the drive. What brings him here? Something dreadful must have happened to induce him to leave his beloved London."

Mrs. Rent rose with a sudden feeling of approaching trouble. It was rare, indeed, for the old family solicitor to come to Devonshire, especially without warning. The elderly man approached the garden-seat and raised his hat. Nothing could be gathered from his austere features except a trace of anxiety on his brow. He murmured something in reply to Mrs. Rent's question, then glanced significantly at Ethel.

"Very well," the girl said. "I see you have come on affairs of state, so I'll run away and finish my flowers. Don't forget that it is very nearly tea-time."

CHAPTER XVI
THE HONOUR OF THE FAMILY

Arnold Rent's mother waited for the lawyer to speak. She scented trouble.

"And now, my dear old friend, what is it?" Mrs. Rent said quietly. "I see you are in great anxiety about something. I suppose it has to do with money. But, in any case, I am sure you are in no way to blame."

"It has nothing to do with money at all," Mr. Westlake replied. "From that point of view, things were never better. Before I go any further, have you had any news of your son lately? Have you heard this morning? I thought, perhaps, possibly— —"

"Arnold!" Mrs. Rent exclaimed. "Something has happened to him! You are keeping me in suspense."

"Indeed, I am not," Westlake protested. "So far as I know, there is nothing wrong with your son, who was perfectly well last night. But it is to consult you about Arnold that I have hurried here to-day. I learnt something yesterday and immediately went out to Southampton last night, where my worst suspicions were confirmed. It struck me as strange that a young man in his position should be telegraphing for money, and I heard one or two rumours in the early part of the week. You must not be too hard upon the boy, because one never knows what temptations unscrupulous women put in the way of impressionable men. And, if I may be allowed to say it, in worldly matters Arnold is a little lax."

All the colour left Mrs. Rent's cheeks. She sat for a moment with her hand pressed to her heart. Then her dignity and courage came back to her. Her voice was tranquil as she spoke.

"Perhaps you had better begin at the beginning, my dear friend," she said. "A mother is always anxious about her child. She has gloomy moments when she fears the worst. I won't say that Arnold has never given me any anxiety, because that would not be true, but I never dreamt he would so far forget himself as to tarnish his good name and honour. Do you mean to say that he allowed himself to get entangled?"

"That would be hardly fair," Westlake said, with lawyer-like caution. "I am told that the lady is exceedingly beautiful and that she has been very unhappy in her married life. She has been described to me as a sweet saint, a kind of Madonna—just the sort of creature who would be likely to appeal to a chivalrous, romantic man like your son. I believe that the husband turned his wife out of the house, or that he sold the house over her head, which comes to much the same thing. Unfortunately, Arnold appeared on the scene at that very moment, and that is how the trouble began. At any rate, the mischief is done and nothing we can say can alter it. The worst feature is that Arnold's career is seriously checked. He will have to delay matters. He will have to abandon his experiments till this fancy is forgotten. No one would listen to a man who had been god in the car to another man's wife. Of course, this sounds very cruel, but, then, you are always so rational and reasonable that I can speak to you the more freely. Believe me, I would have given half I possess if I could have saved the situation before it was too late."

"I know it," Mrs. Rent said quietly. "My dear Richard Westlake, this is a bitter blow to me. As yet I can hardly realise it. He must have been mad. He must have been carried away by impulsive good-heartedness. But we are wasting time. I must see Arnold. I suppose I shall even have to see the woman. I shall have to sit down in the same room with her."

"That is the point I was coming to," Westlake said, almost eagerly. "I want to prevent those misguided people from coming here. That must be avoided at any cost."

"Here!" Mrs. Rent murmured. "Do you mean to say that that woman would have the audacity to come to Alton Lee?"

"I think you will find that that will be the programme," Westlake said shrewdly. "Unless I am mistaken, Mrs. Charlock will pose as a martyr, driven to despair by the brutality of a cruel husband. If she gets a footing here the whitewashing process will be half complete. It will be held that she has the support and sympathy of so great a lady as Mrs. Rent. And even if the other man takes proceedings, as he is sure to do, half the people who read the case will come to the conclusion that Mrs. Charlock is an injured woman. She may be a saint, of course. But that is not a synonym for a fool."

Mrs. Rent looked despairingly across the park. She was beginning to appreciate the full force of the disaster. Her pride was in arms. The strong side of her character began to show uppermost, and there was a depth and force in her moral nature that few people dreamt of. Her duty was plain. If it wounded her to the heart, she must do that which was right and proper.

"I begin to see my way," she said quietly. "I will go and see my unhappy boy and this woman. I will go up with you to-day. It may be that there are extenuating circumstances. Indeed, I shall only be too glad to be able to take a lenient view of this disgraceful affair. But if you will give me Arnold's address I will telegraph to him that on no account is he to come here. It would be an outrage."

"To tell the truth," Westlake confessed, "I have already taken the liberty of sending a telegram in your name. I did it directly I got the news. You see, there was no time to be lost, and they might already be on their way."

"Quite right," Mrs. Rent murmured. "By the way, what did you say was the name of this woman? It sounded familiar."

"Charlock," Westlake explained. "I believe her husband is an artist, or something of that kind."

"I wonder if he is any relation to *the* Charlock?" Mrs. Rent mused. "I have been in correspondence with him. But I suppose that is out of the question, especially as there are two or three Charlocks who are artists."

Westlake glanced at the speaker. She was taking the blow with far greater resignation and courage than he had expected. The colour had crept back into her cheeks. Her face was strong and resolute. Come what might, she would do the right and proper thing; she would vindicate the honour of the family. She rose now and suggested that it was time for tea.

"It seems strange to mention the meal," she said, "but I suppose the world will go on the same, even though this black disgrace has fallen on the family. But fancy having to tell Ethel! My heart sinks at the mere thought of it. And the servants, too, every one of whom was born on the estate. But the thing will have to be done, bitterly as one resents it. Everybody must know. There shall be no attempt at deceit or prevarication. As soon as we have had tea you had better decide to take a stroll in the garden and smoke a cigar. I shall not be able to rest till Ethel knows the story. Now give me your arm."

In silence they passed between the rose-bushes, across the velvet lawns to the drawing-room. The light was subdued, and Mrs. Rent was grateful for it. She had no desire to be under the scrutiny of Ethel's keen eyes. The girl came forward from behind a bank of roses and fern. Something suggested suppressed excitement in her manner.

"Well, are all the secrets told?" she asked gaily. "Or has Mr. Westlake got a surprise in store for us? But, whether he has or not, I have a surprise for you. You know you were talking just now of a famous artist who was to paint my portrait. What would you say if I told you that Mr. John Charlock is in the library at the present moment?"

Something like a groan escaped Westlake's lips.

"The husband," he murmured. "The husband, for a million. Now, what on earth is the fellow doing here?"

There was a startled expression on Mrs. Rent's face.

"This had not occurred to me," she murmured. "Strange that I had failed to notice it. Fancy a thing like this happening in so quiet and respectable a house as Alton Lee! It reminds one of those dreadful plays where extraordinary events take place in the most unexpected quarters. Who could have foreseen the elements of such a drama four-and-twenty hours ago? I should have said this would be the last house in the world to entertain anything like this. But perhaps the misfortune will prove to be a blessing in disguise. Don't you think we might settle matters, now that Mr. Charlock is here, in such a way that there shall be no scandal? I cannot possibly believe that my son is— —"

"An ordinary human being," Westlake said cynically. "My dear madam, when a young man comes in contact with a beautiful woman who is cold-blooded and playing entirely for her own hand, nobody knows what will take place. Believe me, this is not the time for weakness or compromise. It may be that your son is acting from the highest possible motives. It may be that his soul is full of chivalry and all that kind of thing. Nevertheless, I should like to hear what you have to suggest."

Mrs. Rent pondered the matter for a moment.

"Cannot you think of anything?" she asked timidly. "Oh, I don't know how to act. I can't think what to do for the best. And yet it seems as if this were a direct intervention of Providence. On the other hand, you may say that it would be far better if Mr. Charlock left the house without delay."

CHAPTER XVII
"LOVE ME, LOVE MY DOG"

Ethel Hargrave turned with a startled expression on her face.

"What do you mean?" she asked. "Is there anything wrong, aunt? You both look as though something dreadful had happened."

"Never mind that for a moment," Westlake interrupted. "It so happens that I am particularly interested in this Mr. Charlock. Tell me, what is the gentleman like?"

"I like him," Ethel went on, "though he does remind one strongly of a bulldog. He has a tenacious, fighting face. But I always was fond of bulldogs. They are such gentle, faithful creatures when you come to understand them."

"You have been talking to him," Mrs. Rent murmured.

"Oh, dear, yes. We had quite a long conversation. Our introduction was as unconventional as the most bohemian could have wished. Mr. Charlock came up the drive carrying a poor little terrier in his arms. I fancy the dog had been run over, for it was bleeding from a wound in the side, and making a horrid mess of Mr. Charlock's grey flannel suit, which fact I ventured to point out to him. He didn't even take the trouble to reply. He was too busy with the dog. I suppose this incident impressed me favourably. Only a really kind-hearted man would have taken all that trouble about a toy-terrier."

Mrs. Rent and Westlake did not appear to be listening. The solicitor turned to his hostess and elevated his eyebrows.

"This is certain to be the same man," he said. "The circumstance is so extraordinary that it could not be anybody else. I think there is one thing we can count upon—he has not come to make any disturbance. I should not be surprised to find him utterly ignorant of any relations between that lady and your son. It is unfortunate that he should be here at this moment, but it can't be helped. Don't you think it would be as well if I saw him and explained matters?"

"Perhaps you had better," Mrs. Rent murmured. "Naturally, I have a certain amount of sympathy for Mr. Charlock, and I agree with you that he has only come here to talk over Ethel's portrait. If you will be so good as to see him——"

"What is all this mystery?" Ethel demanded. "Why am I being kept in the dark? Not but what I shall know sooner or later, because dear Aunt Helen is one of the most transparent women in the world. It would be impossible for her to keep a secret for more than a day."

Westlake turned to Mrs. Rent.

"You had better tell her," he said. "Meanwhile, I'll go and see what I can do with the artist."

Westlake's tone was so grave that the smile faded from Ethel's cheeks. She placed an arm around her aunt's neck and kissed the white cheek tenderly.

"I know you are in some trouble," she murmured. "Tell me what it is. You have lost all your money?"

"Not a penny," Mrs. Rent replied. "A money loss would be nothing to the trouble I am suffering now. It is difficult to tell you the truth, but it will have to be told. You know how proud I have always been of Arnold. You know how I have boasted that the boy could do nothing wrong. Well, he has disgraced us. There is no other word for it. He has forgotten his duty to God and to himself. He has deliberately broken one of the Commandments."

Ethel's face grew as pale and colourless as that of her companion.

"Do not be afraid to speak," she murmured. "Try to forget that I am not a child. What has Arnold done?"

"There was a woman," Mrs. Rent said incoherently. "She was a married woman, which makes matters worse. And now she has left her husband ... with Arnold. I could not say more if I sat here all night. Of course, one could find excuses for the boy. One could argue that he has acted in this mad fashion from chivalrous motives. But the sorry truth remains that these two have gone off together, and that scandal is bound to follow. Of all the paths of dishonour that my boy might have trodden, I cannot think of one more discreditable than this. Don't press me to say more. Don't ask me for details, for I have none to give you. Mr. Westlake came here at once to break the trouble to me, and I have no doubt that I shall have a long letter from Arnold in the morning."

"What are you going to do?" Ethel asked. She could think of nothing else to say. "You will see him, of course."

"I don't know. I am not sure. I have been a fond and loving mother to Arnold, and I have striven to do my duty by him, but, also, I owe a duty to society. And everything that I possess is at my discretion. If I like to say the word, Arnold will rise to-morrow without a penny. I have not said much, because I hardly realise the magnitude of this disaster. Shame and disgrace like this must not be allowed to go unpunished. I don't wish to be too hard upon anybody, but I cannot believe that that woman would have thrown in her lot with my son unless she had known he had great expectations."

"I see what you mean," Ethel said. "You are going to take a firm stand. But why not wait? Why assume that there is anything really wrong? It is not just to Arnold. You do not mean to disown him?"

"Oh, no, no," Mrs. Rent cried. "I could not do that. That might be the means of sending a poor, unhappy creature headlong to her ruin. We may find Mr. Charlock——"

"Mr. Charlock!" Ethel exclaimed. "Do you mean to say——"

"I am afraid so," Mrs. Rent went on. "I am afraid that the cruel irony of fate has brought the poor gentleman into this house at the most inopportune time. It may be mere coincidence, but that is almost too much to hope for. What was I saying? Oh, yes. You see, when the law gives Mr. Charlock his freedom, it will be a point of honour on Arnold's part to marry this woman. Common humanity will prevent me from interfering. Common decency would compel Arnold to take that step. And do you suppose that that wicked creature would care much, so long as she had money to spend? She would make Arnold take her on the continent. She would drag him down to her own level. The best years of his life would be wasted. But if I say that they must go their own way, without assistance from me, Arnold may pull himself together and live down his disgrace. Don't you see, I wish to find out what this woman is made of? Perhaps Mr. Charlock may be a wretch, and have driven his wife in sheer desperation to take this step."

"I don't believe it," Ethel said firmly. "I don't believe that a man who would take so much trouble over a stray dog could be guilty of unkindness. There is something about his face that I like. But I interrupt you."

"What was I saying? Oh, I want to test the woman. I want to see if she will remain true to the man whose life she has spoilt in the face of adversity. If so, then in the future she has little to fear from me. Meanwhile, I have made up my mind. I will stop Arnold's allowance. He will not receive another penny from me. He is strong and brave and clever. He is equipped for the earning of his own living. All this I will tell him when we meet to-morrow. It will be something for him to find out that I have a side to my character which he has not dreamt of. You may not think that I am right. You may say that I am hard and cruel——"

"You could never be that," Ethel murmured. "I am very fond of Arnold, and this has been a terrible blow to me, not the least so because it has wounded my pride. But I don't want to talk about myself. I am certain you are right, and that, in the circumstances, you could not do anything else. But you will let me go with you to-morrow. I know that Mr. Westlake will accompany you, but a man is so useless in times like these. Besides, I have a desire to see the woman who has come in and wrecked our paradise. I want to judge her for myself."

"That is out of the question," Mrs. Rent decided. "But here is Mr. Westlake."

Westlake came slowly into the room. He could see that Mrs. Rent had told Ethel everything, and that, therefore, he could speak freely.

"It is just as I thought," he said. "This is the husband of the woman who has infatuated your boy. As you may imagine, Mr. Charlock feels the situation acutely. Of course, it occurred to him that you were the mother of Arnold Rent, but he himself is here on business. He says that you invited him to come at the first favourable opportunity, offering your hospitality, which a day or two ago he thankfully accepted. In his letter he fixed to-day, and said he should be here at the time mentioned, unless he heard from you to the contrary. Taking your silence for consent, he came. And, mind you, till I told him a few minutes ago, he had not the faintest idea of this madness between Arnold and his wife. I should like to save you as much pain as possible, but you must see him."

CHAPTER XVIII
CUPBOARD LOVE

Charlock's wife was easier in her mind. When the start was made she could see her way clearly. The long journey was coming to an end at length and the period of inaction was nearly over. Kate Charlock sat in her seat, her eyes half-closed, smiling serenely. Arnold Rent thought he had never seen her smile like that before. It seemed to him that he was one of the most fortunate of men. Hitherto, it had never occurred to him to ask himself a question. He had not paused to debate whether this woman loved him or not. Perhaps he was afraid to face his own vanity. He had made the suggestion on the spur of the moment, carried away by a spontaneous outburst of love and passion, and Kate Charlock had responded without a struggle.

Yet he could not doubt her. It was impossible to doubt her. No woman with a face and smile like that could have done other than follow the dictates of her heart. She had placed herself in his hands, and so long as he had health and strength she should never repent it. No woman had ever been loved before as he loved Kate Charlock.

And she, on the other hand, sat there with beautiful lines of resignation on her face, looking the embodiment of all that was good, and pure, and holy. She seemed to be raised above the level of the common earth. And yet she, too, was thinking as she surveyed Rent under the long fringe of her eyelashes.

He was a nice-looking fellow, she told herself. She regarded him with a certain amount of good-natured contempt. No doubt he would make a man in time, but he would have many lessons to learn first. He would be easy to manage, too, despite his square chin and the resolute lines of his mouth. He would not be surly and self-contained, like John Charlock. On the whole, Kate saw a pleasant prospect before her after the scandal was forgotten and things resumed their normal footing. She knew exactly what the process would be. For a year or so they would be studiously avoided by even the most frivolous of her friends. Then people would languidly inquire whether or not there had been some scandal in the past, and after that others, bolder than the rest, would be calling on Mrs. Arnold Rent. They would come fast enough, provided there were good dinners and entertainments worth sharing, and Arnold Rent would have to provide all those things. It was all very well to talk largely of living in a quiet, frugal way and giving nine-tenths of his income to the poor, but Kate Charlock would see to all that. It was the man's obvious duty to make things smooth for her and pave the way into the pale of Society again. It didn't matter much about the man, for in these matters the man never suffers. It is always the woman who pays.

The prospect was alluring, and accounted for the heavenly smile which Arnold Rent was studying so rapturously. And yet behind it all was a fear that Mrs. Rent might step down from her high place and shatter the fond illusion. Arnold Rent might say that his mother idolised him. It was easy to prophesy that she would come forward and welcome the fugitive with open arms. The elderly lady might be all that her son claimed for her, but she was proud and prejudiced, and had all the conventions of her class. What if she were to put her foot down firmly? What if she refused to see them? The telegram she had sent to her son did not indicate a conciliatory spirit. Still, if once the threshold were crossed, it would not be easy to dislodge the culprits, and Arnold Rent as yet had not seen anything but the mere fringe of the artifices which his companion had at her fingertips. She turned to him presently, a little tired of her gloomy thoughts.

"What is your house like, Arnold?" she asked.

Arnold Rent's face lighted up with pleasure.

"Oh, Alton Lee is a beautiful place," he said. "I don't know what kind of architecture you call it, for it has been built from time to time, as occasion required. Now it is one mass of ivy and creeping plants. To my mind, it is the most beautiful place in Devonshire. It is so restful and peaceful, and I don't believe there are any roses like ours in the world. I suppose, too, there is not a finer collection of antique furniture in the South of England. I have known my grandfather entertain a hundred visitors without the slightest inconvenience."

"How charming," Kate Charlock murmured. "But that kind of thing is very extravagant. I suppose that is why so many of our great families have become so poor."

The speaker uttered the words thoughtfully, as she gazed dreamily out of the carriage window. Rent did not notice what lay behind the simple speech.

"Oh, we are by no means poor," he said. "I don't suppose the Rents have been more mercenary than other people, but it so happens that most of them married money. Our tastes have been fairly simple, too, and we have been very lucky in our advisers. The last time I saw our solicitor, Mr. Westlake, he told me that I should some day have the control of an estate worth nearly a million."

Kate Charlock smiled and murmured something to the effect that money was not everything. Nevertheless, the statement filled her with the keenest pleasure. In her mind's eye, she could see the stately house rising above the sea. Already she was beginning to rearrange the various rooms with their priceless furniture. She saw herself a popular hostess, eagerly sought after and invited everywhere. Arnold Rent was placing his future in her hands now, but it was only like casting his bread on the waters, and the thing would be worth a struggle. It would be glorious to live the scandal down and force the people who regarded her coldly at first to come cringing for an invitation to Alton Lee. For the moment Kate Charlock thought she was genuinely in love with the man opposite. Truly, fortune was favouring her. She was getting her recompense for the five dreary years which she had endured under the roof of John Charlock.

She was quite convinced of the fact, too, that the blame was wholly Charlock's. It *must* be so, since all her friends had said so. She looked back now to the past five years with complacent pride and soothing self-satisfaction. But all that was going to be altered. Before two years had passed there would be no more charming or popular hostess in England than Mrs. Arnold Rent of Alton Lee. If only Arnold's mother——

Ah, there was the trouble. With a subtle instinct all her own, Kate Charlock made no attempt to blind the issue. It was from this quarter the trouble was coming. She felt certain of it. She closed her eyes and feigned sleep. She was getting a trifle tired of the sound of Arnold Rent's voice. She wished he were a little less boyish, a little less certain of his ground. Then, for a while, she sank into oblivion, sitting up with a start when the train stopped at a small station.

"We are here," Rent explained. "It is only a short way to the house, and I will take you a near cut through the grounds. Let us slip away before the station-master comes fussing along."

It was not dark yet. The air was full of the smell of flowers. The peaceful silence was restful and soothing. But Kate Charlock was not thinking about that. Her mind was possessed with the reflection that all this was her companion's property, and that very soon she would be mistress. She had no keen eye for the beauties of the country, but even she was moved to admiration as the path sloped upwards and the great sylvan landscape began to unfold itself. She saw the wide stretch of the park, where the deer were moving like phantoms in the dusk. She noted the outline of the grand old house beyond. For the moment she was touched and thrilled. It was not the first time she found herself in one of the stately English homes. She had always envied the lot of folk who were blessed in this way, and soon she would actually have one of her own.

"Is it not perfect?" Rent said, with a thrill in his voice. "Are you surprised that I should love the place as I do? The time will come when you will be just as fond of Alton Lee as I am myself. Isn't it a paradise?"

"It is, indeed," Kate Charlock said rapturously. "But do not let us think so much of our own happiness when there are others to consider. I am more concerned for your poor mother than anyone else. Do you know, I should be almost thankful if you made up your mind to turn back, even at this moment. Oh, Arnold, do you think that your mother will allow me to stay?"

Arnold Rent smiled convincingly.

"I have no doubt about it," he said. "Of course, I don't disguise the fact that this will be a terrible shock to my poor mother, but, you will see, she will make the best of it, especially when she comes to hear your story. I am going to leave you here till I can make you my wife. That is one of the ways by which we can stifle the breath of scandal. And when you become a member of this household— —"

Kate Charlock quickened her footsteps. Something like a chill passed over her for a moment.

"Come along and let us get it over," she said. "The suspense is more than I can bear. And if your mother fails me in this dreadful crisis, why— —"

CHAPTER XIX
UNBIDDEN GUESTS

Meanwhile, Mrs. Rent was with Charlock in the library. She saw before her a tall, thick-set man, whose hard features and smileless eyes impressed her with a fancy that he was the central figure in some dark tragedy. Yet there was that vague something about John Charlock that appealed to the woman's sympathies, for he, too, had suffered like herself. The same woman who had ruined Arnold Rent had brought shame and disgrace to John Charlock. He stood bowing gravely till Mrs. Rent came forward and timidly held out her hand. Then, at length, he spoke.

"This is a cruel trick that Fate has played us," he said. "Believe me, if I had known what had happened I should not be here this evening. I suppose Mr. Westlake has explained to you how the misunderstanding came about. And I think I know now why you did not get my letter. I had placed it with others on the hall table two days before. It was the day I lost my home. You see, I have been in great money difficulties, due principally to the extravagance of the woman who is my wife. One of my creditors stripped my house of everything, and left me nothing but the bare walls. I am not complaining. I had fair warning, and the money was honestly due to the man. Doubtless, in the confusion of the moment, my letters were lost sight of. But perhaps you will think that I ought not to stay any longer. I daresay I can find some accommodation in the village till the morning."

"Indeed, you cannot," Mrs. Rent exclaimed, all her hospitable instincts on fire. "There is no house of entertainment within some miles of this and the few cottages around are impossible. I appreciate the delicacy of your feelings, but you will have to remain till the morning. And the thing is no fault of yours."

"My wife's friends will tell you otherwise," Charlock said, with a bitter smile. "They will tell you that she is a sweet, saintly creature who put up with my cruel indifference till human nature could bear the strain no longer. Indeed, your son was good enough to tell me so. As a friend of my wife's, he ventured to expostulate with me, a comparative stranger, on the way I treated her."

All the blood came flaming to Mrs. Rent's face.

"He didn't," she said hoarsely. "He never went so far as that. It is incredible. What did you say?"

"I said nothing. I never say anything. The heart knoweth its own bitterness. There is no man on earth who has learnt the wisdom of that saying more than myself. And why should I try to put the world right? In the eyes of most people I am a boor and a brute. I had no business to tie a beautiful woman to a personality like mine. Why should I waste my time in proving to the world that the world is wrong? Why should I proclaim from the housetops that I am a broken and disappointed man, with nothing but my work to fall back upon?"

Charlock appeared to have forgotten himself. The words burst in a stream from his lips as he paced up and down the room. Never before had he shown his heart like this to a stranger. Yet there was something like sorrowful sympathy in the eyes of his hostess that seemed to draw confidences from him.

"I think I understand," Mrs. Rent said gently. "Is your wife, then, so wonderfully prepossessing?"

"I think she is the most beautiful woman I have ever seen," Charlock said, in the same tense tones. "She is outwardly the embodiment of womanly innocence and purity, and I gave her all the heart that a lonely and self-contained man possesses. How she has repaid me I leave you to find out for yourself. And yet, if she were to come back to me now and place her hands upon my shoulders and ask me to forgive her, I should be as wax in her hands. Wait till you see the woman called Kate Charlock before you judge your son too harshly. But, then, you are a woman, and do not know how we men feel when we come in contact with temptation. Mind you, I am not defending myself. I am going to make no defence. When your son came to me and spoke as he did I saw that heart and soul he was the slave of my wife. He did not know it. He did not realise it at the moment, but I let him chide me where ninety-nine men out of a hundred would have kicked him out of the house. But I was patient. I asked him to come four-and-twenty hours later, when I would show him what I was going to do. At the end of that time I knew that my home would be no more than a name. And then I forgot all about my scheme of revenge. And when the time came and my home was no more, I stood within the bare walls and made my wife an offer. There was to be an end of all her shameful extravagance. I was going into a cottage, where we should live without a servant till my debts were paid. My wife refused to go, and in a fit of sullen indifference I turned away and left her in the empty house.... It was then that your son came along.... I can say no more. I leave the rest for you to imagine. And now, if you will permit me, I will seek some lodging for the night."

Gently but firmly Mrs. Rent refused to listen to the suggestion. Till the morning, at any rate, she would not hear of Charlock seeking quarters elsewhere. It would be a dull and dreary evening, but that was inevitable in any case. It was a quiet and somewhat strained meal from which they all rose presently with feelings of undisguised thankfulness. It was barely dark, and the sea shimmered in the afterglow of the sunset. Charlock crossed over towards the French windows and stepped out upon the lawn, followed by Ethel.

"This is a lovely spot," he said. "Isn't there a wonderful walk here through the rose gardens leading to the sea? Would you mind showing it to me? I may never have another chance of seeing it. Won't you come?"

"We will all go," Mrs. Rent suggested. "Anything is better than sitting brooding in the house. Ethel, will you run upstairs and get a wrap for me?"

They started off presently, Ethel and Charlock a little in front of the rest. For a time they were silent, till, at length, the perfect beauty of the scene fell like a charm upon Charlock and he began to talk. It was a new thing for him to have a companion in sympathy with himself. But the responsive look in Ethel's deep eyes seemed to draw him to her. It was not so much what he said as what he implied that led Ethel to believe that he was both a miserable and a misunderstood man. The church clock was striking the hour of ten before they turned and made their way again towards the house.

"I believe I have been talking for a good hour," Charlock said. "I never remember doing such a thing before in all my life. I hope you will not run away with the idea that I am a loquacious man."

Westlake and Mrs. Rent drew up to the rest, and they all stood enjoying the fragrance of the night. Mrs. Rent turned at last with a suggestion that it was getting chilly, and that it would be more prudent to go indoors.

"A few minutes longer," Charlock pleaded. "To an artist such a scene is exceedingly attractive. One could forget all one's troubles in a place like this."

Before Mrs. Rent could make any reply a servant came across the lawn and spoke to her mistress. She seemed to be excited, and her eyes danced with pleasure.

"What is it, Mary?" Mrs. Rent asked.

"Mr. Arnold has come back unexpectedly, madam," the maid replied. "He would like to see you in the library, please. I forgot to say that there is a lady with him."

"Say I will come," Mrs. Rent said faintly.

Now that the crisis had arrived, the unhappy mother felt like shirking it altogether. She had not forgotten what Charlock had said. She was prepared to make every allowance for her son. But, even then, she would have to do violence to her feelings. She only wanted to be just, to do that which was right and proper. And, after all, she only had John Charlock's word as to the way in which he had been treated. And she was bound to confess that he did not look in the least like a man capable of making a woman happy. Perhaps his wife was the injured saint she took herself to be, and her son might be acting from the highest and purest motives. Such things had happened over and over again, despite the fact that the world was cold and critical. But the matter had to be faced, and the sooner the better.

In a dreamy sort of way Mrs. Rent saw her son's smiling face. She noticed the heightened colour on his cheeks. Then she saw the most beautiful woman her eyes had ever fallen upon. Oh, it was impossible to believe that this was a cold, scheming creature playing for her own hand. No one could look upon that face and think her anything but innocent. And Mrs. Rent thought she could vouch for her son.

As she stood there she saw the smile on Kate Charlock's face soften wonderfully. The woman advanced towards her with an obvious intention shining in her eyes.

She stepped back instinctively.

"No, no," she cried. "The time is not ripe for that. I cannot allow you to kiss me—yet."

CHAPTER XX
ACROSS THE THRESHOLD

Kate was in the house at last—in the long drawing-room, where the servants had lighted the lamps. Though pale and agitated, she could not resist the temptation to glance furtively about her. She had not lived under the same roof with a great artist for five years without learning something of the value of beautiful things. She was not slow to appraise the works of art. In her eyes the place was a trifle old-fashioned and out of date. Already she could see her way to make an imposing salon of the room. Then, as she saw Rent looking eagerly towards her, she lowered her eyelids and sighed deeply.

"I ought not to have come in with you," she murmured. "I see that it was a mistake. I ought to have waited outside till you had seen your mother and prepared her for my coming. It would have been so much more——"

The speaker's voice trailed off into a murmur. She was going to say "dramatic," but she stopped just in time. At the same moment there were sounds of voices outside, and the outline of dim figures could be seen advancing across the misty lawn. Instinctively Kate Charlock drew closer to Rent's side.

"My dearest, there is nothing to be frightened of," he said soothingly. "That was my mother's voice you heard. See, she is coming this way. I can't make out who the others are, but one of them looks to me like our solicitor, Mr. Westlake. If so, it is rather fortunate. Westlake always takes such a common-sense view of matters. He is sure to be on our side."

There was nothing more to be said, nothing to do but wait for the coming of Mrs. Rent. And she seemed in no hurry to detach herself from her companions. Why did she not come? Arnold wondered. Usually she was so eager to see him. In the selfishness of the moment it had not occurred to Rent that the ordeal his mother was about to go through would be more distressful than his own. And the cruel shock of finding that he was here in defiance of her telegram was not calculated to make the mother's heart any the less sore and angry. Mrs. Rent stood outside, her hands tightly clasped, looking first from one to the other for support.

"Oh, this is downright cruel," Ethel burst out. "He ought never to have come like this. If he came at all, it should have been alone. My dear aunt, sit down and collect yourself. I know you will be brave and steadfast when it comes to the point, or perhaps you would like Mr. Westlake— —"

"No, I must go through with it myself," Mrs. Rent said. "This is a burden that no one can share with me."

"I am afraid the fault is mine," Charlock said. "I ought to have gone away when I found out whose house I had come into. I should not have hesitated. It is a cruel stroke of fortune, and no one regrets it more than myself."

"It is no fault of yours," Mrs. Rent murmured. "Will you mind talking to Miss Hargrave while Mr. Westlake and I go into the house? I should like him to be near me, though I do not wish him to be present at the interview."

Ethel and Charlock stood alone together, silent and anxious. They watched the others as they went slowly towards the house, then Charlock touched his companion's arm.

"We had better not stay here," he suggested. "We can see and hear too much. Do you know, I feel as if, in a measure, I have thrust this black humiliation and disgrace upon you. I feel hot and cold all over that I should even be discussing the thing with one so young and innocent as yourself."

"And why?" Ethel said. "I am not a child. I have heard of these things before, though I never dreamt that I should live to see the like of this at Alton Lee."

"It is like a romance," Charlock laughed bitterly. "What puppets we are in the hands of Fate! And I thought once that I was a strong man capable of defying the world and shaping my own destiny. I daresay you will say that it is my own fault, and perhaps you will be right. I don't know why I should be talking to you like this. But the peacefulness of the night and the look of sympathy in your eyes invite my confidence. But I will swear to you that if I could have foreseen that this honourable old family would be disgraced in this fashion, I would never have let my home go. I would have worked all the harder to gratify my wife's extravagance. I would have made it worth her while to stay. Perhaps I was too candid, too brutal. Do you suppose she would have left me as she did if she had come back the other night and found the homestead intact? Oh, dear, no. With all her air of purity and sweetness, my wife always had a shrewd sense of business and self-interest."

"Yet you loved her once," Ethel murmured.

"My dear young lady, I love her now. She has only to say one word and the whole past is forgotten. It may seem strange to you, brought up as you have been, that a man should love a woman for whom he has the deepest contempt. But there are many such cases in the world. Call it madness, call it fascination—anything you like. It is possible for a man to love a woman devotedly and yet not to speak to her, though she is under the same roof as himself. That has been my case during the last four years. I have despised myself for my weakness—I, who in other matters can be so strong. I am a self-contained man, and five years ago I thought I had found paradise. Then it began slowly to dawn upon me that I had made a mistake. There was sweetness and melancholy and fascination in my wife's smiling face, but no atom of sympathy behind it. She had no feeling for me. She had no kind of pride in my work. Even when she began to hang the millstone of debt about my neck she had no concern, though on more than one occasion I was on the verge of a breakdown. But I don't ask you to take all these things for granted. I don't even ask you to believe me. You will know my wife later, and it is probable that she will convince you that I am a brute and a boor and not fit to mix with decent people."

Ethel made no reply. There was something in this man's grim tones that moved her strongly. Someone was coming from the house. She could hear footsteps on the gravel. Then the light from the drawing-room windows fell upon the face of a woman who was slowly crossing the lawn. Her features were serene and beautiful. Her eyes glistened with heavy tears. It was only for a moment that Ethel saw the vision before it vanished in the shadows. The girl felt Charlock's hand tighten on her arm.

"My wife," he said hoarsely. "She has come out to leave her lover and his mother alone. Did you see her face?"

"Indeed I did," Ethel murmured. "The beauty of it! And such an air and expression of sweetness and resignation I never saw before. It seems impossible to believe——"

"I see you pause," Charlock said grimly. "I know exactly what you are going to say. It does seem impossible. Before God, it seems to me sometimes that it is impossible and that I am only dreaming. It would go hard with me if we both stood before a jury of our countrymen and she told her tale after I had finished mine. But I won't say more. I will leave you to judge for yourself. You have seen us both, and you must rely upon your own instincts. I won't ask you to give any verdict, because I feel sure it will be against me."

"I am very, very sorry," Ethel murmured.

"Of course you are. But the point is, whom are you sorry for? There is no halfway in the business."

Ethel hesitated for a moment. She hardly seemed to know what to say. A bitter smile crossed Charlock's lips.

"Let me put it plainly to you," he said. "And yet I don't know why I should worry you with this business. I have never spoken to a living soul like this before. At any rate, I am going to be candid now. Let us assume that my wife has a genuine grievance against me. Say that I am too great a bully and savage for any decent woman to live with. I am prepared to admit that I did turn her out of doors in a brutal fashion. It is possible she can justify her conduct in her own eyes and that she is here with the purest and most disinterested of motives. Mind, in her way, she is a good woman—that is, she is highly virtuous. She would never forget herself. She would never step over the border, not even for the sake of Arnold Rent and all the fortune he is to inherit. No doubt she has persuaded herself that she has been right in coming here, that she has a moral claim upon Mrs. Rent's protection. She would argue it all out in her own mind. She would wait for me to commit some blazing indiscretion, and then invoke the aid of the law to release her from such a creature as myself. She would think that the proper thing to do. And after that she would be in a position to marry Arnold Rent and settle here as a county lady. Whether she would keep it up or not is another matter. And now, after I have told you this, let me repeat my question. You said you were sorry just now. Is your sympathy for her or for me?"

Ethel hesitated for a moment, and Charlock watched her with an anxiety which surprised himself.

"I think," she said in a voice little above a whisper, "that I am the more sorry for—you."

CHAPTER XXI
THE HONOUR OF THE FAMILY

Meanwhile, an entirely different scene was being enacted in the drawing-room. All her life Mrs. Rent had lived most placidly. She had never been confronted with a crisis like this. Indeed, the mere suggestion that such a cataclysm could have happened in the family would have moved her to gentle scorn. And now, on the spur of the moment, and almost solely upon her own initiative, she had to decide between her duty and her beloved son. It had cost her an effort to speak as she had done to Kate Charlock, and when she saw the half-wounded expression on the woman's face her heart smote her, and she became, for the time being, almost infirm of purpose.

Still, the situation had to be faced. She had a stern and rigid duty both to her conscience and to the family whose name she bore. There was a curious vein of Puritanism in her blood which came to her aid now. And it was very difficult, indeed, to stand looking at these two, to see her son advance with outstretched hands, and yet to hold back. He would have taken her in his arms and kissed her, but something warned him that the occasion was not opportune.

Under her long lashes, Kate Charlock watched him demurely. Why was he hesitating? It was necessary the fortress should be taken by storm. And Arnold Rent stood there shyly, his face downcast like that of a child detected in some fault.

"Mother," he murmured, "have you nothing to say to me? Have you no kind of welcome to offer to-night?"

The words were pleading and almost passionate, but seemingly they did not move Mrs. Rent at all.

"I am at a loss to understand why you are here," she said.

"Why I am here?" Arnold echoed. "Where else could I go? When you have heard all the circumstances of the case——"

"I have heard them already. Mr. Westlake came down on purpose to tell me. Come and stand here where I can see you—where the light shines full upon your face."

Arnold Rent came obediently a step or two forward.

"Strange," the mother murmured. "You have not altered. To all outward appearances you are still the man of honour and integrity you used to be. And yet you can commit this crime and come here to boast of it without the shadow of remorse, even without a word of apology. It seems incredible."

"But what apology should I make?" Arnold demanded. "What have I done that you should speak to me like this?"

"You ask me what you have done! Are you so blind as not to see the results of your indiscretion?"

Kate Charlock raised her head suddenly.

"May I not be allowed to speak?" she pleaded. "Is it not possible that when you come to hear my story——"

Mrs. Rent raised her hand imperiously.

"Tell her to be silent," she commanded her son. "Oh, I do not know what to do or what to say in such a crisis. Is it not bad enough without bringing your partner in folly under this roof? To think that I should have lived to see a scene like this at Alton Lee! To think that I should be the instrument chosen by Providence for the punishment of my own son! For that is what it comes to, Arnold. I was stunned at first. I was unable to believe the evidence of my senses. But I begin to see my way clearly. The path of duty lies plainly before me."

There was something cold and chilling in the words. They filled Kate Charlock with dismay. All the world seemed to be slipping from under her feet. If the opportunity were lost, the chance would never come again. She darted forward and threw herself in an *abandon* of grief on her knees before the mistress of the house. The ready tears were streaming from her eyes. Her beautiful features were almost irresistible in their entreaty.

"Oh, won't you listen to me?" she said. "You are a kind, good woman; your face tells me that. And yet, though you would be good and generous towards the world, you decline to listen to one poor woman's story. Can't you understand how one may suffer year by year until the strain becomes too great, and, in a moment of passing madness, sacrifice everything that a woman holds dear? That is my case exactly. Oh, it is all very well for you, whose married life has been the path of happiness, to judge humanity from your own standpoint. But there are others——"

The woman's voice snapped suddenly like the breaking of a harp-string. She covered her face with her hands, her whole frame shaking with convulsive sobs.

Nor was it all acting. For the time, Kate Charlock was convinced that she was the unhappy, abandoned wife of a man who had driven her almost to madness in one moment of divine despair. She thrilled with self-pity. She saw her airy castles crumbling to the ground. Unless this old woman could be moved, there would be no rest for the sole of her foot at Alton Lee. The face that she raised once more to Mrs. Rent's dark eyes was stained with tears and broken with emotion. Fighting for self-control as she was, Helen Rent was moved now as she had seldom been moved before.

"Get up," she said, almost gently. "It is unseemly that you should be kneeling here. If you have a story to tell, I may be disposed to listen to it presently."

Slowly Kate Charlock rose to her feet and felt her way across the room to a chair. She had made an impression. On that point she felt certain. If she could only remain here a week, or even a day, she had no fear of the result. Alton Lee was growing nearer. She began to see herself installed. She could hear the swish of the cards on the green-topped tables. She could imagine the rooms gay with the laughter of friends. But not yet, she told herself, not quite yet.

"I will say no more," she murmured. "Indeed, when I came here I had no intention of speaking at all. I see now how wrong it was to come. But in the moment of my madness and despair——"

Once more the pleading voice ceased. Once more the ready tears rained down the beautiful white face. Surely this was no abandoned creature, Helen Rent thought. Surely John Charlock had much to answer for. No woman could be bad with a face like that. If Mrs. Rent could imagine a saint stepping aside from the path of grace, then was Kate Charlock in similar case. And, in common fairness, most of the blame must fall upon the shoulders of her own son. A wave of madness must have come over him, in which he had forgotten everything excepting the features of a woman and his wild desire to sacrifice the world for her sake. Other men, in most respects both great and good, had fallen in like manner. A score of them rose before Helen Rent's mental vision.

Yet she must be firm. She must keep her head throughout this ordeal. Her white lips moved rapidly in prayer for strength and endurance. Kate Charlock noted the flutter of those white lips, and her subtle instinct told her what was passing through the other woman's mind. As a child she had seen her mother at a crisis of her life praying in like fashion. The scene rose curiously before her mind. She could see it all as clear as if it had happened only yesterday.

"It seems to me that we are wasting time," Mrs. Rent said, presently. "I cannot ask you both to leave the house to-night, because that would be impossible, and there is nowhere else to go. But to-morrow will be different. I have made up my mind what I am going to do in your case."

"What is that, mother?" Arnold asked.

"That I will tell you when we are alone. It only concerns our two selves. If you will come with me— —"

"No," Kate Charlock cried. "Let it be here and now. As for myself, I wish to be alone for a time in the open air."

Without waiting for remonstrance on the part of either, she crossed the drawing-room and threw back the windows. She stood there with her face turned up to the purple glory of the summer sky. She saw the golden pageant of the stars; the flower-laden breath of the evening was infinitely cool and refreshing. Here were the wide, trim lawns with their well-ordered flower-beds. Here was the noble sweep of the stone terrace, and beyond it the dim vista of the park, with the trees floating in a mist like ships on a peaceful sea.

And all this was likely to be hers if she had but the skill and patience to play for it. There was no regret in her heart for John Charlock. He had gone his own way. He had left her free to choose her own path. And there was always the chance of renewing the battle again on the morrow.

There were many cards to play, too, and if the worst came to the worst, Kate Charlock would play the great card of self-renunciation. She would offer Arnold back to his mother. She would go out into the world alone, hopeless and penniless, to work out her own salvation. Not in vain had she been studying Helen Rent's features, under the long fringe of her eyelashes.

"I wonder how he will manage it?" she murmured to herself. "I can stand here and listen, and if my presence becomes necessary, well, then, I shall be at hand."

CHAPTER XXII
BREAD AND SALT

Helen Rent thought she should have been conscious of a great feeling of relief when the room was free of the presence of the woman who had brought about her son's delirium. But such a sense was not experienced, nor even suggested.

"Now tell me how this happened," she said.

"Mother, I really cannot tell you," Arnold responded. "The truth is, I do not know. It was all so spontaneous. It seemed so natural and inevitable at the time. Here was one of the most beautiful women in the world, a good and true and pure woman, mind you, neglected by her husband in a manner that was positively shocking. Don't forget that there are some natures to which neglect or hard words are worse than any physical cruelty. Kate Charlock's case is one in point. She was being slowly driven mad by the creature to whom she was tied. She was forced to go into frivolous society, or she would assuredly have lost her reason. It was at the house of one of these Society women that I met her. Even among a gathering like that she was looked up to and respected as none of the rest was. I saw her most cruelly insulted by her own husband in a house where I was spending the evening; in fact, the thing was so brutal that I ventured to expostulate. Perhaps I went too far, but Charlock did not seem to mind. I implored him to treat his wife differently, and it seemed to me that I had made some impression. Then he asked me to call upon him at a certain time in the evening, when he would give me a practical reply. And what did I find when I got there?—the house stripped of everything, and the woman alone, with no better home to go to than a labourer's cottage, where she would not even be allowed the use of a servant. That is how Charlock treated so perfect a woman as his wife. And then, I don't know how, but the whole rest happened on the spur of the moment, and I am here to-night to tell you this strange story. I could not say more."

"It sounds amazing," Mrs. Rent murmured. "Let me put another point to you. Suppose Mr. Charlock had no alternative but to part with his home! Suppose that his wife's extravagance had brought him to the verge of ruin! Suppose that a creditor had removed everything to pay his debt! Do you think, in these circumstances, that the woman was justified in refusing to share the cottage which the man had to offer her? Don't you think it was her bounden duty to make every sacrifice until those debts were paid?"

Arnold Rent waved the question impatiently aside.

"I don't know where you get your information," he said, "though I am prepared to admit, for the sake of argument, that what you say is true. At present other things trouble me. For better or worse, I have cast the die. You will admit that I cannot change my course now."

"I should be the last to suggest it," Mrs. Rent said mournfully. "What are you going to do in the meantime? Your friends will turn their backs upon you. You will have to abandon your career. But I will not dwell upon that. I will confine myself to the moment. What are your plans?"

"My plans are simple enough, mother," Rent replied. "For the present I shall continue my scientific work. Nothing could interfere with that. And from now, until Charlock makes up his mind what to do, I do not intend to see Kate. You will acknowledge I want to prevent all the scandal I can, and in that respect I am looking forward to your assistance. If you will allow Mrs. Charlock to stay here and give her your moral support, I am certain——"

"Oh, the boy is mad," Mrs. Rent exclaimed. "That woman's beauty has intoxicated you. I see now what a mistake I made when I regarded you as unspotted by the world. My friends were right when they said I should have sent you to a public school and university. Do you suppose for a single moment that I could dream of having that woman here? Do you suppose that I could allow her to come in contact with Ethel Hargrave?"

"Need Ethel know?" Rent suggested sullenly.

"She knows already. I had to tell her. No, you shall stay one night here, but to-morrow you must go elsewhere. I have thought this matter out, and I have made up my mind what to do. Your path is plain. You must make this woman see her folly and return to her husband. But did it never occur to you to ask yourself one question before you took this fatal step? Do you suppose that this woman would have thrown in her lot with you if she had not known that you are Arnold Rent of Alton Lee and the heir to a large property? If I call her and tell her that everything is at my disposal, do you think she would not want time for consideration?"

"You malign her," Arnold cried. "I am certain she never gave the matter a thought. For my sake——"

"Ah, for your sake," Helen Rent said. "That is just the point I want to arrive at. For your sake I am going to try that woman in the balance. We shall see whether she is found wanting or not. From this week your allowance ceases. You will receive no more money from me. You will be thrown upon your own resources. You will have to earn your own living, and you will be the better man for it. The same remark applies to Mrs. Charlock, though not to such an extent, because, until the law settles the differences between her and her husband, she will be entitled to an income. Mr. Westlake told me this—I think he called it maintenance. It will not be much, but, at the same time, it will be enough to keep her in a modest way with due and becoming economy. I don't say that my decision is final, because if I find, say, at the expiration of five years that there is likely to be no more of these self-indiscretions and platonic follies, I may change my mind. But I am not going to see Alton Lee made an asylum for social experiments. Had my prayers been answered and you had asked Ethel to be your wife, I might think differently. But this matter is quite another story. I hope I have made my meaning plain. I hope I have made you understand that you will have to face the world now and work for your own living. You little realise how much it hurts a mother to speak in this fashion. Perhaps you will know some day. Meanwhile, I have nothing to add to what I have said. Do you follow me?"

"Oh, I hear right enough," Arnold said bitterly. "I hope before long that you will realise the cruel injustice of what you are doing. And you may be sure that nothing will make any difference to Kate Charlock. She will be only too proud and pleased to have the opportunity of showing the stuff she is made of. I suppose I have to thank Mr. Westlake for all this."

"Indeed, you are absolutely and entirely wrong," Mrs. Rent exclaimed. "The idea is wholly mine. Of my own feelings I have said nothing. I have not alluded to the terrible grief and disappointment that this thing has been to me. To think that a son of mine could so far forget himself—but it is useless to go into that. I am tired and worn out, and this interview has tried me more than I thought. And there is another element in the drama of which as yet you know nothing. It may surprise you to hear that Mr. John Charlock himself is under this roof."

"He came to see you?" Arnold cried.

"Yes, but under the impression that your folly had ceased. You can imagine how distressing it was when the discovery was made. And now, how am I to get out of this dilemma? You will agree that one of you must go. It only remains for you to make up your mind which it is to be."

"I am prepared to do anything you ask," Arnold said. "But what about Mrs. Charlock? What can we do with her?"

Mrs. Rent could only look at her son with troubled eyes.

"It is very strange how perverse women are," Arnold went on. "One would almost think you are wilfully misunderstanding me. Do you realise how much the woman sacrifices, and how little the man gives in return? It has always been a fancy of yours to regard me as a saint. Let me tell you now that I am nothing of the sort. When I first saw Mrs. Charlock, when I first understood how unhappy she was in her domestic life, when I found what that woman really was, it was a revelation to me, and from that moment I laid aside all my selfish aims and ambitions, and I was prepared to make any sacrifice to save her from trouble and affliction. She is good and pure as Ethel Hargrave, and I want you to befriend her for her own sake, if not for mine. To all intents and purposes, Charlock has deserted her. He has been guilty of legal cruelty by turning her out of the house and compelling her either to leave him or to degrade herself by menial work. His next folly will give her the chance of appealing to the law to release her altogether. And then I shall be in a position to make her my wife."

"Mistress of Alton Lee?" Mrs. Rent stammered.

A gleam came into Rent's eyes. There was something almost threatening in his attitude.

"Ay, I mean that," he murmured. "Nothing less. And the sooner you understand it the better."

CHAPTER XXIII
BEHIND THE VEIL

In the purple stillness of the night, Kate Charlock could hear all that was taking place in the drawing-room. It did not occur to Arnold or his mother that there was any chance of the cause of all the trouble playing the eavesdropper. Indeed, the whole situation was so strange, so full of dramatic surprises, that it was impossible to think of anything but the word and the moment.

Kate Charlock had come back to herself with a start as her husband's name was flung at her, so to speak, from the drawing-room. Thitherto she had been listening in a vague sort of way, her mind too full of plans for the future to take much heed. Even now she had not given everything up for lost. She followed with satisfaction Mrs. Rent's declaration of what might happen if only the object of Arnold's infatuation proved to be anything like the woman he declared her to be. It would not be difficult to break down this wall of opposition when she was Arnold's wife. On the whole, it was worth while to take the risk. The struggle might be a long one. On the other hand, Kate Charlock remembered that perpetual dropping wears away the stone. It would be no fault of hers if she were not mistress of Alton Lee at the end of a year. Doubtless she would eat the hard bread of adversity in the interval. But the milk and honey to come would make up for all that. Surely a place like Alton Lee was cheaply bought at the price of a year's poverty.

Then the edifice suddenly crumbled and broke as John Charlock's name was mentioned. There was no mistaking the significance of Mrs. Rent's words. At that very moment Charlock was under the same roof as his wife. But why had he come? What scheme lay at the back of his mind? It seemed impossible he had come to fetch her away. For a moment it flashed across the woman's mind that Charlock had journeyed to Devonshire hot-foot for revenge. He was just the kind of man to shoot Arnold Rent and then take his own life. He would probably leave a long statement behind him detailing his troubles from his own point of view—the sort of statement that the press glories in and publishes in prominent type. If that happened, then, indeed, would she be a marked woman for the remainder of her days. The rest of her years would be spent like those of the heroine of the *Scarlet Letter*.

But it was not for long that these distracting thoughts gripped Kate Charlock. Then she smiled at her own folly. Charlock was a guest. He had partaken of Mrs. Rent's hospitality. No, there must be something deeper and more subtle in his movements than this. And there were other things to think about. It was impossible that she and Arnold Rent and her husband could all sleep at Alton Lee that night. One or two of them would have to go. The air would have to be cleared.

Here was a situation that the turning of a hair might transform into farce or hideous tragedy. The elements of both were strongly in evidence. Something would have to be done, and that swiftly. But if John Charlock was in the house, where was he? Most of the windows of the living-rooms were open. The lamps were lighted, so that it was possible to pass along the terrace in the darkness and examine the various apartments without being seen. Here were the billiard-room, and the dining-room, the library and the morning-room, but all were empty. It was rather disappointing, because Kate Charlock was missing that fascinating conversation in the drawing-room, without any compensating advantage in return. She stepped back swiftly behind a clump of azaleas as two figures came up the steps leading from the rose garden and paused close to her. One was the tall, slender figure of a girl, whom Kate Charlock knew instinctively must be Ethel Hargrave. The other she saw, with a sudden thrill, was her own husband. It was not too dark for her to make out his features. She saw John Charlock hold out his hand, which the girl took reluctantly.

"It seems a pity," the latter murmured, "but, as you say, there is nothing else to be done."

"Of course there isn't," Charlock said in his grim, level tones. "Believe me, had I known what was going to happen, I should never have come near Alton Lee. But who could picture anything so repulsive as this?"

"It is very, very dreadful," the girl murmured. "But what are you going to do? I see you have made up your mind not to stay here a moment longer, but it is impossible for you to sleep out of doors, even on a night like this."

"Sleep!" John Charlock said bitterly. "I feel that I shall never want to sleep again. When I am thinking out a new picture I often walk for hours at a time. I cannot rest. But now that I am thinking out a new life, it is infinitely more serious. Believe me, it would be torture to shut me up in four walls to-night. When I leave here I shall walk as far as Exeter. I shall probably reach there to-morrow evening, by which time my plans will be made. But I am sorry that circumstances have prevented me from painting your portrait. I never saw a face that appealed to me so much before."

Kate Charlock drew a deep breath of relief. Now she understood for the first time what had brought her husband at this perilous moment to Devonshire. He had come to execute a commission, ignorant of the fact that matters with Arnold Rent had gone so far. The thing was a cruel coincidence, but John Charlock was doing his best to clear the situation.

"You will say good-bye to your aunt for me," he said. "I thought at first that I would see her and give her my decision. But, on the whole, it would be much kinder simply to disappear. I will write and let you know where to send my things. And now I will say good-bye. And when, in the future, you come to take the woman's part, as you inevitably will, try to look upon me as not altogether a monster. Try to think the best of me."

"I shall always do that," Ethel murmured. "You have not said much, but I know you are a man who has been deeply wronged. I am certain that I shall never take any other view."

"Oh, yes, you will," Charlock said grimly. "You have no idea what a subtle force you will have to contend with. Beauty and tears are more efficient weapons than strength and courage. You heard what Mrs. Rent said to-night. She would be strong and resolute. She was going to put the woman who had humbled her pride and broken her heart through an ordeal of fire. She meant what she said, honestly meant every word of it. But within a year from now Arnold Rent and his wife will be master and mistress of Alton Lee as sure as I am speaking to you at this moment. The thing is inevitable. And then I will ask you to think of me and my prophecy. As for me, I will know how to act."

Charlock lifted Ethel's fingers to his lips and turned away abruptly. The girl called to him softly as he strode down the terrace, but he gave no heed. Ethel stood there, quiet and thoughtful, until the last echo of Charlock's footsteps died away. Then she turned towards the house. She would have entered one of the open windows leading to the morning-room had not Kate Charlock stepped out from her hiding-place and laid a detaining hand upon the girl's arm. She started back violently and a wave of colour rushed over her cheeks as she saw the woman. There was an involuntary shrinking, a dislike and loathing in her eyes that brought a corresponding glow into the face of Kate Charlock. The lamplight streaming through the open windows picked out the features of each so that there was no disguise.

With all her hatred and repugnance for the author of this mischief, Ethel could not deny the sweetness and beauty and purity of the woman's face. It was the face of an angel, pleading, timid and humble; the tears in her eyes heightened their loveliness and stole like diamonds down her cheeks. Her whole attitude was one of supplication, of appeal to womanliness and pity, and yet so natural and spontaneous that there was not the slightest suggestion of acting.

"You know who I am?" the woman whispered.

"I can guess," Ethel said, still studiously cold. "You are Mrs. Charlock. Is there anything that I can do for you?"

"Ah, there are many things that you can do for me," Kate Charlock whispered. "Oh, my child, I know how you feel. My feelings would be just the same if our positions were reversed. It is always the rich man who is hardest upon the want of honesty in his poorer brother. It is always the woman who has never known trouble or temptation who most reviles her sister who has fallen in the gutter. You think I am wrong. Well, perhaps I am, but I wish I could tell you of my life. I wish I could make you understand how the torment of a whole existence can be crammed into the space of a single month. If I had only had one friend like yourself— —"

The voice broke and trembled. The long, slim hands were pressed to the streaming eyes. The ice round Ethel's heart melted suddenly. Impulsively she came forward and held out her hands.

CHAPTER XXIV
MISTRESS OF HERSELF

Without looking up, Kate felt the girl coming. The capitulation had been even more swift than she had expected. She knew now that she had made a powerful friend in Mrs. Rent's household. In those brief moments the recollection of John Charlock's trouble and the words that he had spoken were wiped clean from Ethel Hargrave's memory. This was not in the least like the picture she had conjured up of Mrs. Charlock. Beauty and grace she had expected, but either the hard, cold beauty of the calculating woman, or the sensuous loveliness of the Circe. And here was a very woman, broken and bent by trouble, who had fallen into dire folly because she could stand the strain no longer. And, after all, it was only natural that any woman should give her heart to Arnold Rent.

"I hope I did not appear to be hard," Ethel murmured. "But, you see, this is really a dreadful business. Nothing of the kind has ever come to Alton Lee before. We never dreamt that Arnold would do anything that was not right and proper. Perhaps we are a little old-fashioned and inclined to take an exaggerated view of the situation. I daresay, in time, when we come to know you better— —"

"Please don't say any more," Kate Charlock replied. "It is enough for me that I have your sympathy. You are acquainted with my husband; indeed, I saw you together just now. Perhaps a little knowledge of him would be the best excuse I could have. It was unfortunate he should have come here at this time, but I will do him the justice to say that he could not have known— —"

"Oh, he didn't," Ethel cried. "And he has gone. He could not remain at Alton Lee— —"

"No, no, I understand. And therefore he has gone. We may leave him out of our reckoning for the present. But that does not make things any the easier for me. I begin to see that it was wrong for me to come here at all. I started on the spur of the moment, not realising till just a short time ago that my presence under this roof is little less than an outrage. Indeed, Mrs. Rent as good as told me so. I could fall at your feet and die of shame when I think how indelicate this must seem to you. And as I stood here just now I could not help overhearing certain words which passed between Arnold and his mother. Her dictates of hospitality are too fine for her to turn us out to-night. But one of us will have to go, and that one must be me."

Ethel murmured something sympathetic. She saw the speaker's point and liked her all the better for it.

"Of course, it must be Arnold," she said. "Indeed, there is no other alternative. There is no accommodation for you in the village. You are a stranger here. Won't you come into the drawing-room with me? and I will do my best to set matters straight."

Kate Charlock shuddered and shrank back as if the mere idea were abhorrent to her. Tears were still in her eyes.

"I think not," she said. "I have been too sorely tried to-night to be able to stand any more, and Mrs. Rent doubts me. Do you know what she is going to do? From to-morrow Arnold practically ceases to be her son. She turns him out into the world to shift for himself. We are to face the future as best we can. Perhaps at the expiration of four or five years, when I have proved my single-mindedness and sincerity, we may be taken back to the fold again. Just as if there were need for doubt, as if the love of a man like Arnold were not enough for any woman."

The words were spoken with sincerity and passion, but they cut into Ethel's heart like a knife.

"I must be loyal to my dear aunt," she said. "It seems to me that she has done quite right, though I am sure it will be a bitter wrench, for she is acting against every impulse of her kindly nature. And if you can show her that she is wrong, why, then, it will be a great triumph for you. It will go far to bring the happiness back to Alton Lee again. And now, if you will come with me into the drawing-room——"

"No, no," Kate cried. "Let me know how you have settled it, and then perhaps you will be so kind as to find me somewhere to sleep, for I am weary and worn out. Let me go into the library and wait till you come back."

There was no more to be said. Kate Charlock flung herself back in an armchair and closed her eyes. When she opened them again she was alone. Her tears had vanished. The fatigue she had spoken of seemed to fall from her like a garment. She crossed rapidly over to the writing-table, and in her clear, bold hand began a letter. It was a fairly long letter, but it was finished at length and addressed to Mrs. Rent. Kate proceeded to put it in a conspicuous place and very quietly passed into the hall and took down her hat and long travelling wrap. A few moments later she was walking rapidly down the avenue in the direction of the road. Her face was clear and bright. There was something like a smile in her starry eyes; her heart was free from fear.

Meanwhile, the conference in the drawing-room was finished. Arnold was standing pale and stern by the side of his mother as Ethel entered. He hardly appeared to notice her at all, beyond a sullen nod which brought the blood flaming to the girl's face. Very quietly she made her explanation.

"Oh, we have settled that," Arnold laughed bitterly. "It is I who am going away. I can walk as far as the station and stay in the waiting-room for the early express. Then, to-morrow, Mrs. Charlock must do as she pleases. I am certain that she will lose no time in ridding you of her detestable presence."

"I do not like to hear you speak like that," Mrs. Rent said. "Ethel, will you go and ask the lady if she will come this way for a moment? I should like her to feel— —"

There was an uncomfortable pause for a few moments till Ethel came back with a letter in her hand.

"I cannot understand it at all," she said. "Mrs. Charlock has disappeared. Her wraps have vanished from the hall, too. She seems to have left this letter behind, which is addressed to you, aunt. After the way she spoke to me just now I am not surprised to find that she has not felt equal to the ordeal of staying here even for a single night."

"It was a fatal mistake," Arnold said hoarsely. "I see it all now. Only it is too late to rectify matters."

Mrs. Rent reached for the letter and slowly broke the seal. She read aloud so that the others could hear:

"All I can say is, forgive me. It was wrong to come, and I can stay no longer. Though I am without friends, I am not without resources, for I have a little to assist me. And yet I am glad to have seen you all, even if it has been only to convince you that I am not the hard, brazen, calculating creature you took me to be. I am going away till I am free. I shall not look upon any of you again till I am ready to send for Arnold. I want no money or favour now, nor in the future. I want to show that I have given my heart to one who will be able to support me without help from anyone. To be in receipt of your favours would ruin the whole romance of the situation. Perhaps later, when I have proved myself, it may be possible—but I can write no more."

The paper slipped from Mrs. Rent's fingers and lay upon the carpet. The eyes that she turned upon her son were troubled and haggard. He turned away with a passionate gesture.

"Ah, yes," he murmured hoarsely, "she was right to go. All the same, mother, you have done a cruel thing."

After all, Mrs. Rent was a woman. She had lived long enough as My Lady Bountiful in that quiet country village to have become imbued with the idea that hospitality and generosity were two of the leading virtues which led directly to the reward of heaven. She had never before listened unmoved to a tale of distress. She had never refused food or shelter to the most undeserving object. And now she had more or less deliberately turned a human being out of her own house to face the night, unaided and alone. And, to make things worse, she had acted with studied cruelty to a woman who, whatever her faults might be, was defenceless.

"I could not have expected this," she murmured. "To confess freely, I had not looked for such pride and independence of spirit. You are right, Arnold."

"Of course I am," Rent said grimly. "But perhaps you will tell me what is to be done."

"You must try to find her," Mrs. Rent went on. "Bring her back here and do your best to induce her to see that I have a point of view as well as herself. There will be plenty of time in the morning to decide as to the future; indeed, it is always well to sleep upon troubles like these."

Arnold Rent waited no more. He strode from the room and out into the darkness of the night, leaving his mother to commune with her own anxious thoughts. She was distracted and torn this way and that. A thousand doubts assailed her.

"What could I have done else?" she murmured. "What other way was there out of this bitter trouble?"

CHAPTER XXV
A PLAUSIBLE SCOUNDREL

We left Ephraim Bark on the landing-stage at Cowes expressing his joy at his good fortune in meeting Tanza once more. But, despite his appearance of engaging candour, the little man seemed to have some difficulty in swallowing a large lump which had risen at the back of his throat. His muddy features had turned pale. He glanced about him as if looking for some avenue of escape, presenting at the same time a ludicrous resemblance to a jackdaw recently encaged. On the other hand, Tanza appeared to be enjoying the interview. His features beamed with good-nature. There was a kindly smile upon his face. But, as a great many criminals had discovered to their cost, this was just one of the moments when the Italian was most dangerous.

"You fill me with pleasure," he said. "It is always a happy thing to find an old acquaintance so ready to resume friendship. But come along, we are wasting time. We shall be much more comfortable and sociable on board the yacht."

Bark protested that there was nothing he would like better. Nevertheless, his bluster was forced, his air dejected, and, for the time being, he had lost all his swagger. Even when he found himself seated in a luxurious cabin chair, with a famous brand of cigar in his mouth and a well-filled glass by his side, he presented the same apologetic appearance. There was very little resemblance to the man who had accosted Malcolm Grey so shortly before. Tanza beamed on his guest.

"Now we are going to be really happy and comfortable," he said. "Let us talk about old times. Have you been in Paris lately? And, if so, how are the old people? The last time I was in Paris a most extraordinary thing happened. It chanced that one night, as I was walking along——"

"Oh, drop it," Bark broke out suddenly. "Never was a gentleman like you. You play and play with a chap, and just when he thinks everything is nice and snug you drop down upon him and he doesn't know where he is. Reminds me of a boy with a cockchafer on a pin, it does. I've never done you any harm, and I am ready to answer any questions you like. But don't sit there smiling in that friendly way just as if you've got nothing on your mind. I can stand punishment, but I like to know where it is coming from. Just say what you want to say and get it over."

"That's candid, at any rate," Tanza smiled. "Very well. If you are ready to take it lying down, we'll come to the point at once. There are certain matters going on here that interest me greatly, and on those matters I am sure you can throw some light. I shouldn't have identified you with the business, only my friend Mr. Grey told me that he met you at Mr. Rent's office. Just now Mr. Rent and his doings fascinate me. How long have you known him?"

"I'll tell you everything," Bark said. "On and off, I've known him for the last five years. And, between ourselves, he isn't a bit better than he ought to be. A regular mixture of a man, I call him. One day he is going to give up the world and go into a monastery, and the next day you find him enjoying himself in some fast set as if he had been accustomed to it all his life. I never knew a man who was more guided by the feelings of the moment. But this last game of his beats all. Fancy a man who has ten or fifteen thousand a year before him running the risk of losing the lot simply for a woman who cares no more for him than the cigar I've got in my hand."

"You are speaking of Mrs. Charlock," Tanza said quietly.

"That's right enough. Not that it is any business of mine, but there are ways and means of doing things which even I don't approve of. Rent is a clever fellow, but no man can manage to make love to two women at the same time without getting into trouble."

Tanza's eyes gleamed.

"Ah, now you are speaking about that French maid?" he exclaimed. "I mean the poor woman who was called Hortense."

Bark glanced at the speaker with unfeigned admiration. It was not for him to know that Tanza's quick mind had grasped the point like a flash of lightning, but, for aught he could tell, Tanza might have been working on the problem for some time.

"Quite right," he said. "Between ourselves, Rent is a bit of a blackguard. He has never put his foot into it because there never has been any occasion. He has always had more money than he needed, or you may be sure that he would have gone to the dogs long ago. But he is not a bad fellow as men go. He would stick at nothing as far as his interests were concerned. A clever chap, too, and one who, with any luck, will make his mark in the world of science. But he is cruel and vindictive. He is making a fool of himself over Mrs. Charlock now. He has got a rare handful to deal with there. Still, it is a brazen thing to be making love to the mistress and the maid at the same time. That's what he was up to."

"Oh, ho," Tanza said gently. "We are getting along. I suppose this is where you come in. What do you know about this lady's maid?"

"She was my sister," was the unexpected reply. "You see, we are as much French as English. Hortense spoke the language like a native. She was a Parisienne to her finger-tips. That is why she called herself Hortense and passed herself off as a Frenchwoman. French maids are much more sought after than English ones and get much more money."

"No doubt. Now, how long had your unfortunate sister been in Mrs. Charlock's employ before she met with her accident?"

"I suppose about two years," Bark explained. "But why?"

"Oh, we shall come to that presently. Perhaps you can tell me who put it into your sister's head to steal her mistress's jewels? That is the point I want cleared up."

Bark looked at the speaker with open-mouthed admiration.

"No use trying to keep anything from you," he said. "But, as a matter of fact, I don't know. I am telling you the truth. Indeed, I would have nothing to gain by lying to such a clever gentleman as yourself. But my sister is dead, and anything I say can't do her any harm. She wanted to return to Paris. She was finding things very slow with Mrs. Charlock, and I suppose the idea of taking her mistress's jewels was her own. They were a pretty fine lot, I understand, but the trouble was to get them away without arousing suspicion. My sister wrote to me about it and told me what she was going to do. I don't mind admitting that I gave her the best advice I could, because I am sure you won't use this evidence against me. I came over to see my sister and Mr. Rent at the same time. I had had a bit of bad luck lately, and I knew that Rent would help me out. I had only got to mention a little thing that occurred in Paris some years ago and he was good for a hundred pounds at least."

"Blackmail," Tanza suggested.

"Oh, blackmail be hanged!" Bark said vigorously. "I was never properly paid for my share in the job, and Rent knows it perfectly well. He has been keeping out of my way lately. But it's only putting off the evil day. It is a small world, and I wasn't surprised to find that my sister knew Rent as well as I do. I wasn't long in finding out that he was making love to her for some purpose of his own. And perhaps it is a good thing for him that Hortense is out of the way. She was a fine hater when she chose."

"We are getting wide of the point," Tanza suggested. "What I want to know is where your sister put those jewels."

Bark protested by all his gods that he hadn't the faintest idea. Tanza did not press the point, though, from his view, Bark was lying strenuously.

But there was nothing to be gained for the moment, and Tanza changed the conversation. It was perhaps an hour later that Bark left the yacht, on the whole not displeased with his visit. He was palpably afraid of Tanza. He had expected to find himself closely cross-examined as to certain dark passages in his life, and he was only too thankful to get off so easily. He thought he had parted with no information of the slightest value to himself; indeed, he flattered himself that so far as the missing jewels were concerned he had led Tanza astray.

He might have been less easy in his mind if he could have lingered behind and listened to what took place as soon as he had left the yacht. Grey turned to his companion.

"You are a most extraordinary man," he said. "You don't seem to have learnt anything from that scamp, and yet you appear to be absolutely satisfied. Tell me what you are driving at."

"No, no," Tanza said good-humouredly. "Let us keep to our bargain. We are both working from different points, though we both have the same object in view. A little time ago it was your opinion that Hortense, Mrs. Charlock's maid, had died from an accident. On the other hand, I was convinced that she was the victim of foul play. If you have not changed your mind— —"

"I have," Grey said curtly. "But go on."

"Perhaps I have changed my mind, too," Tanza continued. "I begin to see the possibilities of suicide. It was only to-day that Fortune placed in my hand a clue to this conclusion. But perhaps I had better show you what I mean. Wait here a moment till I go and fetch it.... Now what do you think of that? Isn't it strange that I should gain possession of it?"

CHAPTER XXVI
THE JEWEL CASKET

As Tanza spoke he laid on the table a small, brass-bound, mahogany box, the patent lock of which had been forced; indeed, the whole thing appeared to have been so badly used that even the neatly made hinges were out of place. Inside were drawers and trays lined with crimson velvet, all wet and saturated as if they had been soaked in water for some time.

"You see what it is, then?" Tanza observed. "This is a jewel box. On the lid you will notice a little glass frame behind which is a sheet of paper inscribed with a list of the articles which at one time formed the contents of the box. When this casket was brought to me it was empty as you see it now; indeed, one of my men found it at low tide not very far away from the landing-stage, half imbedded in the sand. It is easy to guess whom it belongs to, seeing that the owner's monogram is on the outside, together with an address. Beyond question this once belonged to Mrs. Charlock. Mind you, I haven't heard that Mrs. Charlock was robbed of her jewels. I am simply deducing the thing from the condition this casket is in at present. In the first place, you see the casket has been forced open. Now, nobody but a thief would do that. In the second place, the casket was thrown into the sea, which is also what a thief would do. Now, who would be the most likely person to commit a crime of this sort? Who would be in a position to do so? But you know that my deductions are correct, because that rascal Bark told us who the thief was. Where the stones are is another matter. That will be something for us to find out when the mystery of the woman's death is cleared up. Meanwhile, we had better stick to the original mystery and do one thing at a time. I am bound to confess that I have slightly changed my mind, and should not be surprised to find that this lady's maid committed suicide. It is possible that Mrs. Charlock discovered her loss and traced it home to the thief. On the spur of the moment the latter goes off and drowns herself in the fountain by the sundial."

"And there," Grey said emphatically, "you are wrong. I shall be able to prove that to you before long. I, on my part, have not been altogether idle. Still, we will keep to our bargain, as you say, and each go his own way. Clever as you are, and much as I respect your opinion, I am prepared to back myself to get to the bottom of this mystery before you do. Within a week I promise not only to solve the mystery of Hortense's death, but also to produce the missing jewels."

"Ah, that's all right," Tanza exclaimed. "You are a pupil after my own heart. Do you mean to say you suspect the place where the jewels are hidden?"

"I don't suspect anything," Grey said quietly. "I know. I could put my hands upon the jewels within four-and-twenty hours."

Tanza nodded approvingly. It was characteristic of the man that he displayed no curiosity and asked no further questions. Nor had it occurred to him that Grey was speaking in a boastful spirit. He made no effort to move when Grey rose from his chair, saying he had important business on shore which might detain him to a late hour.

"All right," he said. "I presume you are on the same business still. You will be able to tell me what has happened in the morning. Well, good-night and good luck to you."

It was very late when at length Grey skirted the town and proceeded along the shore to the small block of buildings where Rent was carrying on his experiments. The buildings were in darkness. But that did not seem to trouble Grey, who threw himself down upon a bed of sea pinks and proceeded to light a cigarette. He had barely finished two before a tiny speck of light appeared in one of the windows, followed by a brilliant illumination behind the blinds as if some one was turning on the gas. As a fact, it was electric light, as Grey very well knew. He moved forward almost immediately until he stood under the shadow of the buildings. The main door was slightly open, and Grey hesitated whether he should enter or not. There was no one about, so far as he could see, though he could hear voices in the room where the light had been turned on. There was nothing to gain by timidity, so he pushed his way into the building and felt cautiously along the corridor. The door of the room where the light was stood ajar, and the intruder could see Swift standing on one side of the table and Bark opposite.

"And now you have got me here," Swift was saying, "what do you want? Why all this mystery? Why couldn't you have come to my lodgings like any other man? Instead, you drag me here as if I were a thief or something to be ashamed of."

"What else are you?" Bark said brutally. "And what else is that employer of yours, for that matter, either? Look here, my friend, I know too much about both of you to stand any nonsense. I don't want to put the cat among the pigeons, but unless I have this money by midday to-morrow somebody is going to get into trouble. That is all I have to say."

"But I haven't got it," Swift said passionately. "I haven't got a tenth part of it. Mr. Rent will be here to-morrow and you had better see him for yourself. I am sick of all this business. I begin to wish I had never come here at all. And now the sooner you clear out the better."

"I'm going when I like," Bark said sullenly. "And, mind you, I won't be played with any more. I can say too much and I can prove too much to be treated as if I were some tramp trying to beg a copper or two. If you take my advice you will leave Arnold Rent to his own resources. No man ever yet trusted him without repenting it afterwards. Poor as I am, I wouldn't be under a favour to that man unless I was obliged to, and it is possible that I may not have to come here to-morrow, after all. I have a scheme on, and if it turns out trumps you can tell your employer that he isn't likely to see me for a bit. What are you up to here? What's the little game?"

"We came here on a purely scientific errand," Swift said coldly. "And, in any case, our experiments will not be of the least interest to you. And now, as I am busy— —"

"Oh, I'm off," Bark laughed. "I don't want to pry into your secrets; I've plenty of my own to worry about. Good-night."

Bark turned away and swaggered down the passage, so close that Grey could have touched him as he passed. He emerged into the road and went off towards the town with the air of a man who has much to do before he seeks his bed. Grey followed him at a respectful distance until he came to the lodge gate leading to the house recently occupied by John Charlock. Bark pushed through the gate and made his way along the grass towards the lawn at the back of the house. Here he stopped and produced a box of matches from his pocket. There was little or no wind, so that the match flamed out clearly, so clearly that the watcher could see Bark's evil face carefully examining a piece of paper which he had in his hand. So still was it that Grey could hear Bark's muttered comments.

"Hang me if I can make it out. What an awful fist she wrote, to be sure. Now, is it on this side or the other? And what does she mean by a hundred and fifty to the right? And where the dickens is the right supposed to begin? I wish I had a tape measure. Not that it would be much use on a dark night like this. Still, it won't do to work with a lantern."

The match went out and Bark's musings came to an end. Grey had been gazing so steadfastly at the match that when it was extinguished suddenly he could not see anything for the moment. Then, when his eyes became accustomed again to the gloom, he found that Bark had vanished, leaving not the slightest trace behind.

The incident was annoying as it was unexpected. There were trees all about the lawn standing back in dense shadow, so that it was almost impossible to make out in which direction Bark had gone. Grey could do nothing but go back to the road and wait till Bark came back again. There was, of course, a chance that his time might be wasted. But he had gone so far now that he did not care to abandon his search. He went slowly and cautiously back to the road and stood by the lodge gate for the best part of an hour. He was thinking of giving up the adventure when Bark came down the avenue muttering to himself and groaning as if he were in considerable pain. He did not appear to think it extraordinary that Grey should be there. On the contrary, he grinned knowingly and inquired affectionately after Tanza's welfare.

"You are wasting your time to-night, anyway," he said. "So am I, for the matter of that. There is something wrong with this place. Never mind why I am here. I stumbled over a fountain arrangement in the garden and fell with one hand in the water. It was only for a second, and now look at my fingers. Painful! Well, rather. But what the devil is it? Strike a match and look for yourself."

Bark held up a shaking hand in the light of the match. His fingers were shrivelled and blue, as if they had been badly scalded. There were blisters here and there, and Bark writhed with the pain he made no effort to conceal.

"What do you make of it?" he groaned. "Tell me what you make of it."

CHAPTER XXVII
KATE COMES BACK

Grey was startled, but Bark was in too great pain to notice that. It was some time before the former trusted himself to speak. When he did so, his tones were clear and distinct.

"I shouldn't like to say," he remarked. "Probably you are suffering from some irritant poisoning which the water has excited. This is rather out of my line, and you had better go into the town at once and see the doctor. You really ought not to delay. My studies of medicine did not go far enough to enable me to deal with a case like this. But I should like to know how you get on. And I hope you will come aboard the yacht to-morrow afternoon."

"I might just as well," Bark growled. "It is evident you don't intend to lose sight of me. I suppose that is why you followed me to-night."

Grey deemed it prudent to make no reply. Without further words, Bark turned sullenly away and walked down the road. Grey went back to the yacht as soon as possible. He felt that he had not wasted his time, though, on the whole, the events of the evening had not turned out quite so successfully as he had hoped. For the best part of the next day he waited on the yacht in expectation of seeing Bark, but the latter did not put in an appearance. Another day of almost enforced idleness followed, and it was not until after dinner on the next evening that Grey received a letter from John Charlock asking him to call at the house and favour him with a few minutes' conversation. He handed the letter to Tanza, who had been out all day and had only come back in time for dinner. The little Italian chuckled as he read.

"Now what is the meaning of this?" he said. "In the course of my investigations I have made a few inquiries, and was under the impression that Charlock had gone into Devonshire. I thought Arnold Rent was in Devonshire, too, but was surprised to see him this evening going off towards that laboratory of his. To make the matter even more complicated, I had a telephone message to call at the Queen's Hotel and see Shiplake. Imagine my astonishment when the first person I saw was Mrs. Charlock. Now there is a nice problem for you. What do you make of it?"

"I think I understand," Grey replied. "I believe Rent has been playing the chivalrous fool over Mrs. Charlock. I don't believe he was thinking about himself at all. He was going to take her down to stay with his mother till some arrangement could be made. Now I happen to know a good deal about Mrs. Rent. She is a splendid woman in many respects and a rigid Puritan at heart. You may depend upon it that she told Rent pretty plainly not to look to her for anything until he had got out of the scrape he had walked into with his eyes open. Rent, not being a fool, had to explain to the lady, and she, not being a fool, saw the difficulty at once. I shouldn't mind betting that Mrs. John Charlock has resolved to return to her husband. At any rate, that is the only logical explanation I can offer."

"It sounds plausible," Tanza said. "But you will know better when you have seen Charlock. He may want you to be present when he meets his wife. If he has a friend, you are probably that remarkable person."

"He is a queer man," Grey said, as he turned the letter over in his hand, "but not to blame. However, I'll let you know what happens."

Half an hour later Grey was walking up the drive to the deserted house. Lights were burning in one of the windows, and behind the curtainless casement Grey could see two candles standing on a table. There was a litter of papers on the table and a chair on each side. As Grey rang the bell the clang of the metal sounded hollow in the empty house. Charlock came to the door.

"I am glad you have come," he said. "I take it very kindly of you. I daresay you wonder why I am here and why I wrote to you. Perhaps this letter from my wife will explain matters. Yes, I want you to read it. There is no reason why you shouldn't."

With some reluctance, Grey took the letter and read it. It was from Mrs. Charlock, in her own neat handwriting, written as carefully and regularly as if it had been a serious business communication. There was no sign that it had been written in a hurry, or that it had been inspired in a moment of anxiety and emotion. There was no heading to it and nothing at the foot but the writer's signature. As to the body of the letter, it might have been read by anybody. It pointed out that there had been a difference between husband and wife, and that perhaps there had been faults on both sides. The writer regretted that in a rash moment she had been so foolish as to take a step which might have compromised her in the eyes of the world. But she pleaded in extenuation that her husband's harsh conduct had driven her to retaliate. On thinking the matter over, she had decided it to be her duty to return home and place herself in her husband's hands, only stipulating that residence in the cottage should be restricted to a definite period. The writer concluded by asking an interview and stating that she had returned to the neighbourhood for that purpose. Grey laid the letter down with a murmur to the effect that it seemed to him to be right and proper.

"You think so?" Charlock said, with a hoarse laugh. "You are more confiding than I am. Do you know what has happened? That woman bewitched Rent. For the time she made him forget his own selfish schemes. She wanted to pose as an injured woman, though that was not a new *rôle*. She wanted to get rid of me. She wanted to force me to some crowning folly, so that the law might release her, and then she would have every claim to marry Arnold Rent. Doubtless it struck her as a fine thing to become a county lady of unlimited income. But, then, you see, she reckoned without another woman in the person of Rent's mother. Mrs. Rent displayed a firmness which upset her calculations altogether. And Mrs. Rent played exactly the right card. She told these two platonic fools that her son had nothing to expect from her. Perhaps in five years' time she might hold out her hand to help them. But they were to understand that meanwhile Arnold Rent was no better off than any other penniless man of good education. I know all about it, because I was on the spot. The irony of circumstances took me to the house. And when those people fully realised what was to happen, their common sense came back to them. Mind you, I am going on supposition now. But I don't think events will prove me to be far wrong. Otherwise, why is my wife here again? Why has she asked me for an interview? And why has she agreed to listen to my terms? It suited my mood to grant that interview at this hour of night. It was my whim to ask you to be present. You will see for yourself that what I have said is literally correct. And now, will you be good enough to open the front door for me? She may be here at any moment."

Grey went off obedient to Charlock's request. He stood outside for a moment in the stillness of the evening until Charlock joined him. They were quiet for a little while. Then Charlock began to speak in the bitterness of his heart. But Grey did not appear to be listening. He raised his hand as if to impose silence.

"Hush," he said. "Didn't I hear a cry?"

Charlock shook his head. He had heard nothing. A moment later the cry was repeated, so far as Grey could judge, from the bottom of the garden. It was not a loud cry. It sounded as if from someone in dire pain. Grey moved hastily forward.

"It is nothing," Charlock said, "nothing but mere fancy. One's nerves get out of order sometimes."

But Grey was not to be moved. He knew that his imagination had not played him false. He could hear a stifled moan again. Almost like an inspiration he traced the sound to its source and raced across the lawn.

"Bring one of the candles," he cried, "and follow me to the sundial. I am certain that is where the cry came from."

Charlock muttered something in reply, but presently Grey saw the light twinkling across the lawn. He waited till Charlock came to his side, then with a trembling hand snatched the candle from Charlock's fingers. He bent down over the clear water of the fountain and saw something black and limp, something that seemed in parts to glow and glisten in the flickering light of the candle. Then, a moment later, the mysterious something lay motionless on the grass, and Grey was wiping his fingers as if they stung him. But he was not thinking of the physical pain.

"There," he said hoarsely, "I told you so. Take the candle and hold it down so that we can see the poor creature's face. Good heavens! To think that she should come to this!"

Charlock held the candle low. He appeared to be singularly quiet and self-contained. He made no sound as the light fell upon the dead white face.

"My wife!" he said. "What is she doing here? Grey, what does this mystery mean? What curse lies on this place?"

CHAPTER XXVIII
A STARTLING CONTRAST

Mrs. Bromley-Martin's rooms were well filled as usual, for she was giving one of those bridge parties of which she and her set never seemed to tire. It seemed strange that they had not become weary of their pursuit. But, then, the element of gambling entered largely into their calculations, and of this they never tired. It was a perfect night out-of-doors. The long French windows leading to the lawn were invitingly open. But probably few of the guests appreciated the beauty of the night. The rooms were hot and stuffy and there was a cackle of conversation and high-pitched chatter without which no smart function is complete. There were a dozen tables going, and from time to time those whose hands lay on the table were gathered together round the fireplace discussing choice morsels of scandal. The hostess herself, resplendent in blue and silver, was being listened to with rapt attention, for she had something especially fresh and piquant which she was relating to the motley throng around her. Her shrill voice rang through the room.

"I assure you it is perfectly true," she said. "I saw her myself at the station. She came back this afternoon and went straight to the Queen's Hotel."

"Did you speak to her?"

Mrs. Bromley-Martin laughed.

"My dear, of course I did," she screamed. "Did you ever know me do anything like other people? Did you ever know me care two straws for what folk said? Oh, I know I ought to have walked by with my head in the air and my skirts drawn about me as if I feared contamination from her very touch. But I did nothing of the kind. Behold in me the Good Samaritan!"

A wild cackle of laughter followed this suggestion.

"Oh, you may laugh," Mrs. Bromley-Martin went on good-temperedly. "Besides, I was desperately curious. And there she was, looking more saint-like than ever; indeed, I felt quite a sinner by contrast. Besides, she is no worse than the rest of us. The only difference is that she has been found out."

"But has she been found out?" a tall man asked seriously. "Can you mention one single thing against Mrs. Charlock? Here is a woman married to a boor, who is supposed to ill-treat her because he can't have his own way; he sells the house over her head, and says she can remain if she please. A woman ought to be able to get rid of a man for less than that. Upon my word, I think it was one of the most chivalrous things I ever heard of. Then there is Arnold Rent, whom we all regard as a clever fellow, who, apart from his science, is living entirely for himself. I have heard it said that he has no heart and no feeling. And yet he makes a deliberate sacrifice for the sake of a woman who apparently cares nothing for him. Really, in these prosaic times, for a man to go out of his way to offer a suffering woman the shelter of his mother's roof is touching. This kind of thing an author might make into a book. I suppose nobody has heard anything of Rent?"

"Indeed, they have," a voice interrupted. "It is my turn now to contribute to the harmony of the evening. Our charming hostess has given us the first act of the comedy. Now I can proceed to write up the second. What the third act will be like is a matter for speculation. Anyway, as I was coming here to-night, I saw Rent going along the shore to his offices. He wouldn't allow me to stop him; he would hardly allow me to speak to him. At any rate, he is back again, and the Charlock-Rent romance is at an end. I am sorry to spoil sport in this way, but I am bound to speak the truth. It looks to me as if the story had a commonplace ending, after all. Probably Mrs. Rent threw a cold douche of common sense upon her son's argument, and Mrs. Charlock has made the best of it by coming back to her husband. That is my conclusion."

"I don't believe a word of it," Mrs. Bromley-Martin cried. "I refuse to have my illusions scattered in this way. If I had only known Arnold Rent was here I would have asked him to come round this evening. His appearance would have created a sensation. And sensations in these times——"

The speaker paused, conscious that there was something wrong. Her back was to the door. She did not see that someone had come into the room. That everything was not quite in order she could gather by the expression on the faces of her guests. No one was sneering or smiling. Most of them were looking blank, and one or two decidedly uncomfortable.

"What is the matter?" Mrs. Bromley-Martin asked. "Have I said anything so very *outré*, or have you all suddenly become——"

"It is a pure matter of conscience," a cold, clear voice said. "You have every right to your own opinion. But on this occasion, gracious lady, you are absolutely wrong, much as it grieves me to tell you so."

A little spurt of colour flamed to Mrs. Bromley-Martin's face. Possibly it was the first time she had blushed for years. She forced her voice to a higher pitch as she recognised Rent.

"Talk of an angel and you hear his wings," she cackled. "How dare you stand there and listen to what I was saying! Why, bless my soul, a set like ours, if we all knew what our neighbours thought of us, would be deadly enemies in a week. Still, my dear boy, I forgive you, because it was so thoughtful of you to come round this evening to make my party a success. But did you hear what I was saying?"

"Every word," Rent said gravely.

"In that case, it would be foolish of me to apologise. We were talking of Mrs. Charlock and yourself. I believe it was under this roof that you met her for the first time. It was here that the tender romance had its initiation. It was here, also, that John Charlock behaved in such a brutish way and played into the hands of his wife. I daresay you recollect the occasion."

"Perfectly well."

"What a sphinx it is!" Mrs. Bromley-Martin remarked, with a shrug of her shoulders. "Why don't you try to help me out? You must know what conclusion we came to. We all give you credit for acting the part of the cavalier without fear and without reproach. But when both parties came back in this prosaic fashion, why, naturally——"

"One moment," Rent said coldly. "Loth as I am to spoil your recreation, I must speak. You are all mistaken. It is true that chance gave me the opportunity of befriending Mrs. Charlock when she was badly in need of advice, but there the thing begins and ends. I might have been wrong in offering Mrs. Charlock a temporary home with my mother; I am not prepared to say that I had given the matter due consideration. However, Mrs. Charlock has thought the matter over and come to the conclusion that she cannot do better than fall in with her husband's wishes. That is why she is here, and you can guess why I have returned, also. It will be just as well in future to drop this subject."

There was something so cool and self-possessed in the speaker's words that no one in the group round the fireplace ventured even to smile. Rent flashed a challenge from one to the other, but no one offered to take it up. There were one or two murmurs of approval, and Mrs. Bromley-Martin thought it wise to change her ground.

"I am sure, I beg your pardon," she said. "I had no idea you would take it in this way. You see, it is so seldom that anybody in our set is serious that one forgets that there are real responsibilities in life. Now let us go back to the tables and devote ourselves to the business of the evening."

Rent bowed gravely. Mrs. Bromley-Martin had gone as far in the way of an apology as she was likely to go. Before he could say anything there was a further commotion at the door, and another man entered, apparently bursting to relate some item of news. Mrs. Bromley-Martin heralded the intrusion at once as a godsend. Here was a speedy and graceful escape from the position she had taken up, and she hastened across the room.

"Well, colonel, what is it? What fresh scandal is afoot? Positively, we are so dull here that anything, even if it is deliberately untrue, will be welcomed."

"Oh, this is true enough," the man replied. "I was coming past Charlock's house just now, and I met that fellow Grey coming out of the gate in a hurry. You know the man I mean—he is staying with that clever Italian, Tanza, on his yacht. At first, I could not make out what was the matter with him. It appeared he was asking me to fetch a policeman, as something terrible had happened in Charlock's grounds. Mrs. Charlock had fallen into a fountain, or something of that kind. At any rate, when Grey and Charlock found her she was lying there quite dead."

A sudden exclamation broke from Rent's lips. He turned a white, set face towards the speaker.

"In the fountain?" he asked hoarsely. "By the sundial, do you mean? Oh, the thing is incredible."

"All the same, it is quite true," the newcomer said. "I saw it for myself before I went off for the police. And the strange part of the whole thing is that mistress and maid perished in the same way. There seems to be a fatality about that sundial."

CHAPTER XXIX
A LAPSE OF MEMORY

Arnold Rent seemed to be striving for words to express his feelings. He pressed his hand to his throat, as if something had risen and choked him. There was a deadly pallor on his face, too, which some of the guests did not fail to notice. They were quiet now, for this *dénouement* was calculated to suppress the frivolous spirits even of Mrs. Bromley-Martin's guests.

"Tell us some more," the hostess murmured.

"There is very little to say," the man who was telling the story went on. "I met a policeman within a few yards of Charlock's lodge gate and sent him off headlong to bring his inspector and a doctor. Then I went back to the scene of the tragedy to see if I could do anything. I heard voices in the garden and went down towards that now famous sundial. I had heard of the thing before; in fact, I remember reading a paragraph or two in the papers when Charlock bought it. At any rate, there it was, looking pale and ghostly in the gloom, and by the side of it stood Charlock and Grey bending over an object on the grass. As a matter of fact, they had no business to disturb the body at all. Still, the thing was done, and I helped to carry the poor creature into the house. I came away as soon as I decently could, because it was no place for an outsider."

"Dreadful!" Mrs. Bromley-Martin shuddered. "What a fate for a beautiful creature! And what did John Charlock say? How did he seem to take it?"

The man who was telling the story shrugged his shoulders.

"Don't ask me," he murmured. "Charlock is not like other people. You see, he is a genius, and geniuses are allowed to express their feelings in their own way. So far as I could see, the discovery made not the slightest difference to him; excepting that he lives and breathes like most of us, he might have been carved out of stone. There was no expression whatever on his features, not one word escaped his lips. I was glad to get away."

Arnold Rent listened to this recital with the air of a man who dreams. More than once he appeared as if desirous of asking a question. Then he changed his mind. By this time it had already reached those who were deeply immersed in cards. As the various rubbers were finished people began to gather by the fireplace and discuss the tragedy. The first feeling of awe had passed away and everybody was talking at once.

Rent was unnoticed. He seemed to have fallen into the background, and before anyone was aware of the fact, he had slipped out of the drawing-room into the hall, where he donned his coat and hat. Then, without the formality of saying good-night to Mrs. Bromley-Martin, he walked down the spacious drive into the road. He came presently to the lodge gate of Charlock's house, where he paused. Now and again he passed his handkerchief over his forehead to wipe away the beads of moisture which had gathered. The night was warm, but not sufficiently so to account for the water trickling down his face.

"I've got to do it," he groaned. "Lord, what a coward I am!"

The last words came with an accent of bitter self-reproach. It seemed as if Rent were taking hold of himself and impelling his feet unwillingly forward. He came at length to the house, where the lights were still burning in the front room, where he could see John Charlock and Grey standing facing each other across the table. There were other shadows in the background, but of these Rent took no notice. He would have liked to knock at the door and make inquiries, but even his audacity shrank from going so far. It was not the time to face John Charlock. The only thing was to wait until Grey came out.

The young scientist emerged presently and closed the door behind him. He turned very coldly, almost offensively, to Rent when the latter accosted him.

"What can I do for you?" he asked.

"I have just heard the news," Rent said hoarsely. "I had gone as far as Mrs. Bromley-Martin's when Colonel Suffield came in and told us. He was the man you sent for the police. It seems incredible. It seemed all the more impossible to grasp because it was told before that frivolous lot yonder. I could not wait a moment. Suffield told me you were here. Of course, I could not ask for Charlock in the circumstances."

"That would be playing the blackguard," Grey remarked pointedly.

"You are altogether unjust," Rent murmured. "If you knew the whole story you would not blame me in the least. I only acted on Mrs. Charlock's behalf as any other man would have done. Surely, a good and pure woman is above scandal. But I am not going to discuss that. I want to know what has happened."

"There is very little to tell you," Grey said. "I came here by appointment to see Mr. Charlock. He wanted me to be present because his wife was coming back, and he deemed it best to have a third party at the interview.

We heard a cry of distress from the bottom of the garden and immediately proceeded in that direction. To make a long story short, we found Mrs. Charlock's dead body lying in the fountain by the sundial, precisely in the same way as her late maid's was discovered. Beyond that I can tell you nothing. What more would you know?"

It appeared as if Rent could have known a great deal more, but he restrained his feelings and walked silently down the drive by Grey's side. The two parted at a turning in the road, and Rent made his way across the foreshore to his offices. There was no light, so far as he could see, and this seemed to fill him with relief.

"I suppose Swift is away to-night," he muttered. "Well, perhaps it is for the best. And yet I told him particularly that I wanted him at eleven. That accursed drink again, I suppose! I shall have to get rid of him."

Rent struck a match and fumbled with his key in the lock. He left the front door open on the off-chance of Swift coming back. Then he proceeded to the inner office and switched on the electric lights. From a safe let in the wall he proceeded to take out some electrical appliances, and with these in his hand he turned rapidly towards the door. Then he stepped back with an oath and a cry of vexation as he saw someone standing there. The intruder's face wore a wide grin, but his dark eyes were set in stern determination. Ephraim Bark was not pleasant to look at.

"What the devil are you doing here?" Rent demanded.

By way of reply Bark closed the door and took a seat. Then he produced a cigarette, which he lighted coolly.

"What is the good of talking that rot to me?" he said. "I have been looking for you for the past week, and you have been keeping out of the way because you were afraid to meet me. Oh, it is all very well to smile, but if you weren't afraid, why didn't you toe the scratch like a man?"

"I have been away on business," Rent said, lamely enough.

"Business be hanged! Now, look here, I am not going to waste words with you. After that little affair in Paris you promised me two hundred pounds, not a penny of which I have had yet. Why should I be walking about on my uppers while you are rolling in money? A rich man like yourself— —"

"I am not a rich man," Rent protested. "As a matter of fact, I have an allowance which is quite insufficient for me, and, apart from that, I am dependent for every penny upon my mother, who can leave it all away from me if she pleases. Yes, and she would do it, too, if she knew the sort of life I have been leading."

"I know all about that," Bark grinned. "I make every allowance. But you must have something to spare. I tell you, I am penniless, desperate almost, and I am going to have a hundred pounds or its equivalent before I leave you to-night."

Rent burst out into furious epithets.

"I tell you, I haven't got it," he protested. "I have never been so hard up as I am now. There are particular reasons why I cannot appeal to my mother just now. In the course of a fortnight or so I may be able to accommodate you."

Bark laughed insultingly. He made use of expressions which brought the blood flaming to Rent's cheeks, but he dared not retaliate openly. He was in this man's power, as he reflected bitterly. A murderous instinct rose within him. He reached out and grasped a heavy ruler, and ere he knew what he was doing he was holding the weapon threateningly over Bark's head. There was no mistaking the gleam in his eyes. There was no time for further argument, as Bark saw. He closed at once with Rent. He crooked his foot dexterously behind the latter's heel and Rent fell heavily to the ground. He staggered as he fell, so that his head came in violent contact with the corner of the iron fender of the fireplace. He lay still and motionless, with Bark bending over him.

"Lord, I've done it now," the latter said ruefully. "I believe I've killed the beggar. Well, if I have— —"

Bark paused suddenly and lifted up his head like a hare. He seemed to hear footsteps coming closer. If he had dealt Rent a fatal blow, he had no mind to be caught red-handed. And no one had seen him come. He darted from the room like a flash and raced across the sands as if the Powers of Darkness were after him.

CHAPTER XXX
"THOU ART THE MAN"

It was some time before Rent came to himself and sat up, wondering what had happened. His brain was dizzy and confused. His head was aching violently. In some vague way he was haunted with an idea that he had come down to the office on some important errand which had life or death behind it. But, cudgel his brain as he might, he could not recollect what it was. There was no mark of violence on his forehead. He could not remember how he got there. He would have found it difficult, indeed, to put a name to the man who had brought this catastrophe about. He sank down into his chair, a profuse perspiration breaking out on his brow. He had utterly forgotten the past up to a few minutes ago. Yet all the time he was haunted with an insistent feeling that he had something to do, that he had something to obliterate, or suffer consequences disastrous to himself.

"I suppose it will pass off presently," he muttered. "Let me see, wasn't there somebody with me? Was Bark here, or did I dream it? Yes, he certainly was here. But what happened? Why did I come to myself lying in the fireplace? And what was it I had to do? Perhaps Swift can tell me."

But, though Rent sat there with his head in his hands for half an hour, his treacherous memory did not come back to him. He looked up eagerly as he heard a step in the passage and Swift came in. With a certain feeling of thankfulness he recognised Swift. But all that had taken place during the past week was a blank complete and absolute. Swift gazed into the face of his employer with uneasy surprise. He had not been drinking to-night. His faculties were clear.

"What on earth is the matter?" he asked. "You look so white and wild. What have you been doing?"

"Oh, I don't know," Rent groaned. "I came for a special purpose a little time ago, but what brought me I haven't the remotest idea. I suppose I had a fainting fit or something of that kind, for when I came to myself I was lying in the fender, and now I can recollect nothing that has taken place during the last few days. I have heard of brain lapses of that kind, but I have never believed in them before."

"Did you come alone?" Swift asked.

"That I can't tell you. And I don't know how long I have been here, either. Oh, my head is dreadful!"

Swift shrugged his shoulders indifferently. He had his own idea as to what had taken place, but saw that it would be a waste of time to cross-examine Rent further. He glanced about him. The man smiled cynically as he saw the end of a cheap cigarette in a saucer on the table. It was not the sort of cigarette that Rent would smoke. Possibly that kind of tobacco might appeal to a man like Bark. Swift did not require to be told any more. He had reconstructed the whole scene in his mind's eye.

"I am very sorry," he said. "Unfortunately, I can do nothing to help you. If you take my advice, you will go back to your hotel without delay and send for a doctor. It is uncommonly awkward for a man who leads your sort of life to forget all that happens for the best part of a week. An accident like that might lead to unpleasant consequences. Now let me take you back."

Rent raised no objection. He was too thoroughly frightened and broken down to heed his assistant's sarcasm. And all the time he was filled with a haunting dread that he was leaving some work unfinished, some task which, if neglected, might involve him in a veritable catastrophe. He submitted quietly to follow Swift. No words passed as they walked through the deserted town. Near the harbour they met Malcolm Grey on his way to the yacht, but neither seemed to observe him, though he recognised them plainly enough.

"I wonder what these two fellows are up to?" Grey mused. "I would give something to see into the back of Rent's mind at the present moment. But, still, I know how to act now."

When he reached the yacht he found Tanza awaiting him, the little man's eyes sparkling, as usual. He appeared to be on excellent terms with himself.

"So you have been busy?" he exclaimed. "Well, I have not been idle, either. But tell me all about this extraordinary accident to Mrs. Charlock. You needn't be surprised to find that I know, because, for the last hour or so, I have been at the police station. Is this another case of suicide?"

"Pure accident, I should say," Grey replied. "But one can never tell. You are going your way and I am going mine, but it is odd if we can't arrive at the truth between us."

"And how did Charlock take it?" Tanza asked.

"Well, he didn't take it at all," Grey replied, "if I may put it in that way. For all the emotion and feeling he displayed we might have fished a dog out of the reservoir instead of his wife. But his feelings are so keen and intense that he keeps an extra tight hold upon them. I am to see him in the morning.

I want an excuse for going over his house, and, if I am not mistaken, I shall make a sensational discovery or two in the course of to-day or to-morrow. I'll have one of your cigarettes, after which I'll go to bed."

There was no change in Charlock when Grey reached the house on the following morning. He found the artist in the same quiet, self-contained mood. There was nothing to show that his feelings had been played upon, except for certain hollow rings under his eyes.

"I am glad you have come," he said. "It is dreadful being here alone. I have got a few things in the house and furnished a sitting-room for the time being. They tell me the inquest is at ten o'clock. I shall be glad when it is over, for the police are worrying me with all sorts of questions more or less impertinent. I have the greatest difficulty in keeping my hands off some of them. Ah, here is another. It is the inspector this time. He rather wants to see you. Meanwhile, I'll get out of the way till he is finished."

Charlock slipped quietly out of the room as the inspector came in. He was a pompous little man with a heavy manner, who appeared to think that he had the care of the universe on his shoulders. Nevertheless, when he began to speak his questions were very much to the point.

"I don't want to bother you, Mr. Grey," the inspector said, "but I think you can give me certain information. I have been talking the matter over with Mr. Charlock and he has shown me his wife's letter. It appears that the lady came here last night at her own suggestion. It was Mr. Charlock's idea that you should be present at the interview. Of course, we don't want to go into the details of a domestic quarrel, but it must be admitted that the relationship between husband and wife was exceedingly strained. I suppose you know that?"

"You are stating it fairly," Grey said cautiously.

"Exactly. Mr. Charlock was inclined to be harsh, and the lady, I understand, was terribly extravagant. There had been a serious quarrel before Mrs. Charlock made overtures for reconciliation. It doesn't matter why Mr. Charlock decided to call you in, seeing that you were here. Now, have you any reason to believe that Mrs. Charlock was in the house alone with her husband before you came? Did you see any evidence of it?"

The question startled Grey.

"Indeed, I didn't!" he said. "I understood from Mr. Charlock that he had not seen his wife. He put it plainly to me that I had been asked to go round an hour before Mrs. Charlock was expected, so that in the first place he could explain to me why I had been sent for. I feel sure I am right."

By way of reply the inspector produced a light dustcoat, which he held out for Grey's inspection.

"I think I shall prove that you are wrong," he said. "I traced Mrs. Charlock's movements all yesterday, and I am prepared to show that the lady was wearing this dustcoat at the very time that she left her hotel last night. She was seen by several people to whom she is personally known. You will perceive for yourself that this cloak is quite dry, and that it is not in the least stained, as it would be had it been immersed in water. Now, last night, after I came here at your suggestion, I went all over the house, and in the drawing-room, by the side of one of the French windows, I found this cloak. The window was unfastened, so that anybody could get in who liked, and I came to the conclusion that Mrs. Charlock was either in the house when you came or she had been here before. As a matter of fact, the cloak proves it."

"I am afraid it does," Grey was fain to admit.

"Thank you," the inspector said. "But I have not done yet. I have been examining the lawn for footmarks, and I find traces of a pair of boots, or rather of tennis-shoes, which go right round the side of the lawn to the back of the sundial. These shoes were worn by Mr. Charlock and yield distinctly the same impressions as were given by the shoes which marched side by side with yours when you were on your way to the fountain last night. Now, can you explain this?"

"It is very awkward for Charlock," Grey murmured.

CHAPTER XXXI
AN UNEXPECTED FRIEND

Inspector Battley nodded his head gravely.

"I suppose I ought not to tell you these things," he said. "But I understand you are a friend of Mr. Charlock's; in fact, so far as I know, you are the only friend he has. Of course, this may not be more than a mere coincidence, but you might mention the matter to him, and no doubt an explanation will be forthcoming. I could not take any action at present."

"Of course you couldn't," Grey exclaimed, "especially in view of the evidence which I have already given you myself."

"That is exactly the point," Battley said eagerly. "According to what you say, you heard a cry of distress and hastened off at once in the direction of the sundial. There you found the unfortunate lady lying dead in the fountain. I suppose you are quite sure that it was her voice you heard?"

"Well, that's rather a large order," Grey said. "But, on the other hand, if it wasn't Mrs. Charlock, who could it have been? I am pretty sure that I am right, and that my evidence would convince any jury that Mr. Charlock had nothing to do with his wife's death."

"It is a good point," the inspector said. "Still, the lady was in the house before you came, beyond all doubt. It would be a good thing if we could ascertain what brought her here. I hope you will recognise that I am doing my best to help Mr. Charlock."

"Oh, I quite see that. And as to Mrs. Charlock's presence here before I came, that can be easily explained. There is no secret in the fact that Mr. Charlock and his wife were on exceedingly bad terms, owing to the wife's extravagance. So far as I can gather, she did not seem to have the least idea of the value of money. She spent all she could get in reckless fashion, and she did not hesitate to pledge Charlock's credit to the utmost capacity. Rightly or wrongly, she became possessed of the idea that he was merely a money-making machine, a kind of slave to minister to her wants. Charlock is a peculiar, self-contained man, like most people with deep-seated feelings, and this reserve has given him the reputation of being an unfeeling brute who did not deserve such a wife as Mrs. Charlock. At any rate, that is the view that most of their friends take, and at one time, I confess, it was my opinion, too. Of course, it was foolish of Charlock to turn his wife out of the house——"

"Did he do that?" the inspector asked.

"Well, that is what it came to. He had made up his mind to sacrifice everything with a view to getting out of debt. He had taken a small cottage, where he intended his wife to do the domestic work, and where he meant to remain as long as a penny was owing. Perhaps it was natural that Mrs. Charlock should refuse to fall in with this suggestion. Charlock took the bull by the horns by stripping the house entirely, and when Mrs. Charlock came back one evening she found the place as bare as you see it now. Two courses were open to her—either to go to her own friends or follow her husband. There was one more alternative, and that was to live for the time being on the sale of her jewellery, of which she possessed a considerable quantity. But the jewellery had been stolen, or, at least, so Charlock tells me. He seemed to be under the impression that the French maid, Hortense, had had some hand in the robbery. My impression is that Mrs. Charlock came an hour or so before the time appointed for the interview in order thoroughly to search the house for the missing gems. I think you will find that Charlock hasn't the slightest idea that she has been here at all."

"Oh, it is possible," Battley remarked. "Perhaps you will be good enough to mention this matter to Mr. Charlock. I don't want to allude to it for the present. I have been candid with you, and perhaps you will do your best to get an explanation of this peculiar point."

Before Grey could reply, Charlock returned. He asked impatiently how much longer Grey would be. He seemed to be put out about something.

"I am coming now," Grey said. "By the way, I have had an interesting conversation with Inspector Battley. He wants to know why Mrs. Charlock was here for some time before I came in response to your letter."

"Who says she was here?" Charlock demanded.

"Inspector Battley is in a position to prove it," Grey said significantly. "Lying on a chair yonder is the wrap she was wearing when she left her hotel last night, and the wrap was found on a chair by the French window, perfectly dry, so that it must have been discarded before she found her way into the water. You were also wearing a pair of tennis-shoes last night, the prints of which Inspector Battley says he traced to the back of the sundial. Of course, the inspector doesn't suggest——"

Charlock burst into a hoarse laugh.

"Oh, no, he doesn't suggest anything," he cried. "He hints all sorts of mysterious things, which is a great deal worse. He will be saying next that I had a hand in removing the woman who was such a hindrance and encumbrance to me. Not that it in the least matters, because if he doesn't say so, somebody else will. There are scores of people who regarded my wife as an injured saint and myself as a monster of cruelty. I didn't see my wife last night. If she was here, as you say, I know nothing whatever about it. She had her own reasons for coming, no doubt, and her visit was made in absolute secrecy. Possibly she was looking for her lost jewels, of which she had a quantity. I ought to know, because I paid for them, like the fool that I was. I understand that the jewels were stolen, and I don't mind admitting I was very pleased they were. They were bought at a time when I had no means of paying for them; they were the final cause of all my trouble. But that doesn't matter. You may depend upon it, my wife came back to have another look for the missing stones, and, for certain reasons of her own, she didn't want me to know it. And now, if you have anything else to say, perhaps you will say it to me honestly and straightforwardly."

There was something truculent in Charlock's expression. A gleam of defiance lighted his eyes. The inspector reddened slightly.

"I beg your pardon," he said. "I am bringing no accusation against you. I merely remarked that your wife was here last night, and that you had said nothing about the fact. I admit now that you did not know of it. You may regard this as a mere detail, but in our profession trifles often turn out to be of the greatest importance. I asked Mr. Grey to mention this matter to you in an entirely friendly spirit. I did not expect that he would have done so just yet."

"There was nothing to be gained by delay," Grey said.

Battley curtly agreed, and took himself off without delay. In his queer, sardonic way, Charlock seemed to be amused about something, for he chuckled to himself as he walked up and down the room.

"What foolish things clever men can do sometimes," he said. "Now, you see perfectly well what that fellow has got in his mind. Nothing will persuade him that I hadn't a hand in my wife's death. He is convinced that I had an interview with her before you came into the house. It is lucky for me that you can give evidence to the contrary."

"Are you not a little foolish yourself?" Grey ventured. "You might have taken what the inspector said in a more friendly spirit, and you admit that there are plenty of people who regard you as a most undesirable man to marry any woman. Of course, I know I am going rather far— —"

"My dear fellow, nothing of the kind. I know you are only too ready to help me, and in my own way I am grateful. Besides, I am certain that I am right. Let us assume for a moment that Hortense stole those jewels. The night my wife left here on her foolish mission with Arnold Rent she intended to take her diamonds with her. With all her saint-like purity and innocence, she did not forget their value. But the diamonds were gone. It did not matter so very much, however, seeing that my wife was to find an asylum with Mrs. Rent and remain under that lady's roof till I should generously make a fool of myself and give her the chance of getting rid of me altogether. But when Mrs. Rent figures as a woman of firmness and determination the whole situation is changed. Then it becomes necessary to secure those gems. That is why my wife came here. And you needn't be afraid about what people say of me. What does it matter what they say? What does anything matter? My life has been blackened and ruined because I was fool enough to mistake a cold-blooded, self-seeking creature for a good and true woman. If they like to say that I had a hand in her death, they can if they please. They ought to be grateful to me for giving them something to talk about!"

It was in vain that Grey protested, for Charlock turned a deaf ear to him. Then the artist walked out of the room across the grass towards the sundial.

CHAPTER XXXII
SWIFT COMES OUT

As was only natural in the circumstances, the tragic death of Mrs. John Charlock created a profound sensation. The accident to the French maid had set most people talking, but the unfortunate end of the mistress in the same mysterious fashion bade fair to become a general topic of conversation. The whole thing was so simple, and yet so strange and out of the common. A score of theories were set on foot, but not one of them worked out in a satisfactory manner. The police were plainly at fault, and though Inspector Battley was reinforced by a colleague or two from Scotland Yard, the end of the week found the authorities no nearer the solution of the trouble than they had been at the beginning of the inquiry.

As for Grey and Tanza, they went their own way, which was by no means the way taken by the police. Ephraim Bark was still in the neighbourhood, and his movements were watched by Tanza and Grey with a patient care which would have astonished that worthy had he only known of it. Grey had his own theory, which he was developing slowly. It was an integral part of his theory that Bark could have said a great deal more had he chosen to do so. And there was yet another person whom Grey was keeping a close eye upon. He had by no means forgotten the torn photograph he had found in the French maid's room. He did not ignore the information as to Arnold Rent's strange friendship with the dead Frenchwoman. And there was another item of which, as yet, Grey had said nothing to anyone. He was coming to his conclusions now—conclusions so strange and startling that he hardly dared trust himself to believe them. A week passed slowly, during which nothing particular had happened, and Arnold Rent appeared to get no better. So far as Grey could gather, his brother scientist had had a nasty fall, which, for the time being, had affected his intellect. There was a good deal of mystery about the affair, and Grey was at some pains to make the acquaintance of the doctor who was attending Rent. The thing was accomplished at length through Tanza, who made some pretext for inviting the doctor to dine aboard his yacht. Very cautiously and patiently Grey led up to the subject which was next his heart. The thing was so naturally done, and Tanza played into his hands so cleverly, that the doctor fell into the trap at once.

"Oh, so you know Mr. Rent," he said, as he lay back in a deck-chair smoking a cigar. "An exceedingly clever fellow, who, unless I am much mistaken, will make his mark in the world yet. A strange illness that of his, by the way."

"I was going to ask you about that," Grey murmured. "I hear he is suffering from the effects of a severe fall. I hope the accident won't leave any permanent injury."

"I don't think so," the doctor said. "I had a specialist down to-day and he takes a very sanguine view of the case. All that is wanted is rest. For the moment my patient has a partial lapse of memory—a sort of hiatus of a week. In other words, he can recollect everything perfectly well, except that the past seven days are a complete blank to him. And during the last day or so before his fall he had been engaged in some experiment, the results of which ought to be placed on record at once. This seems to worry him terribly. It has affected him to such an extent that he is making himself seriously ill over it. Imagine a man who has some great commercial deal on and has to buy or sell at a given moment suddenly forgetting the very thing he has to do. That appears to be Rent's case. Anybody might suppose that he had committed murder and had forgotten to hide the clue, by the way he goes on."

A sudden exclamation broke from Grey, which he checked immediately. The doctor looked up inquiringly.

"A twinge of pain," he muttered. "Nothing much to trouble about. A most interesting case, doctor. And you think that in time Rent will be quite himself again?"

"Oh, I am certain of it. If I could only prevent him from worrying, I should have had him right by this time. Of course, what I am saying to you is in strict confidence."

Grey and Tanza gave the desired assurance, and the conversation became more general. When the doctor left he was accompanied by Grey, who said he had business on shore. He left the man of medicine at the corner of a street leading up from the quay and proceeded along the shore to Arnold Rent's workshop. He stood for a long time making a mental calculation after which he walked several times round the building, examining the ground carefully as if in search of something. Apparently, nothing had rewarded his efforts, for he shook his head impatiently and crossed over to the office, in the window of which a light was burning. Someone inside was singing a snatch from a comic opera in a loud, blustering voice. An unsteady, flickering shadow crossed the blind once or twice, and Grey's features broke into a grim smile.

"Friend Swift has broken out again," he murmured. "What a pity so clever a man should be the victim of a curse like this! Still, his misfortune is my opportunity, and if there is anything he can tell me, now is the time to learn it."

Without further hesitation, Grey pushed his way into the office, which was flooded with half a dozen powerful electric lights. The large slate-topped table had been cleared of all kinds of electric appliances. There were the remains of a supper at one end, flanked by two or three empty bottles. The reserved and saturnine Swift seemed to have changed altogether. His dark features wore a look of reckless gaiety; his sombre eyes were shining. He did not appear to be in the least surprised to see Grey; in fact, he might have been expecting him. His unsteady gait and thick speech, however, told their tale.

"Hallo!" he exclaimed. "So you have come to pay me a visit? You have come here to learn the secrets of the prison-house? Ah, my dear fellow, you are very clever, but your tuppenny discoveries are nothing compared to what we are on the track of here. For we've got it, my boy, we've got it. You remember the dream you used to indulge in at school?"

"Intermittent electricity," Grey exclaimed. "A wireless current. You don't mean to say you have got to the bottom of that!"

Swift seemed to be sober for the moment. A sullen, obstinate look came over his face, but he did not appear to be half so agitated as was his visitor. Only for an instant did it occur to the dull brain that secrets were being betrayed, and in the same instant Grey saw that he had gone too far. He changed the subject with a quickness that fogged Swift.

"What did I say to you?" the latter asked, as he passed his hand across his face. "I hope I didn't make a fool of myself?"

"Not at all," Grey hastened to say. "Besides, I haven't come here to-night in the guise of a spy."

"Quite right," Swift said, with a sudden change to amiability. "Of course, you didn't. You are too much of a gentleman for that. Now, Arnold Rent isn't a gentleman, for all his pretence. He treats me like a dog. He uses my brains and then passes off my discoveries as his own. He knows that no one else will employ me, that nobody else would look twice at a man who is often drunk a week at a time. But I can't help it, Grey. Upon my word, I can't. I inherit it from my father. I fight against it and fight against it till the sweat runs off my forehead and my limbs refuse to carry me. Then, all at once, everything grows misty and I can't recollect anything more till I am gloriously drunk. That's why Rent puts up with me. But he is a blackguard, all the same, and he will come to a bad end. Don't you trust him, Grey.

Don't you trust him, or it will be all the worse for you. Now come and sit down and make a night of it with me."

Grey declined the tempting offer.

"I can't stay many minutes," he said. "I merely looked in to see how Rent was getting on."

"He is bad, downright bad," Swift said, with a chuckle. "And he has got something on his mind. There is something he has to do, some piece of infernal rascality to conceal, and his brain fails him, and he can't for the life of him think what it is. And all the time the trail is open for anybody to pick up, and he might find himself in trouble at any moment. That is what's wrong with Arnold Rent, and I can't say I'm sorry. Do I know what he has been doing? No, I don't, and I don't care. You think that his accident is the result of a fall. Nothing of the kind, my boy! He and that blackguard, Ephraim Bark, had a quarrel the other night and Bark knocked him into the fender. How do I know that? Well, you see, I came in directly afterwards and Rent tried to persuade me that nobody had been here. Unluckily for him there was a cheap cigarette on the table, and I guessed at once Bark had been smoking. But why don't you sit down and make yourself comfortable? You are different from me. You always know when to leave off—when you have had enough."

Half-defiantly, Swift helped himself to another strong glass of whisky, and a moment or two later was lying back in an armchair, more or less asleep. It was a good chance for Grey to get away and he seized it promptly.

"That's a lucky call," he muttered. "Now I see what it was that puzzled me. Rent has learnt the secret of the intermittent current and he has been using it. It will be my turn next."

CHAPTER XXXIII
A WORD IN SEASON

Mrs. Rent might have possessed all the strength and determination for which she gave herself credit, but she lost no time in responding to the call of duty directly she heard that her son had met with an accident. She had waited till nearly daybreak for Rent's return on that eventful night when he had gone out in search of Kate Charlock. She had waited, too, with an anxiety which she strove in vain to conceal. But there came no sign of Rent until a letter reached her in a day or two saying that he had reconsidered the whole position and had come to the conclusion that she was right and he was altogether wrong. The letter was couched in terms of due filial affection, and was none the less convincing for being a tissue of lies from beginning to end.

But Mrs. Rent read it all the more lovingly because she wanted to believe that her son meant every word he wrote. He told her how he had talked the matter over with Kate Charlock and how the latter had agreed that his mother had acted entirely for the best. No doubt she had appeared to be harsh and cruel, but she was only cruel to be kind. Mrs. Charlock was going back to her husband and she and Arnold Rent were not likely to meet in the future. Meanwhile, the writer would work as he had never worked before and try to wipe out every suggestion of his folly.

For the next two or three days life had resumed its old peacefulness at Alton Lee. Then came a few curt lines from Swift to the effect that Rent had met with a nasty accident and that it would be as well if his mother came at once. Within twenty-four hours Mrs. Rent was installed by her son's bedside, with Ethel Hargrave in close attendance. It never struck either of them that there was anything sinister about the patient's constant complaint that he had something to do which he could not remember. There were hours and almost days together when he sat in sullen silence, taking no notice of anybody and apparently trying to work out some problem in his clouded mind. At such times Mrs. Rent preferred to be alone with her son, and urged Ethel to go out of doors as much as possible.

It was lonely for the girl, but she had not forgotten the events of the last few days, and found herself thinking a good deal about John Charlock. There was a romantic vein in her nature which rendered her different from most girls, and her solitary life at Alton Lee had given her plenty of time to think and form her own conclusions. From the very first she had taken a fancy to John Charlock. His rugged austerity and reserve did not repel her as it did most people. She saw beneath it a depth and sincerity of feeling with which she was in absolute sympathy. And simultaneously with the appearance of John Charlock her idol in the form of Arnold Rent had fallen to the ground. She had been asking herself many questions lately, and when the first shock was over she knew in her heart of hearts that she did not care for Arnold in the way in which a woman should care for the man she hoped to marry. She had heard both sides of the question, too. She had interviewed John Charlock and his wife, and the more her mind dwelt upon the matter the more convinced she was that the woman had been to blame. Of course, Ethel had heard of the tragic death of Kate Charlock, and now that she was in the neighbourhood she felt herself irresistibly drawn towards the house where Charlock had spent some of his unhappiest days. Ethel thought that it would be safe to stroll through the beautiful grounds, for the house was still empty, and she had not the least idea that Charlock was in the district.

On the third day of her visit she ventured to pass the lodge gate and walk down the drive towards the house. The place looked blank with its staring windows, but there was no sign of neglect in the garden. Here the lawns were cut and trimmed, and there were beds luxuriant with flowers. Here, too, gleaming in the sunshine, was the white marble of the sundial on the fountain, near to which those two terrible tragedies had taken place. It was impossible to connect so fair a spot with mystery and horror. As Ethel was standing almost fascinated, she heard a step on the gravel behind her, and when she turned she saw John Charlock watching her.

"You startled me," she said, a faint wave of colour tingeing her face. "I am ashamed you should find me here."

"And why?" Charlock demanded in his imperious way.

"Well, it seems so unfeeling. It suggests impertinent curiosity. Believe me, I would not have come had I known you were here."

"Well, I am glad you didn't know," Charlock retorted. "You see, I have to stay here for the present. I am doing my best to let the house, but so far without success. It is possible that I may come back again. My wife is dead and I must say nothing about her, but I think that, seeing I have no longer any reason to fear her extravagance, I might manage with economy to remain here until I am free of debt. I suppose you came with Mrs. Rent to look after your invalid. I hope he is progressing favourably."

"Well, no," Ethel said. "He doesn't seem to get any better. To all appearances he is well, but he seems to be suffering in his mind. There is something which he has to do, but he can't remember what it is. Mrs. Rent and I are taking turns nursing him. The doctor says the cloud may lift at any moment and then Arnold will be himself again. What a lovely place you have!"

"I thought so at one time," Charlock said. "I had dreams of being happy here, but, in fact, it is here I have passed the most miserable days of my life. Oh, I am not complaining. I am not blaming the place. But, tell me, did you happen to see my wife after I left Alton Lee?"

Charlock asked the question in his abrupt fashion. His eyes were fixed steadily upon his companion.

"Yes, I saw her," Ethel said. "A beautiful woman."

"No fairer on God's earth. And I suppose she managed to persuade you that she was an injured innocent and I an absolute monster. Still, I am glad you saw her, because it is well to hear both sides of a question. And yet I am conceited enough to think that you cannot imagine so much evil of me, or you would not be talking as you are at this moment."

"I am still of the same opinion," Ethel murmured. "I think your wife had the peculiar temperament which can sincerely make out that wrong is right. Certain men justify dishonourable actions in the same way. I might have been prejudiced. I might have been offended by your wife's coming to Alton Lee at all. But I told you that night in the garden that I was sorry for you and I see no cause to change my opinion."

The words cost Ethel somewhat of an effort, but she uttered them bravely. Then she turned away as if the conversation were ended, and Charlock sought to detain her no longer. There was that in his silence, a suggestion of delicacy of feeling, for which the girl was grateful. She shook hands with him by the lodge gate, and the favourable impression he had created in her mind was not lessened by the absence on his part of any suggestion that they should meet again.

But all thoughts of Charlock faded from the girl's mind when she reached home and saw how pale and worried Mrs. Rent was. The doctor was coming down the stairs and was urging his patient's mother to rest for an hour or so. Ethel cordially supported this suggestion.

"I ought to have been back before," she said contritely. "Oh, surely you can leave Arnold to me for a little while. It isn't the first time that I have had him in my care."

With obvious reluctance Mrs. Rent gave way. There was little or nothing to do, for the patient was sitting in his armchair, with his head in his hands as usual, pondering the problem which occupied his mind to the exclusion of everything else. He made no reply to Ethel's question as to how he felt. The girl picked up a book and gradually became interested in the story. She was roused presently by a loud exclamation on the part of the patient. He was standing upright, his eyes gleaming, a peculiar fixed smile on his face. He crossed the room with rapid strides and proceeded to open a cupboard door with a key which he took from his pocket. Somewhat alarmed, Ethel watched him with dazed astonishment. She saw he held in his hand a mass of india-rubber bandages and something that looked like a pair of gloves. From the expression of his eyes and the way he looked over her head he seemed to be oblivious of her presence. Yet he held the gloves out towards her.

"Come along," he said hoarsely. "Thank Heaven, I recollect it at last. But we have not a moment to lose, for the secret might be discovered at any moment. Why are you standing there staring? Why don't you do what I tell you? You have been drinking again."

Ethel sprang to the wall and rang the bell. At the same moment Rent dropped his burden on the floor and once more lapsed into the old sullen state of mind.

CHAPTER XXXIV
A BLACK SUSPICION

There was no occasion for Ethel Hargrave to be afraid. There had been no suggestion of violence on the part of her patient, but yet, in some unaccountable way, she felt her heart sinking and her nerves throbbing as if the shadow of a great disgrace was hanging over her. She had ceased to care for Arnold Rent; indeed, she was almost grateful to him for showing her that she had made a mistake in her estimate of his character. All these years she had lived so quiet a life, she had seen so few men, that she had come to regard Arnold Rent as typical of what was best in his sex. In this she had been encouraged by Mrs. Rent's pride and delight in the progress of her son. Ethel thought she was fortunate above women, inasmuch as she would some day become the wife of Arnold Rent. The whole thing had been a tacit understanding, and at first when disillusion came the pain had been smart and keen.

But this was due to wounded vanity, though Ethel did not know it. It was her first contact with the meaner side of human nature and it left its mark. Despite the fact that Ethel had lived so long alone, she had read a great deal and knew much of the world and its ways. It did not need anyone to teach her that Arnold Rent had behaved foolishly in the matter of Mrs. Charlock, and since then one or two little things had opened Ethel's eyes.

She was glad the disclosure had come before it was too late. She could only regard Arnold Rent in the light of a friend, and found herself contrasting him with John Charlock, much to his detriment.

And now she could not rid herself of the idea that there was something more than mere hallucination here. The blow which Rent had received would be hardly accountable for his acting in this fashion. Undoubtedly, the man had something desperate on his mind. He had every appearance of it in the uneasy, haunted expression of his face and the gleam of his eyes. Something was fearfully wrong, and Ethel felt her heart sink as she watched the moody, disconsolate figure seated in the chair opposite her. What it was he had to conceal she did not know, nor could she manage, with all the patience at her command, to find out what was amiss.

"Is there nothing I can do for you?" she asked.

Rent shook his head sulkily. The mass of matter which he had removed from the safe lay on the floor, but he took no notice of it. The cloud had fallen again.

"Don't bother," he said. "It has all gone again. There was something I had to do and I can't for the life of me think what it was. I had to go somewhere. There was a little thing— —"

He broke off abruptly and smote his forehead passionately with his hand. Ethel watched him curiously.

"Surely there is some way I can help you," she said.

"No, there isn't. You know nothing about it. Besides, in any case, it is not a woman's work. Swift will be all right. But, then, you can't trust Swift, because you never know when he is going to give way to one of his drunken bouts. The most useful man I know is Malcolm Grey. He can manage it."

Rent was speaking rationally enough. It was only the uneasy gleam in his eyes which proved to Ethel that he was still wandering. But she caught at the suggestion.

"Would you like to see Mr. Grey?" she asked. "I understand that he is here; he has called to ask about you once or twice. He is staying with a friend who has a yacht in the harbour."

"That's the idea," Rent said eagerly. "Send for Grey at once. Well, why don't you go and do it? Why do you sit looking at me in that extraordinary way?"

Rent's voice was harsh and hard and his face wore an angry look. Ethel rose from her seat, but before she could leave the room Rent sprang up and detained her.

"You are not to go," he whispered. "Do you hear me? You are to stay where you are. What do you mean by making such a suggestion to me? Do you want to get rid of me? Why, if Grey so much as guessed, I should never know a moment's peace again."

It was hard to tell what to do in the circumstances, and Ethel could only regard her companion with astonishment. He dropped back in his seat and the same sullen silence fell over him. There was nothing to do but to humour the patient, and, to her great relief, a little later Ethel saw that he was asleep. She slipped from the room into that of Mrs. Rent, which adjoined, but that lady lay on her bed without sign or motion. No doubt she was asleep also. It was with a sensation of relief that Ethel heard the doctor coming up the stairs presently. As his quick glance took in the state of affairs, he crept quietly from the room and beckoned to Ethel to follow him.

"I am glad to see that," he said. "Whatever you do, don't disturb him. The more sleep he has the better."

"Mrs. Rent is sleeping, too," Ethel said.

"That is right," the doctor murmured. "I am sure she wants it. If we could only induce a sleep like this on the part of the patient oftener he would get better much the sooner. It is impossible for him to recover so long as he keeps on worrying his brain as he does. And now, at the risk of being impertinent, I am going to ask a personal question. I understand you have known Mr. Rent for a long time. Is that so?"

"I have known him all my life," Ethel said.

"Then you'll be able to tell me what I want to know. Of course, I recognise that he is an exceedingly clever man and that he has a very active and intelligent mind. I am told that he sits up half the night working out problems and fascinating experiments. These men make the most difficult patients when there is brain trouble. Tell me, do you think Mr. Rent has anything weighing heavily on his mind?"

Ethel hesitated. She was startled to find the doctor's train of thought very like her own. He put the question with a gravity which impressed her. But he was the doctor in charge of the case and had every right to the information of which he was in search.

"I am afraid so," she said. "It has been dawning upon me for the last day or two that there is something very wrong. Arnold Rent seems to be full of the idea that he has left some task unfinished. He is dreadfully afraid lest somebody should find out certain information which his illness prevented him from concealing. It may be that he has hit upon a new invention—something startling in the way of a discovery. On the other hand, it may be that he has done something to be ashamed of and does not want it known. I was going to ask his assistant, Mr. Swift, about the matter, but Mr. Rent never trusts him with anything of importance, because the latter has a weakness for drink. I feel pretty sure that the secret has something to do with a scientific discovery, because, a few minutes since, your patient was anxious to send for Mr. Malcolm Grey, a brother scientist. Then he suddenly changed his mind and told me to do nothing of the kind. I can't make it out at all."

The doctor looked grave.

"It is a most puzzling case," he said. "The best thing to do is to fall in with every wish the patient expresses. Never mind if he changes his opinion the next moment; humour him to the top of his bent, and don't disturb him in any case. The same remark applies to Mrs. Rent. Let the poor lady have all the rest she can get. I will look in again later."

The time passed slowly. It was growing late, and there was no sign of Mrs. Rent. Ethel sat in the sick-room waiting the advent of the doctor, who did not come, though it was now past eleven o'clock. Probably he had been detained somewhere. But, since Rent was slumbering in his chair, it did not matter. He moved uneasily in his sleep once or twice, and Ethel caught the name of Grey on his lips. Unconscious as he was, his mind was working away at the problem which puzzled him so sorely. Then Ethel closed her own eyes and for a little while was oblivious to all that was going on. When she came to herself she heard a clock striking the half-hour after eleven, so that she knew she had been asleep some five-and-twenty minutes. She wondered if her patient was awake, but was surprised to see that he was no longer seated in the chair. Possibly he had gone back to bed.

But the bed was empty. The door was closed and locked on the inside. Ethel rubbed her eyes in astonishment. She was not yet conscious of the full extent of the catastrophe. Then she roused herself with an effort. She began putting the pieces together in her mind. The door was locked on the inside, and yet Arnold Rent had vanished. Where had he gone to, and how had he contrived to obliterate himself? The window was open, and, as Ethel looked out, she saw it was a short drop to the garden. Beyond question, Arnold Rent had disappeared in that way. It was the kind of furtive exit a man with a diseased brain and perturbed mind would make. His clouded intellect had pointed to secrecy. He had deemed it prudent not to show himself in the house. But where had he gone? And why?

For the moment Ethel stood thinking the puzzle out. Then she unlocked the door and walked quietly into Mrs. Rent's room. The latter still lay on her bed fast asleep.

CHAPTER XXXV
THE SEARCH

It was a cruel dilemma for the girl, but her courage and intelligence returned and she began to see how to act. Nothing was to be gained by rousing Mrs. Rent. Possibly before she woke Arnold would be found. But where to look for him, and which way to turn, Ethel did not know. Perhaps the best thing would be to go at once to Rent's workshop on the shore. No doubt what was troubling him was in some way connected with his researches, and it was an obvious inference that he had gone in that direction. Ethel slipped into a wrap and, without waiting to put on a hat, walked into the darkness.

She knew which way to go, because the workshop had already been pointed out to her. She did not mind the dark and lonely journey. She flew swiftly over the broken ground and gave a gasp of relief when she saw a light in one of the offices. Her search seemed to be finished almost before it had begun. Taking her courage in both hands, she opened the door of the office and walked in.

But she did not, as she had expected, see Rent. The office was not deserted, for Swift was present. There were strange appliances on the table, weird-looking apparatus and receptacles which conveyed nothing to the girl, and over one of these Swift was bending with a critical eye. In spite of her trouble Ethel saw that his face was deadly pale. She saw how horribly his features were twitching, and how the pupils of his eyes were dilated. She had never in her life before been face to face with a man verging on *delirium tremens*. But she instinctively recoiled, feeling that something was very wrong. It flashed across her mind how Arnold Rent had said that Swift was given to prolonged bouts of drinking. She wondered if the repulsive aspect of his face had anything to do with the dreadful weakness. The girl was frightened. She knew there was something akin to danger here. But it was not the time to hang back, not the time to show the terror which set her trembling from head to foot. She had to find Rent. She had to forget her own risk.

"I beg your pardon," she said firmly, "but I am looking for Mr. Rent. Has he been here?"

A queer sort of laugh came from Swift's lips. He pushed his curious-looking appliances aside and came a pace or two nearer to the questioner. She stood her ground.

"Do my eyes deceive me?" he said hoarsely, "or is this a vision that I see before me? Speak again, bright spirit, and let me know that I am not dreaming. I swear if these delusions only came in this form I would never willingly be sober again. But you can never tell. Sometimes it is a swarm of bees, sometimes an army of pink rats, or an array of black and grinning devils. But in the shape of loveliness like this— —"

The speaker paused and his features twitched horribly. Ethel remembered having read of such cases. The man was on the brink of collapse, though he had sense enough to know what was going on. His madness might take a dangerous form. At any rate, it would be perilous to show fear.

"My name is Hargrave," Ethel said. "I live with Mrs. Rent. Mr. Rent has disappeared and I came to see whether he was here. I am sorry to intrude— —"

"Don't mention it," Swift said. "It is not often that I have a pleasure so charming as this. And so you have come to look for my master. Fortunate Arnold Rent, who can command the services of so fair a friend. I suppose that you and he— —"

"Certainly not," Ethel said. The colour flamed painfully into her cheeks. "Nothing of the kind. I am merely a friend of Mr. Rent's. I am helping to nurse him and am concerned at his disappearance."

"I beg your pardon," Swift said, with some show of humility. "And I congratulate you. Don't have anything to do with Arnold Rent. Keep him at arm's length, for, between ourselves, he is a precious scoundrel, as a good many people have found out to their cost."

"Has he been here?" Ethel demanded.

"Oh, no, he hasn't. And, what is more, I don't think he is in the least likely to come. I am sorry to disappoint you. It cuts me to the heart to see that anxious expression on a fair face. If you want Arnold Rent, why don't you try John Charlock's place? I know it is late and the grounds are lonely, but I am giving you good advice."

Swift accompanied this remark with a leer so malicious that Ethel recoiled in disgust. In spite of the man's muddled brain and besotted intellect, he had certain information of which Ethel was ignorant. It would not do to show that he filled her with disgust.

"I am greatly obliged to you," she said. "I will go there at once. There is no time to be lost."

"No, don't go," Swift pleaded. "Give me your company a little longer. I am all right if I am not alone. But directly I am by myself those grinning faces peep at me out of every corner—there, can't you see them? Don't you notice their ugly heads sticking out of the row of bottles along that top shelf? Horrible! Horrible! Don't go."

The few last words rose to a wailing cry, which filled Ethel with pity, frightened as she was. She could stand it no longer, but turned and made her way to the door. She flew along the passage into the open air, glancing over her shoulder to see if Swift were following. It was good to be alone, to feel the fresh breeze blowing on her face, and to know that she had escaped that danger. For Swift had made no attempt to follow. She could see his lank shadow crossing and recrossing the blind. She could hear him singing hideously to himself.

"Poor wretch," she murmured. "Surely, he is more to be pitied than blamed. And now what am I to do next? I suppose I had better follow his advice. Fancy being involved in an adventure like this! I should have smiled at the mere suggestion a month or two ago. Still, my duty is plain."

It was, indeed, a strange position for a young and unprotected girl. She found herself presently walking up the avenue to John Charlock's house, with no definite plan in her mind. What she expected to see and what she expected to gain it would have been impossible to explain. But Rent might be wandering in the grounds. It occurred to Ethel in a fantastic way that his trouble might be connected with the sundial. Everything seemed to centre round that mysterious monument, and it was possible that Arnold Rent's state of mind might be due to the tragic death of Mrs. Charlock. The notion might be illogical and absurd, but Ethel could not get it out of her mind. She passed round the garden twice without any sign of the object of her search. Then, half ashamed of herself and her own simplicity, she turned to leave.

As she passed the house she saw, to her surprise, that a light was burning in one of the windows upstairs. Perhaps Rent was there. Possibly in his madness he had elected to call upon John Charlock. Ethel knew that the latter was camping in the empty house for the present.

Acting on the spur of the moment, she crossed the drive and rang the bell. Even now she was half inclined to go back, but she forced herself to remain until a light appeared in the door and Charlock in person answered the summons. He held a candle, the light of which fell on Ethel's pale, anxious face. He staggered.

"Miss Hargrave!" he said. "What does this mean?"

"What must you think of me?" Ethel asked unsteadily. "What excuse can I have for knocking you up at this hour? I can only plead that I am in trouble."

"You need not say more than that," Charlock murmured. "Now, tell me how I can help you."

"It is Arnold Rent," Ethel stammered. "He has disappeared from the house. I was looking after him while his mother was asleep, and I dozed in my chair. When I came to myself he had vanished. I did not know what to do or how to act. It seemed to me that my best course was to try to find him before he was missed. From something he said in his delirium I fancy he was anxious to see Mr. Grey. Then it struck me that perhaps he had gone off to his workshop. I went there and saw a man called Swift. I don't know but I think he had been drinking, for his manner was strange and wild. He frightened me terribly. And I was glad to get away. I should not have come here, only he made a strange remark to the effect that I could not do better than look for my patient here. There was such an expression of cunning on Mr. Swift's face that I felt bound to come. For the last quarter of an hour I have been wandering about the grounds. Then I saw your light and some irresistible impulse forced me to ring the bell. I know it is much to ask, but I am sure you will help me."

"Help you!" Charlock exclaimed. "Of course I will. I will do anything in my power. Wait a moment till I go in the house and get an overcoat."

CHAPTER XXXVI
AN UNSEEN DANGER

Somewhat later, Ethel and her companion were walking rapidly along the road towards the town. During part of the time Charlock had been quiet, almost taciturn. But now he began to speak more freely.

"I have been thinking the matter over," he explained, "and I think there is a good deal in what that poor creature, Swift, said. It may come with a bad grace from me, but I have a shrewd suspicion that Arnold Rent is no better than he should be. I have heard rumours of certain statements made by Swift when under the influence of drink, and they have not impressed me favourably. It is possible that Swift is right and that Arnold Rent set out to-night to try to find Mr. Grey. Frequently people, otherwise demented, display a wonderful tenacity of purpose and clearness of mind when they have a definite object in view. I know a man hopelessly insane who is one of the best military tacticians in Europe. Keep him to his hobby and he might lead an army to victory. But trust him in any other capacity and you will make a fatal blunder. Now, I propose, late as it is, to go off to Dr. Tanza's yacht and see whether Arnold Rent has been there."

Ethel expressed her gratitude and waited in the shelter on the quay for Charlock's return. He came presently, accompanied by Grey, and the information that the yacht had seen nothing of the missing man.

"I am exceedingly sorry for you, Miss Hargrave," Grey murmured. "It is plucky of you to have come——"

"Won't you say foolish?" Ethel murmured. "You don't know how ashamed I feel of myself. It is very thoughtless of me to give you all this trouble for nothing."

"I beg you won't mention it," Grey said eagerly. "I admire the way you have behaved beyond measure. I am sure you are fearless, and it is only consideration for other people that brings you out alone at this time of night. As you have proved your mettle so clearly, I am not afraid to speak plainly. You will have to be prepared for an unpleasant shock before long, and if you have formed a high estimate of Mr. Rent's character——" "That illusion has been dispelled lately," Ethel said quietly. "Mr. Rent is nothing to me except that his mother has been more than kind, and if you have anything unpleasant to say, I implore you not to hesitate on my account. Let me know what it is."

"Ah, that I cannot do," Grey went on. "It is a matter of suspicion for the moment. And now let us see whether we can find your patient. Mr. Charlock has told me everything which you confided to him, and I am of opinion that Swift is not far wrong."

"Then we are going back to my house?" Charlock asked.

"That will be best," Grey replied. "Possibly we are on a wild goose chase, but we ought not to neglect a single chance."

The trio turned in silence and made their way to Charlock's residence. Charlock invited Ethel to come inside and wait while he and Grey searched the grounds.

"I would rather come with you," Ethel said. "I have not quite as much bravery as you give me credit for. I don't think I could stay alone in this deserted house."

"Oh, nonsense," Charlock said, with a return of his old peremptory manner. "Really, you must do as you are told. We shall not be very far away. And after what you have gone through to-night this will be a mere trifle."

Ethel was about to demur, when she met Charlock's steady glance. There was something in the look that checked the words on her lips and summoned her fleeting courage. From the first Charlock had fascinated her in this way. She seemed to know that she would be compelled to do almost anything he asked her. And she knew, also, that there was nothing he would require her to do that would not bear the light of day. She seemed to be comforted and uplifted, and a smile came to her lips.

"You are arbitrary," she said, "not to say rude. But I will be obedient. Only don't keep me waiting longer than you can help. I am ashamed to think that I have given you so much trouble."

Charlock turned upon his heel without reply. He seemed to take it for granted that Ethel should do exactly as he asked her. Possibly it gratified his vanity to notice how implicitly she placed herself in his hands. Charlock produced a couple of candlesticks from a cupboard and proceeded to light them and place them on the mantelshelf. There was a solitary chair in the room, upon which he asked Ethel to be seated.

"There," he said. "Try not to worry. We sha'n't be long."

Ethel smiled bravely in reply. As a matter of fact, her courage was oozing out rapidly again. She was not in the least anxious to be left alone in that echoing house. Half-ashamed of herself, she crept to the front door to see if the two men had gone, and flung it open. Anything was better than that gloomy prison, where she could hear her own heart beating, and the scratching of a mouse behind the panel sounded loud and menacing. There were queer noises, too, here and there, as if the girl were surrounded with unseen people who were wandering about the bare floors. A sudden draught of air caused a door upstairs to slam with a noise which set the whole fabric quivering. It was almost more than the girl could stand. She felt that if she remained much longer she must cry aloud. She tried to reproach herself with her own timidity. She tried to imagine that it was merely fancy which caused her to believe that someone was creeping up the stairs with stealthy steps.

But the feeling would not be fought down. The stealthy steps were far too real. It was impossible to sit there longer; she must satisfy herself that her nerves were playing her false. In an access of anger she snatched a candle from the mantelpiece and rushed into the hall.

It was no fancy. Somebody was actually creeping up the stairs. She saw the dim outline of a man. She forgot herself and her prudence in the terror of the moment. A scream escaped her lips. The man turned and regarded her with eyes that shone green and threatening out of the gloom. Then the steps were retraced and Ethel was conscious that a heavy hand was laid upon her shoulder.

"Stop that noise," the stranger said hoarsely. "Do you want to betray me? What brings you here, Ethel?"

At the mention of her name the girl looked up. To her intense surprise she saw Arnold Rent. He was fully dressed. He carried something that looked like a lever in his hand. The strange, uneasy light was still in his eyes, but there was a resolute look upon his face which spoke of directness and determination of purpose.

"What are you doing here?" she faltered.

"Never mind," Rent whispered. "That is no business of yours. If you make a fuss, if you call those men back, you will be sorry for it all the rest of your life. I am not doing any harm. It isn't as if I had come after Mrs. Charlock's jewels."

Ethel started at the suggestion. What connection could there be between Arnold Rent and the missing jewels?

"You are not a thief?" she stammered.

"Not in that way," Rent said in the same hoarse whisper. "But there are other things besides jewels. There is that Frenchwoman and her papers. I did not know at the time. I did not guess that she had been cunning enough.

But what am I doing? What am I saying? If you dare betray me I will take you by the throat— —"

Rent broke off in a whisper. An expression of malignant fury convulsed his face. Ethel could stand it no longer. With a sudden cry she burst from Rent's detaining clasp and fled into the garden, calling for help. As she crossed the lawn towards the sundial she could hear Rent's footsteps behind her. She was very near to the fountain now, when Rent closed with her and, lifting her high in the air, dragged her to the side of the lawn.

"Not there, not there," he said in the same hissing whisper. "If you value your life, keep away from here. I don't know what the danger is, though I could have told you a day or two ago. If my mind was only clear I could explain. But, as you value your future, don't come here any more."

The words might have meant a great deal, or they might have meant nothing. There was no time to inquire or explain, for out of the gloom emerged the figures of Grey and his companion. No sooner did Rent see them than his manner changed. He withdrew his hand from Ethel's arm and darted off to the house, muttering something about papers and diaries. Ethel would have staggered and fallen had not Charlock caught her.

"Did you see him?" she asked.

"Oh, we saw him right enough," Charlock said with unexpected tenderness. "He has gone into the house. And now let me take you home. This is no place for you."

CHAPTER XXXVII
A DARK SUSPICION

Ethel Hargrave did not appear to hear what Charlock was saying. Her mind had gone back to the moment when Arnold Rent had laid violent hands upon her and spoken so harshly. She thought there was something more than madness here, something in the nature of overpowering fear. Rent had cast away his peculiar vagueness of manner and appeared calm and rational. If he had only been an acquaintance snatching her from some unexpected peril his words could not have rung out more truly and sensibly. Yet, on the face of it, it seemed absurd that there could be any danger in simply walking on the lawn, though lately two tragedies had occurred there. It was small wonder, then, that Ethel trembled from head to foot with a sense of some great impending discovery. Charlock repeated his remark twice before the girl appeared to heed him.

"I am frightened," she whispered. "I don't know what to make of it. Did you see what happened?"

There was a peculiar thrill in her voice and her eyes filled with tears. Charlock looked slightly puzzled, but if anything could be gleaned from the expression of Grey's face, the mystery was no sealed book to him.

"I saw," he said curtly. "Everything will be explained in due time. Meanwhile, Mr. Charlock is right in saying this is no place for you. You must go back to your lodgings."

There was almost a command in Grey's tone, but Ethel did not offer to move.

"But it is impossible," she persisted. "How could I leave Arnold Rent? What would his mother say when she heard what I had done?"

"Nevertheless, you must do exactly what I tell you," Grey went on. "There is a mystery which must be solved, even thought it breaks Mrs. Rent's heart, and you suffer into the bargain. And if you will allow Mr. Charlock to take you quietly home, I will pledge my word that Arnold Rent shall come to no harm. Within an hour I will see that he is back."

Ethel would have ventured some protest, but the stern, hard expression on the speaker's face checked her. She turned almost imploringly to Charlock, as if seeking his protection.

"I don't understand," she murmured. "The whole thing is inexplicable. Still, if you must have your own way, I will bow to the inevitable. Mr. Charlock, would it be too much trouble to ask you to come as far as— —"

"Not in the least," Charlock said eagerly; "it would be a pleasure. And I hope you won't think Mr. Grey censorious. He is acting for the best."

"I pledge my word to that," Grey said, with a stern ring in his voice. "Believe me, Miss Hargrave, I am not here on pleasure bent. But the truth must be told, even only for the sake of innocent people. I will do my best not to abuse the trust you have put in me. I promise you that before long Arnold Rent shall be safe back in bed again. Meanwhile, there is one thing I must ask you to do. As you go along the quay you might stop and tell the boatman who is waiting to row me back to the yacht that Dr. Tanza is wanted at once. Don't say more than that, for Tanza will know what I mean. I don't think I need say more."

Silently Charlock offered his arm to Ethel Hargrave, and they vanished into the darkness. No word passed between them till after they had interviewed the sleepy boatman and sent him off on his errand. Then Ethel turned to her companion and faced him resolutely.

"I think you are a good man," she said, in a voice that shook a little. "At any rate, I know you to be generous and truthful. Now, Mr. Charlock, kindly tell me what all this means. What is the object of so much mystery? Why could not Arnold Rent have accompanied us home instead of staying behind in that gloomy old house? It is hardly fair to two defenceless women to make them puppets in a game like this."

"I swear I cannot tell you," Charlock said passionately. "I really don't know. But I am sure Grey knows what he is doing and will never rest till he gets to the bottom of the mystery."

"What is the mystery?" Ethel asked.

"Surely a superfluous question," Charlock said quietly. "Within a few days my wife and her maid have both met with strange deaths. It may be coincidence. On the other hand, it may be crime of a terrible, if ingenious, character. I should not have suspected it myself, but Mr. Grey does."

"It seems impossible," Ethel murmured.

"Oh, it does. I agree with you. But one never can tell. The whole thing is maddening. Is there nothing mysterious, think you, in this strange illness of Arnold Rent's? Mind you, I am trying to speak without prejudice. I am trying to think the best of that man. But there are moments when the most awful suspicions come into my mind, and I have literally to expel them."

Ethel was silent for a while. She could not forget her own haunting suspicions. They came back to her now with vivid force—Arnold Rent's violence, the unsteady terror in his voice as he snatched her from some unseen danger. His conduct and his manner were not consistent with innocence and integrity.

"What do you think?" she asked timidly.

"I don't know what to think," Charlock burst out. "As I said before, I have my suspicions. But I am prejudiced. I decline to believe that Arnold Rent is the upright, honourable man people believe him to be. But it is hardly fair to speak of a man in this way when he is in trouble. I think the best thing we can do is to drop the subject."

For some time the two walked side by side in silence until they reached Mrs. Rent's lodgings. To Ethel's surprise, the door was open and Mrs. Rent was standing in the hall. There was a look of stern displeasure on her face. She spoke to Ethel with a harshness which she had never used before.

"What is the meaning of this?" she demanded. "What has become of my son? And why is Mr. Charlock here?"

"I am very, very sorry," Ethel faltered. "I went to sleep, and when I woke Arnold had gone. Of course, it was exceedingly careless of me to allow myself— —"

"Careless? Is that the only word you have for it? It seems strange there is no one whom I can trust. But where have you been? Why do you waste your time like this— —"

"I assure you she had not been wasting her time," Charlock said coldly. "You can rest easy in your mind, Mrs. Rent, for your son is found. He will be here by-and-bye. Meanwhile, it will be well not to make any noise at this time of night. There is no occasion to arouse the good people here, unless, indeed, you have already done so."

There was something so curt and incisive in Charlock's voice that Mrs. Rent's manner grew quieter and more subdued.

"I am only just downstairs," she explained. "I went into my son's room just now and, to my surprise, found it empty. But if my boy is all right there is nothing more to be said. Perhaps I said too much to you, Ethel, but I was speaking on the spur of the moment— —"

"Oh, please don't apologise," Ethel said. "I feel that I am to blame. When I discovered what had happened I went to Arnold's workshop, and Mr. Swift told me where I might find him. He is coming later with Mr. Grey, and I don't think you will find he is any the worse for his adventure."

A faint smile passed over Mrs. Rent's face.

"Then there is no more to be said," she murmured. "My dear child, how white and tired you look! I insist upon your going to bed at once. Mr. Charlock will perhaps keep me company till Arnold comes back."

Ethel was only too glad to be alone. She shook hands somewhat timidly with John Charlock and made her way upstairs. Then Mrs. Rent turned to Charlock and suggested that it would be better if they talked the matter over in her sitting-room. Once inside, the lady's manner changed. She grew agitated and distressed; her face was white and haggard.

"Now tell me what this means," she said. "I implore you to be candid with me. I am not the first mother who has worshipped a golden idol only to find that it has feet of clay. This is the punishment for my pride in my son. It was my fancy to regard him as something better and more upright than other men, and I begin to see different, now that he has deceived me. People come to see him who fill me with dread. I know that he is deeply in debt and that he has been deliberately deluding me. I suppose he is afraid to tell me, lest I should stop his allowance and perhaps leave the bulk of my money to some worthier object."

"There is nothing novel in the situation," Charlock said grimly. "You are by no means the first parent who has been deceived in the same way. I have known scores of such instances."

"That does not render the discovery less bitter," Mrs. Rent said sadly. "But I am sure that is not all. There is something worse behind. And if you will tell me what it is— —"

"I cannot," Charlock said, "because I do not know. But you will need all your courage and strength before long."

CHAPTER XXXVIII
THE EMPTY ROOM

Malcolm Grey sat himself down to wait grimly and patiently for Tanza. From his position on the lawn he commanded a view of the front of the house. He had the satisfaction of knowing that Rent was safe and that he could not leave without being seen. In one of the rooms at the top of the house the light flickered from time to time, so that Grey had a fair idea of where Rent was and what he was doing. The better part of half an hour elapsed before Tanza appeared on the scene. Grey hailed him in a whisper, and he crept noiselessly across the grass. For once he appeared to be curious.

"What is on foot now?" he demanded. "Why did you send for me in so mysterious a fashion? Why is there a light at the top of the house? Is the problem solved?"

"To all practical purposes it is," Grey replied. "I know what took place, and why. But precisely how the mischief was brought about I cannot say. Possibly before daylight the thing may be explained. But that depends upon luck. At any rate, I am going to take you into my confidence and tell you what I have discovered."

"I am glad to hear that," Tanza murmured.

Tanza inclined his head to listen, and for the next quarter of an hour followed Grey with the most careful attention. He was more interested than perhaps he had ever been before in his life. The strangely tangled web which Grey was unfolding was the most complicated of all the affairs in which he had ever been engaged.

"Wonderful," he murmured. "Really, a work of art. Perhaps it is rather cold-blooded of me to regard these puzzles in the way of a recreation. But there is a peculiar horror about this affair which has rarely been equalled. So that's the way the thing was done, eh? Well, I suppose I must leave the matter in your hands. What do you propose to do next? But, by the way, you have not yet told me who is in the bedroom overhead."

"You will be surprised when I tell you," Grey murmured. "The intruder is no other than Arnold Rent."

An exclamation of genuine surprise broke from Tanza's lips.

"Is that really a fact?" he demanded. "But what brings him here? What has he come after?"

"Ah, that I can only conjecture. I don't think my theory is far wrong. Although Arnold Rent is the son of a rich woman, he has by no means the command of unlimited money. Mrs. Rent is rather simple in her ideas and inclined to be somewhat of a Puritan. She is quite capable of leaving her money elsewhere if she thinks her son will waste it. Therefore, it has been a necessity on Rent's part that his mother should be deceived as to his mode of life. To put it plainly, he is more or less afraid of her. And when a man lives in a smart set, and has no control over his expenditure, he is bound sooner or later to find himself in difficulties. That is the matter with Rent. He did not know which way to turn for money. He did not dare to go to his mother and ask her to set him on his feet again. Therefore he hits upon another plan. He makes violent love to Bark's sister Hortense with a view to securing her mistress's diamonds. At first I don't believe that Rent cared for Mrs. Charlock at all. What he meant to do was to get hold of her jewels, but when he came to know the woman intimately she fascinated him to such an extent that he lost his head. He was prepared to sacrifice everything for her sake. Witness that mad idea of his taking Mrs. Charlock to stay with his mother. I give the fellow credit for honesty in that respect. I believe his affection for Mrs. Charlock was absolutely pure and good—perhaps the only disinterested impulse he ever had in his life. Meanwhile, he had talked Hortense over and between them they laid hands upon Mrs. Charlock's jewels. You will ask what became of the jewels. They were hidden in a place of safety, so that they might be available when they were wanted."

"That sounds logical," Tanza said. "Is it part of the problem to find the jewels, or do you know where they are?"

"I know where they are," was the unexpected reply. "They are within a stone's throw of us."

The little Italian whistled softly.

"Oh," he said, "I shall have to hand my mantle over to you, I see. But hadn't we better secure the plunder while we have the chance? It would be folly to miss the opportunity."

"Oh, the gems are safe enough," Grey said, with a grim chuckle. "You can almost touch them with your hands. And yet they are as safe as the Crown Jewels in the Tower of London. Indeed, they are safer, seeing that an attempt on the National Regalia would only end in imprisonment, while a determined attack upon Mrs. Charlock's gems would end in sudden death. I won't gratify your curiosity yet. I have told you enough for the present, and the truth, too. The first hand that rests upon that jewel case will be the hand of a corpse in the twinkling of an eye. In a day or two, perhaps, it may be safe to rifle the hiding-place. But not yet, not yet."

Grey spoke with a thrill in his voice that had something of horror in it. Tanza had seen too many mysteries in his time to express anything in the way of incredulity. On the contrary, he nodded his head solemnly.

"Does anybody else know?" he asked.

"Anybody besides Arnold Rent, you mean?" Grey replied. "Well, yes, one other person knows, and that is Ephraim Bark. His information came to him from his sister, who wrote and told him all about the affair when she discovered that she had been made a tool of by Rent and that he did not care two straws for her. We shall know presently how Rent managed to silence that jealous woman's tongue and leave the field clear for himself."

"You mean to say," Tanza began, "that Arnold Rent— —"

"My dear fellow, I mean to say nothing. I shall have a repulsive enough task later when I am compelled to speak plainly. Meanwhile, I have told you pretty well all there is to know. We had better go up and see what Arnold Rent is doing. You will not be surprised to hear that he is in Hortense's bedroom, probably looking for papers. Oh, by the way, there is one thing I forgot to mention. It is a photograph I found in the French maid's room. It gave the clue to the greater part of my discovery. Perhaps I had better show it you."

"I should like to see it very much," Tanza murmured.

Grey produced the torn photograph from his pocket and, with the aid of a match, exhibited it to his companion. He would have liked to know who was the other figure in the photograph. But that did not much matter, and it was a point which was not likely to be elucidated. Then the two friends crept quietly into the house. It was not easy to grope their way upstairs in the dark, but they managed it without noise, and presently stood outside the room, watching Rent at work. He seemed to be wrapped up in his task to the exclusion of everything else. He was pacing round and round the room, tapping on the panels and measuring distances with an iron lever in his hand. He was muttering to himself, too, but it was by no means easy to catch what he said. A quarter of an hour passed in the seemingly futile task, and then the searcher appeared to come to some definite conclusion. With a muttered exclamation he drove the point of his lever into one of the panels, and with a crackling, splintering sound the timber gave way. So far as the watchers could see, there was a space behind the panel more or less filled with letters. These Rent stowed away in his pockets. Beyond question, the object of his search was satisfied, for the expression of his face changed and a gleam of gratification sparkled in his eyes. He turned to the door so abruptly that Tanza and his companion had barely time to fall back into the doorway of an empty room before Rent began to descend the stairs. They watched him carrying the candle till he reached the basement of the house.

"What are you going to do now?" Tanza asked.

"Follow him," Grey said curtly. "In point of fact, I promised to take him home. Practically, though behaving like a sane man, the cloud is over his brain still, and I doubt very much if he knows what he is doing. Of course, there is a good deal of method in his madness. Still, we have to deal with a man who is not altogether accountable for his actions."

"And where do I come in?" Tanza asked.

"Oh, you'll go back to the yacht and wait further developments. It won't be very long before I am there again. And when I do come I may bring one if not two visitors with me. It might be necessary to do a little amateur kidnapping, but I am not sure about that yet. And now you had better leave me."

"All right," Tanza said cheerfully. "I am content to leave matters to you. Good luck to you!"

Grey walked after the other figure. He laid his hand upon Rent's arm and accosted him.

CHAPTER XXXIX
IN THE BAR

Morning was beginning to struggle with night when Grey turned his footsteps from Mrs. Rent's lodgings towards the quay. He was more than satisfied with his work, despite the fact that the most unpleasant and most repulsive part of it was yet to come. He was tired and weary by this time, but there was something to be accomplished before he returned to the yacht. One or two facts had to be verified. He turned aside for a bit and walked along the foreshore to Rent's workshop. But it was in absolute darkness, and no doubt Swift had gone to his lodgings. It was Swift whom Grey wanted to see, and, rather than go to the yacht before his task was altogether finished, Grey loitered about the streets till daybreak. He took a short cut through a series of dingy streets and past the fish-market, where one or two public-houses flaunted their garish lights across the pavement. Grey wondered at this infringing of the licensing act, until it dawned upon him that these were free houses specially retained for the benefit of the fish-dealers and hawkers and certain crews of yachts which landed in the early morning. It was a survival of old times. For the most part they seemed to be doing a certain amount of business.

There was something inviting about the lights and the open doors. It suddenly occurred to Grey that it was six or seven hours since he had partaken of food. He turned into one of the houses, where he saw piles of thick but appetising sandwiches laid out in plates upon the long table. He called for three or four of these and a small glass of whisky-and-soda, which he proceeded to dispose of in the snug seclusion of one of the little oak cabins which still obtain in some old-fashioned taverns. The cabins were by no means well-lighted, so that one could sit practically unseen in the darkness and yet see everything that was going on in the bar. Grey had barely finished his repast and lighted a cigarette before the swing door was thrown open and Ephraim Bark swaggered in. There was nothing surprising in the appearance of the little man; in fact, this was just the kind of place that such a thirsty soul would patronise, seeing that it was possible to obtain strong drink at any time of the day or night. All the same, it was a coincidence, and Grey determined to make the best of it.

But Bark had not come solely with the intention of consuming drink. He asked a question of the sleepy-looking man behind the bar, then looked at his watch impatiently. Grey smiled grimly to see that Bark was in possession of a watch again. Evidently he was in funds once more. For nearly half an hour Bark stood exchanging pungent chaff with the barman, until the door opened and Swift came in. No doubt this was the man for whom Bark was waiting. Bark scowled at the newcomer and intimated that a few moments later and he and the public-house bar would have been complete strangers. Swift did not appear to heed. He swayed unsteadily to and fro. His face was ghastly white and twitching. There was a queer, fitful gleam in his eyes.

"Something to drink," he said hoarsely. "A large glass of brandy with nothing in it. I'll pay the next time I come in, upon my honour I will."

The barman laughed contemptuously. Evidently Swift was an old customer and his promise carried but little weight in the eyes of the management. Bark looked curiously at the dreadful wreck opposite him with his head cocked on one side.

"Shall I risk it or not?" he asked. "You are on the verge of a bad breakdown, if ever man was, and it is a toss-up what the stuff will do for you. It will pull your wits together and make a man of you; on the other hand, it may send you climbing up the gaspipes under the impression that you are a monkey. I know all about it. I have been there myself."

This coarse badinage passed over Swift's head. He pressed his hand to his burning throat and once more asked piteously for drink. Bark relented.

"All right," he said. "Let him have it. We have all got to take risks sometimes. There, do you feel better now?"

Like a man dying of thirst in a desert, Swift reached out an eager, trembling hand for the potent yellow fluid and poured it down his throat at one fell swoop. Then gradually but surely a little colour crept back into his cheeks. His hands ceased to twitch and the horrible spasmodic jerkings of his lips left his mouth firm and straight.

"Ah, that's better," he said, with the air of a man escaping from physical pain. "Now I am ready to talk. What is it you want? Haven't you done mischief enough already? You have managed to knock Arnold Rent out of time, and that ought to be sufficient. What can I do for you?"

Grey started as these words fell upon his ears. He knew now how the latter's state of mind had been brought about. He saw Bark and his companion cross the bar and take their places in one of the cabins higher up the room. Bark called for more refreshment, but he was careful to specify the exact quantity which Swift was to consume, with the promise of more when their business was concluded. There was a certain amount of risk attached to it, but Grey felt he must establish himself in the next cabin so that he might hear what was going on. While the barman's back was turned, Grey crept noiselessly across the floor and disappeared in the cabin next to that occupied by Bark and his companion. The little man apparently was bent on business only, for the first words he uttered took him straight to the point.

"Oh, you know what I want," he said. "I want you to tell me how that affair was managed. It doesn't matter so long as I can get about without any danger. Now, you needn't look at me like that, pretending to be innocent, because you know where the jewels are hidden."

"What jewels?" Swift asked. "What do you mean?"

"Mean!" Bark echoed. "Why, what I say."

"There seems to be some misunderstanding," Swift murmured. "I give you my word, I don't know anything about any jewels. This is the first time that I have heard them mentioned. Oh, I am all right now. My head is as clear as yours. But, so far as any gems are concerned, you are talking clean over my head."

Bark hesitated for a moment, then laughed with the air of a man who is rather pleased with himself.

"So much the better," he said. "Sometimes a little knowledge is a dangerous thing. I believe what you say, and, seeing that you don't know, I am not going to enlighten you. And now we come to another matter. You are a scientist and so is Arnold Rent. It wouldn't be any exaggeration to say that you are two of the cleverest of the new school of investigators in England. If you kept off the drink and Arnold Rent had not been an extravagant fool you might have startled Europe before now. You could have made Edison look like an ignorant schoolboy. But I didn't bring you here for the purposes of flattery. I mean to ask you questions and see that you answer them. Question number one—did you ever hear of intermittent electricity, and what does it mean?"

A sharp exclamation broke from Swift.

"You don't know what you are talking about," he cried.

"Ah, well, that's just why I am asking questions, my friend," Bark sneered. "But, as it happens, I have dabbled in science and am not quite such a fool as I look. I know you can send messages by wireless telegraphy, and before very long wireless telephones will be a back number. This being so, why shouldn't we have wireless electricity? Suppose you put a battery of five hundred volts over yonder where the barman is—— Oh, by the way, would five hundred volts cause a fatal shock to anybody who came in contact with the current?"

A choking sort of sound proceeded from Swift. Evidently he had some difficulty in getting out his words. Grey, listening behind the partition, understood him to say that the shock of five hundred volts would be fatal in certain conditions.

"Well, I know that," Bark said impatiently. "What conditions would the force be fatal under?"

"Some people might suffer with impunity," Swift said hoarsely. "On the other hand, it would simply shrivel up others, and, in any case, no one could withstand it if they stood——"

Swift paused. It seemed almost impossible for him to speak further. Bark laughed in a sneering manner.

"Well, go on," he said encouragingly. "Don't be afraid. I suppose what you mean to infer is that the dose would be absolutely fatal if any one was wet or stood on wet ground?"

"That's it," Swift replied. "Quite correct."

"Very good," Bark replied. "We are getting on. Now listen to me and answer me carefully. On your oath, have you discovered the secret of wireless electricity or not?"

CHAPTER XL
"INFIRM OF PURPOSE"

The affair was getting interesting. The conversation was proceeding, too, on lines more or less as Grey had expected. He had thought the whole matter out, weighing up the pros and cons of the situation, but the more he debated the thing in his mind the more sure was he that he was on the right track. But for a miscalculation on the part of certain people the mystery of the sundial might have sunk into eternal oblivion. By the irony of fate the very man who could piece together the tangled sections of the puzzle was at hand to do so. For the most part, people regarded the tragedy which had involved the lives of mistress and maid as little more than coincidence. But there were others who, from the first, had insisted that there was mystery calling for solution. Grey was now in possession of information calculated to startle the public, and plenty of newspapers would have been only too pleased to pay a fancy price for what he had to sell. There was one flaw, and only one, in his line of argument, but that for the present was absolutely fatal—he was still in the dark as to how the thing had been brought about.

As to the main issue, he was clear enough in his mind. He knew that to all intents and purposes his information was not of the kind which would have been likely to satisfy a judge and jury. But it seemed that he was about to pick up the missing link, and he listened all the more eagerly to what was going on in the next compartment. Bark put his strange question again. He still appeared to be anxious to know if there was such a thing as intermittent electricity. And still Swift preserved the same strange silence. But Bark was not to be put off by the sullen reticence of his companion.

"Take your time, my buck," he said. "Don't hurry. Don't commit yourself to anything likely to be used in evidence against you afterwards."

"Why do you want to know?" Swift demanded fiercely.

Bark laughed in a wholly good-natured manner. He appeared to be exceedingly sure of his ground.

"Well, let us say that I am a humble seeker after knowledge," he said. "Because I am a wanderer on the face of the earth it doesn't follow that I lack scientific yearnings. If I had been caught young enough I should have been an eminent scientist myself before now. I have worked out many clever little things which would astonish you if you knew. But ever since Marconi invented wireless telegraphy and the other man hit upon telephones without lines I have been dreaming of wireless electricity. Mind you, it is bound to come sooner or later, and it is all the more likely to arrive because it is so impossible."

"Then why worry about it?" Swift murmured.

"My dear fellow, you have answered your own question. Because the thing is impossible, it is so easy. I don't mind admitting that I have tried a few experiments myself, but hitherto without success. Still, it won't be so very long before the whole world is lighted with a fluid which will supply burners without wires. Sounds fascinating, doesn't it? At any rate, it fascinated me to the exclusion of everything else. I tried to puzzle it out in the same way that Marconi puzzled out his invention. In my mind's eye, I could see a big fire station, say where my glass is, and a big factory where yours stands. By the use of powerful induction coils it seemed to me that I could force the power into the factory lamps without the aid of wires. Isn't that the way they propose to work telephones?"

"I don't know anything about it," Swift said sullenly.

"Oh, yes, you do," Bark said, with sudden impatience. "You know all about it. And, what's more, a successful attempt has been made within a mile or so of this very spot. More than once, when I was trying my experiments, it occurred to me to come to England to discuss the matter with Arnold Rent. I didn't do so for reasons which I will not go into now. But when business compelled me to come to this country and see Rent, I wasn't surprised to find that he was working on precisely the same thing. But you know that just as well as I do. What is the good of pretending you don't?"

"It pleases you to say so," Swift murmured.

"Yes, and it will please me to prove it before long, if you take that line. Mind you, I should not have known it if it hadn't been for a mere accident. Perhaps you will deny that there is any connection between what we are talking about and the mysterious death of my sister, to say nothing of Mrs. Charlock?"

A sudden exclamation broke from Swift. He seemed to be startled and alarmed. From his hiding-place Grey could almost imagine the satisfied grin on Bark's face.

"Take your time," the latter said playfully. "I won't hurry you, for we sha'n't part till I get to the bottom of this business. I asked you a plain question and I mean to have a plain answer. Have you or has Arnold Rent made any startling discovery in the direction of intermittent electricity? Is the thing within the range of practical politics?"

It was a long time before Swift replied. Grey could hear him playing with his glass. He could hear the uneasy shuffle of the unfortunate man's body. When the electrician did speak his voice was both timid and hesitating.

"You have no business to ask me this," he said. "If we have made the discovery you speak of, it lies entirely between Arnold Rent and myself. A discovery like that means a huge fortune to the author. The richest man in the world would be a pauper alongside the man who could reduce such a discovery to practical uses."

"What a chap it is to talk!" Bark said impatiently. "Why don't you come to the point? You know perfectly well that you dare not refuse the information I am after."

"We won't go into that," said Swift, with some attempt at dignity. "You will, perhaps, be disappointed to hear that I know nothing about intermittent electricity. If there has been a discovery in that direction, it is Rent's and not mine. He is a far cleverer man than I am. I am a child compared with him."

"Not if you kept off the drink," Bark said impatiently.

"Well, I didn't keep off the drink. What's more, I never shall. And eventually it will be the death of me," Swift said, with a snarl. "For a long time past I have known that my employer was on the verge of a fresh and startling plunge into the sea of discovery. To some extent Rent confided in me, but exactly what he was after he kept to himself. But by piecing one or two little bits of information together I arrived at the conclusion that wireless electricity was the goal. I could tell that from certain new pieces of machinery which were set up in the office. Of course, I said nothing. I knew it was useless to ask questions. And, besides, I felt that sooner or later I should be taken into my employer's confidence. I gathered that things were progressing in a satisfactory manner, when, all at once, the whole scheme of experiments was abandoned and the machinery was destroyed. And now you know pretty well as much as I can tell you."

Bark chuckled unpleasantly.

"I don't think so," he replied. "Still, I am going to take your word for it as far as it goes. I should like to know the exact date that the machinery was destroyed."

"How could I tell you that?" Swift demanded. "It happened some time ago."

"I have no doubt," Bark went on, in the same sardonic way. "That I am quite prepared to believe. But let me refresh your memory. Isn't it a fact that the machinery was destroyed and the experiments came to an abrupt conclusion on the day following my sister's death? Didn't Arnold Rent come down to the office that same day and break up all his machinery, with the excuse that he had made a mistake in his calculations and would have to begin all over again? I don't say that those were the precise words, though I am prepared to swear that that was the purport of them."

"Rent told you himself, then," Swift exclaimed.

"No, he didn't," Bark chuckled. "But you have just done so. Come, don't pretend you are ignorant of what I am driving at. Tell me all I want to know, and it will be the best day's work you ever did in your life. If you will make a clean breast of the whole thing I will put a thousand pounds in your pocket. A little later I'll pay you double that sum. Think what that will mean to you! You could set up for yourself. You could go off to America and make a fortune. All you have to do is to keep straight and you'll be a millionaire in five years. That is the prospect, on the one hand. But there is another point of view which I want to present to your notice. Which would you rather have—the career I have indicated, or find yourself laid by the heels, charged with being accessory before and after the fact to a deliberate and cold-blooded murder? I don't want to speak more plainly."

A strange, inarticulate cry rose from the compartment; there was a sudden rush on the part of Swift, and a moment later he blundered headlong through the door into the darkness.

"That's all right," Bark said, *sotto voce*. "I think I've touched him on the raw. The next time we meet he will tell me everything. He will be like wax in my hands in future."

CHAPTER XLI
DAMNING PROOFS

Morning had come at length, and, so far as Ethel Hargrave could judge, Arnold Rent appeared to be none the worse for his adventure. He had been brought back the night before by Grey, who did not wait to afford any information, but merely said that he had found the sick man wandering at large. Mrs. Rent was satisfied with this explanation, being only too glad to have her son back again. It would be a lesson to Ethel in future. As to the rest, the unfortunate lady decided that she would look after her son, at any rate, between the hour of his return and daybreak. All through the night Arnold Rent slept with the fatigue of a man who is physically exhausted. When he awoke he did not appear to have the smallest idea of the commotion he had caused on the previous evening. Ethel crept into the room, anxious to see what she could do to wipe out her failure of the night before. Mrs. Rent smiled at her indulgently.

"I think I can leave him to you," she whispered. "I don't suppose you'll be so careless again."

"Indeed I won't," Ethel said earnestly. "You can trust me, I am sure. Go downstairs and get some breakfast and then lie down. Does he seem to be any better?"

Mrs. Rent shook her head sadly.

"Not in the least," she murmured. "He is in the same sullen mood. He seems still anxious over some trouble worrying him. My dear child, we made a great mistake in coming here at all. At any rate, we ought to have left at once and taken Arnold with us. He would have been far better at our quiet house in Devonshire. All I can hope and pray for now is that his memory will be quickly restored. And yet there are moments when it seems to me that we are better off as we are. I begin to dread the future. I am in hourly fear of some shocking exposure. I do not know what it is, but I am sure that we are all going to suffer before many days pass."

Ethel said nothing. She was not without the same dread herself. And, moreover, she had information of which Mrs. Rent knew nothing. It was impossible to hide from herself that the shadow of disgrace hung heavily over the house of Rent. With a vivid recollection of last night's scenes she could not delude herself with the feeling that all was going right. What had Rent been doing in that silent and secretive way under the roof of the man upon whom he had inflicted such a deadly injury? Possibly he had not intended to do John Charlock the slightest harm. He may have been actuated by the highest and most honourable intentions. But the facts pointed in another direction. Moreover, why had he gone off in his madness to the house of the man who should be his worst enemy? It might be argued that the whole thing had happened in a moment of frenzy, but there was no getting away from the fact that there was a good deal of method behind it. And it was impossible, also, to pretend that Arnold Rent's present mode and manner did not lack a shadow of guilt or a suggestion of fear. The man was palpably frightened about something. He acted very like a criminal who expects at any moment to feel the grip of the law upon his shoulder. Ethel tried to put these gloomy thoughts out of her mind. She spoke cheerfully to her patient, who was already dressed and seated in an armchair, looking into the fire.

"Do you feel better this morning?"

"There is nothing whatever the matter with me," Rent said moodily. "I feel as well and fit for work as you do. Since I have been up I have thought out a whole train of new experiments. I remember all that happened to a certain point, and then for a few days everything is blank. There is something I ought to do, something that I have left undone which I dare not neglect any longer. If I could only think of it! Oh, if I could only think of it, what a relief it would be!"

The words came from Rent in a tone of positive anguish. He paced up and down the room with his hands locked behind his back. Ethel could see how drawn and contracted his brows were. Beads of perspiration stood on his forehead, his lips quivered, his whole body shook.

"You must try to put it out of your mind," the girl said. "You cannot hope to get better as long as you distress yourself in this fashion. And, besides, I don't suppose it is of any importance. If it is business, somebody is bound to remind you sooner or later."

Rent laughed in a hollow fashion.

"Oh, it isn't business," he explained. "It is worse than that. It is something that I am desperately afraid of, though I can't tell why. Do you know what I feel like?"

The speaker paused abruptly in his walk and came to a standstill in front of Ethel. He grasped her hands in his and pressed them with a certain passion which filled her with pain.

"I feel like a man who has committed murder," he said. "I am like one who has made away with a fellow-creature and hidden the body hurriedly till I could find time to dispose of it. It is like some hideous nightmare, some chapter from a weird novel. Imagine a man who has killed a fellow-creature. Imagine that nobody knows who this fellow-creature is. Try to think of a person who, once got rid of, no one would be any the wiser for the loss. You may say the woman came to my house late at night, if you like, after everybody had gone to bed.... And then she dies and is laid in a quiet spot, which is not so quiet but that people go there sometimes. The murderer dare not proceed further at present, but in the morning he promises himself that he will sink the body in a deep pool and then he will have no more anxiety on the matter. And when he wakes up on the morrow he has forgotten what he has done with the body. Don't laugh at me."

"I am not," Ethel said, trembling from head to foot with a fear she could not repress. "I swear I am not laughing at you. But why let your mind dwell upon such morbid subjects? You are the last man in the world who is likely to be mixed up in a terrible thing like that. Try to compose yourself."

But Rent was not to be turned so lightly aside.

"I don't know," he said. "There are thousands of cases on record of sudden lapses of memory. Haven't you read of people whose minds suddenly become blank as they are walking along the street? Why, I am a case in point. What is the meaning of this extraordinary lapse? And why do I feel this hideous impulse to go out and hide something? Why am I haunted by the terror that I have brought myself within reach of the law? Oh, the whole thing is ghastly, almost unbearable."

Rent broke off suddenly and flung himself headlong into his chair. There was a change to sullenness in his manner. He waved Ethel aside with the curt intimation that he wanted to be alone. Involuntarily he had placed his hand in the breast-pocket of his coat and drawn thence what appeared to be a packet of letters tied up with string. The packet seemed to start some train of thought, for a bright light shone in his eyes now, and he seemed on the point of grasping something which had eluded him.

"Can I do anything for you?" Ethel asked.

"Leave me alone," Rent said hoarsely. "Where did I get these things? How did they come into my possession? I thought they had been destroyed long ago. Now, why don't you do as I tell you? Why are you standing there gaping? I beg your pardon if I seem to be rude. But I am hardly accountable for what I am saying. Now please go."

There was nothing for it but to obey, and Ethel went off to her own room, the door of which she left open. Nothing unusual could happen so long as she kept watch and ward and listened to what was taking place in the opposite room. She had plenty to occupy her thoughts. She felt incapable of sitting down to read or write. She could not forget what Rent had been saying. She could not dismiss his burning words. She began to wonder if he were mad, after all, or if, perhaps, there was some dreadful chapter in his life which was still left unfinished and which might sooner or later bring him into some serious trouble. And he had not spoken like a madman, either, but rather like one who was consumed with remorse, terror and anxiety. For the moment it seemed as if he had torn aside the veil and allowed Ethel a glimpse into the past. For a long time the girl sat deep in her own troubled thoughts and anxious speculations.

An hour or two passed, then she felt the need of society, the necessity for human companionship. Probably Mrs. Rent was down by this time. She looked into Arnold's room as she passed. She saw that he was lying back in his chair, fast asleep. He had untied the bundle of letters, which seemed to have slipped off his knee and had fallen in a heap on the floor. Mechanically, Ethel stooped to pick them up, her action dictated simply by love of tidiness. Then a word or two caught her eye, and before she knew what she was doing she was reading the letters.... When she crept down the stairs, presently, her face was pale, her eyes were dazed as if the light were too strong for them. She did not go into Mrs. Rent's sitting-room. On the contrary, she put on her hat and jacket mechanically and turned out of the house towards John Charlock's residence.

CHAPTER XLII
THE FIRE

Late as it was, Malcolm Grey found Tanza still awake when he reached the yacht. The little doctor was seated in his cabin smoking a strong cigar and reading a scientific treatise, which he put aside directly Grey came in. There was a gleam of pleased expectation in the Italian's eyes as if he were looking forward to something in the way of information.

"Well," he said, "you are very late. It is daylight, and yet all this time I have been sitting up for you. Something told me that it would be worth the trouble, so I refrained from going to bed. Now, tell me what you have been doing and what adventures have you had."

"Oh, they were exciting enough," Grey laughed. "And now that I have taken you into my confidence I might as well finish my confession. I have been passing an hour or so in the company of that engaging rascal Bark and the unfortunate Swift."

"The three of you together?" Tanza asked.

"Not exactly together. I have been playing the part of eavesdropper. It isn't a pleasant recreation, but 'needs must when the devil drives.' Nor was my occupation without meet reward, because the discourse was a most interesting one. Try to guess what they were talking about!"

The Italian's eyes twinkled brightly.

"You must give me a lead or two first," he said. "You must tell me whether I am hot or cold, as the children used to do in the game we played when I was a boy. In the first place, did they meet by appointment, and did the meeting take place in a public-house? On consideration, I am sure it took place in a public-house."

"Right," Grey smiled. "An old-fashioned public-house, with the bar divided into compartments, where one can listen comfortably. Bark was waiting for his victim, who came more or less unwillingly; in fact, I don't think he would have come at all, except that he was desperately hard up and in urgent need of liquid refreshment. He appeared to be on the verge of an attack of *delirium tremens*, but was in possession of his faculties. And now I think I have told you enough. You may be able to guess what they were talking about."

Once more Tanza's eyes twinkled brilliantly.

"Well, perhaps they were discussing Arnold Rent," he ventured. "I don't suppose his name was mentioned, but no doubt he was the chief topic of conversation."

"You are getting warm," Grey laughed. "Go on."

"You encourage me to proceed," the Italian said. "Of course, Bark wanted information. Like the child in the story, he wanted to see the works of the watch. He was very desirous to know exactly how certain things were brought about. I suppose he wanted the very latest information on the subject of electricity."

"Wonderful man!" Grey murmured. "You have hit it exactly. That is precisely what he did want. Not that he got much information out of Swift. On the whole, I should say that Bark found him very disappointing. It appears that some time ago Arnold Rent began a series of experiments in electricity——"

"Intermittent electricity," Tanza interrupted.

"Once more, wonderful man!" Grey laughed. "That is what Bark was driving at. He wants to know all about those experiments, and no doubt it was exceedingly exasperating to discover that Rent had abandoned his researches and broken up his machinery. By a singular coincidence—at least, you and I will call it a singular coincidence—that machinery was broken up on the very day that the French maid's body was found in the fountain by the sundial. Let me tell you that it was Bark who elicited this information; in fact, he fished for it. From our point of view, this is a most important discovery, as you know. Still, it is practically the only real point that Bark made, and it turned his head to such an extent that he made the mistake of frightening his man. A moment or two later Swift bolted like a hare, and Bark remarked, *sotto voce*, that next time they met his man would be as wax in his hands. But if we play our cards correctly, the next time Swift has an interview with anybody it will be with us two and not with Bark. I know that Swift always works from eight till ten o'clock at night, and it struck me that the best thing we could do would be to call to-morrow night and have it out with him."

"A good idea," Tanza said. "But suppose the same idea occurs to Bark. He knows as well as we do what Swift's habits are, and there is nothing to prevent him from turning up at the interview. Wouldn't that be rather awkward?"

"Oh, it might," Grey admitted. "But I have a plan for dealing with Mr. Bark. Leave him to me. We can afford to take it easy to-morrow, and after dinner we will go as far as Rent's offices and get to the bottom of this business. We can see Rent's place from our anchorage as soon as the office is lighted up. We can go then and interview him. If you don't mind, I should like to turn in between the sheets for an hour or two, for I am dead-tired."

The two friends dined comfortably, then lingered for half an hour over a cigar, until the twilight began to fall and the houses and shops along the sea-front were picked out picturesquely with tiny points of flame. It was possible to discern the outline of Rent's workshop from the deck of the yacht, and presently Grey's quick eyes made out the square of flame which burnt so brilliantly in the office window. Swift was at work, and there was no occasion to waste further time. Tanza rose to his feet and tossed the end of his cigar into the water. He seemed alert and vigorous.

"Now I am ready if you are," he said. "I suppose there are no preparations to make. Shall we order the men to wait for us, or shall we leave it and take a shore boat back?"

"I think the men had better wait for us," Grey said. "And, if you don't mind, we'll pull round the bay and land opposite the workshop. Your boatmen may have a burden to bring back with them, so I shall be glad if you will choose two who are devoted to your interests and are not too fond of asking superfluous questions. I don't think there will be any risk in the matter, but I will take a small bottle of chloroform."

Tanza asked no questions. He gave Grey credit for knowing what he was talking about. He picked out two of the most discreet of his crew, who, he declared, were ready to commit every crime in the Decalogue, and ask no questions, if only he ordered them to do so. The boat set off presently, and was moored at length on a spit of sand opposite the low block of buildings which formed Rent's workshop. The two friends stole over the sands and made their way into the buildings. It seemed to them that there was more than one person inside, for they could hear the sound of voices, which, however, presently resolved themselves into the voice of Swift, who was singing wild snatches of incoherent verse. Grey looked at his companion significantly. Then Tanza suddenly paused and complained of the closeness of the atmosphere. A moment later a puff of acrid smoke filled the corridor, and there came the snapping sound which speaks unmistakably of fire.

"The madman!" Grey explained. "He has set the place ablaze. Come, there is no time to lose."

They burst into the main workshop, which was now full of smoke and flame. There was a heap of highly inflammable materials on the floor, round which Swift was dancing wildly, singing jubilantly as he leapt. The light of insanity blazed in his eyes. Evidently he was no longer responsible for his actions. Seizing a heavy ruler, Tanza proceeded to beat down the flames, which Grey finally extinguished with a bucket of water which he discovered under a tap in a corner of the room. Then the windows were flung open, and it was possible to breathe freely again. Swift glanced vacantly at the intruders. He did not seem to have the least idea whom he was addressing. He continued to journey round the smouldering ashes, singing and shouting in the same meaningless way.

"Burn the whole place down," he screamed. "Destroy it and wipe it out altogether, then you will be safe. But not till then, not till then. Burn it down, I say!"

"What is to be done with him?" Grey whispered.

"Bromide and strychnine," Tanza said curtly. "Get him on board the yacht, and I'll guarantee to put him right in twenty-four hours. But if I were you— —"

Tanza paused and the door opened, and Bark came staggering in. He appeared disconcerted at the sight of strangers. He would have turned and vanished again, but Grey was on him like a flash. There was a slight struggle between the two men, and then, before Bark could realise what had happened, a saturated handkerchief was pressed to his nostrils and he sank placidly to the floor in a state of blissful unconsciousness. As if nothing had happened, Swift still revolved round the charred ashes, singing his weird, incoherent song. Tanza glanced at his companion.

"It is all right," Grey said. "Help me to carry Bark to the boat and we'll send him on board. Then they can come back for this poor fellow. When you bring him to his senses I shall be able to tell you how we can put our hands upon Mrs. Charlock's jewels. That will be something gained."

CHAPTER XLIII
A ONE-SIDED CONTEST

Tanza's eyes gleamed. The little man was enjoying himself immensely. He was beginning to grasp the situation. Already he knew more of what had transpired than Grey gave him credit for. Nevertheless, there was warm admiration in his glance as he looked towards his younger companion.

"You appear to be in charge of the expedition," he said. "I should like to know what you propose to do next. Taking one consideration with another, this is, perhaps, the most interesting case I have ever been connected with. I never had a clever set of antagonists. But isn't there something more important than spending half the night in regaining possession of Mrs. Charlock's jewels? Surely, that is a minor point in comparison with bringing the criminals to justice."

"We shall bring the criminals to justice before long," Grey replied. "One event follows the other. In all probability, if there had been no jewels there would have been no crime. At least, that is my view of it."

"And what about the French maid?" Tanza asked.

"You really are a wonderful man," Grey exclaimed. "I believe you know as much about the thing as I do."

"I have been putting two and two together," Tanza said modestly. "Besides, you have given me such an excellent clue to work upon. But it is a sad business, Grey, and I am almost sorry I ever touched it. If those innocent women were not mixed up in the affair I should not mind so much. Just think what a terrible shock it will be to Mrs. Rent when she learns the truth. And either you or I must tell her."

A shadow crossed Grey's face.

"I have not forgotten it," he said. "Meanwhile, we are wasting time. But we must wait till the boat comes and then take the unfortunate Swift along with us. He will be safe in your hands. If there is one man living who can put him right, you are the man. You see, it will be necessary to confront Swift and Bark before we get to the root of things. I shouldn't wonder if Bark showed fight."

"Action for damages and that kind of thing, I suppose," Tanza chuckled. "Forcible abduction of an honest British citizen. Heavy damages, presumably. Oh, I have no doubt we shall have trouble of that kind, but if you leave Bark to me I think I can find a way to reduce him to reason. Give me a few hints when we get back, for when I talk to Bark I wish to let him know that I am well posted in what has taken place. Practically, I could write a history of the whole transaction, though I am in the dark as to the way in which this business has been engineered."

"Electrically engineered, I suppose?" Grey asked.

"That's it," Tanza said eagerly. "That is the point on which I am somewhat dubious. If you enlighten me I can tackle Bark efficiently. It had best come through me."

"It shall," Grey said curtly. "Here is the boat and we have Swift to deal with."

In the inner office Swift was still walking round the charred remains of the fire, muttering to himself and quite oblivious that he was no longer alone. He stared vacantly at his companions. It seemed impossible to beat anything like sense into his head. He was palpably on the verge of a breakdown. What he needed was a powerful drug and sleep, which, evidently, he had been without for some time. Tanza shook his head gravely as he watched the unhappy man.

"A bad case," he muttered. "Look at the pupils of his eyes. If that man doesn't sleep before long he will be a raving maniac. But it is not too late to save him if he is properly looked after. I don't envy his feelings when he comes to himself. What a pity it was you didn't warn me about this, so that I could have brought my drugs with me."

"I am sorry," Grey murmured. "But what are we going to do? There is little to be gained by hanging about like this."

There was nothing for it but strong measures. And, despite his struggles and protestations, Swift was carried to the boat, shouting and singing as he went. Fortunately, it was a quiet spot, and there was not much chance of attracting the attention of the passers-by. But Grey drew a deep breath of relief when the boat touched the yacht side and Swift was hauled unceremoniously aboard. A few minutes later Tanza got to work with his drugs and hypodermic syringe, and gradually Swift's cries and protestations died away. The dilation of his pupils narrowed and lessened. The wild look on his face gave place to a more placid expression, then by degrees his breathing grew more regular, his head fell forward on his breast, and he slept. Tanza watched him with satisfaction.

"That's all right," he said. "Now let us get the poor fellow to bed. He is not likely to wake for eight or ten hours, and when he does so I don't envy his feelings. I daresay I can keep him in hand with a judicious application of drugs. But the pity of it, my dear fellow, the pity of it! Fancy talent like that being frittered away in this foolish fashion. Upon my word, I had a great mind to devote the best part of six months to Swift's mental regeneration. I think it would be worth the trouble, and he could repay me by initiating me into those scientific mysteries so essential to the pursuit of my hobby."

"I wish you would," Grey murmured. "I am sure that Swift would do you credit. It isn't as if the poor chap had a natural weakness for drink; but he has no friends and he has drifted into this terrible habit. It is a good thing you have a crew you can rely upon. Otherwise we should have been hard put to it to carry this daring scheme into execution. Now let us get this fellow to bed and send for Bark."

Swift was put to bed at once and Bark fetched. A grinning sailor came up in response to Tanza's summons with the information that Bark was in a state of furious indignation and demanded to be released without delay.

"He seems to be annoyed, then?" Tanza asked pleasantly.

"Carrying on something awful, sir," the grinning sailor responded. "But, seeing as the orders were yours, we just let him talk and took no notice. Do you want him here, sir? Certainly, sir."

The sailor vanished, and a moment later a pair of unseen hands pushed Bark violently into the cabin. He came in staggering and rolling, making, however, some attempt at dignity, which was lost upon his captors. Tanza closed the door and turned the key in the lock. Then he wheeled round and faced the infuriated Bark, who stammered and stuttered with rage.

"What is the meaning of this?" he demanded. "Why this outrage? Why couldn't you have sent for me as a gentleman would have done? Am I a free British subject, or am I not?"

Tanza smiled.

"I will answer your questions one at a time," he said coolly. "You ask me why this outrage. Now, I put it to you as a far-seeing man with more than the ordinary share of brains—would you have preferred us to bring you on board the yacht, or would you rather have had the thing done through the medium of a policeman?"

"You are talking rubbish," Bark blustered.

"My good Bark, I am not in the habit of talking rubbish, as you very well know. It suits Mr. Grey and myself to work this matter out in our own way, without fuss or bother. Besides, we wanted to remove you beyond reach of temptation. So long as you were free to go your own way there was always the danger of Mrs. Charlock's jewels falling into your hands. And we objected to that. You will stay here just as long as we like, and, if I am anything of a prophet, you will be thanking us before long for the interest we have taken in your welfare."

"I am a free British subject," Bark cried.

"No, I beg your pardon, you are nothing of the sort. You are a prisoner on board this yacht, and here you are likely to remain for the present. Besides, how long would you be free if you once got ashore? I have only to mention one or two matters which we know of to the police and your boasted freedom would come to a speedy end. You may as well take it quietly. You will gain nothing by bluster, and you can't frighten my crew. If I were to put you in irons and take you a voyage round the world, not one of my men would interfere. But you need not be alarmed. I have not the least desire for your company on a voyage of circumnavigation, and that, singularly enough, is why you are here to-night. I know the remark sounds illogical, but you will see how sensible it is before long."

"Go on," Bark said theatrically. "Keep it up. I see that you are enjoying yourself."

"I am," Tanza said crisply. "Nothing gives me such pleasure as the elucidation of a crime. It is a positive joy to me to bring a scoundrel to book. And yet I am really the best friend you have, because I am saving you later from being charged with the murder of Mrs. John Charlock!"

CHAPTER XLIV
BROUGHT TO BOOK

Bark quailed visibly before the eyes of his companion. He ceased to stand upright. His back was bowed and bent, his head was buried in his shoulders. His jaunty air vanished. The cynical smile faded from his lips. The pallor of his face and a shadow of fear in his eyes told their story.

"I swear I don't know what you mean," he said hoarsely. "For God's sake, don't talk like that, doctor. Oh, I am a bad lot, and I own it. Call me a scamp if you like, and I'll not deny it. You know all about me, doctor. But I am not as bad as all that. It had never occurred to me—no, not for all the money in the world—to do violence to a fellow-creature. I am innocent of bloodshed, if this is the last word that I am ever allowed to speak."

"Ah, now you are coming to your senses," Tanza said. "It is one thing to feel sure of a man's innocence, but it is another thing to prove it. Now, let us regard this matter from the point of view of the Crown Prosecutor who is opening the case against you. You have a sister who was Mrs. John Charlock's maid. This sister was carrying on an intrigue with a celebrated chemist whom we will call—but why make a parable of it? Let us call him by his proper name of Arnold Rent. This Rent was simply making a tool of your sister, because he wished to get her mistress's jewels. He is a far-seeing young man and, to use a common expression, has a pretty good notion of his own interest. Like many a clever young man before him, he has gone a bit too far. He is up to his eyes in debt and difficulty and dare not tell his mother, who is a bit of a fanatic in her way and quite capable of leaving her money elsewhere if she thinks her son is likely to make a bad use of it. Therefore he conceives the idea of getting hold of Mrs. Charlock's jewels. We won't go into the love affair, because that does not concern either of us, though it has a bearing on the story. Your sister Hortense acts as this man's tool and robs her mistress of her diamonds. For the present the stones are hidden in a secure place, which is known only to the thief and to Arnold Rent. It is just at this time that the thief discovers that she is merely a pawn in the game; it is her mistress who is the object of Rent's affections. The girl is beside herself with jealousy, though Rent manages to soothe her to a certain extent. For her own protection, however, she writes a letter to her brother, telling him how he can find the jewels in case anything happens to her. She is not too explicit as to the hiding-place, and this brother has to exercise his ingenuity as to the way in which the stones may be brought to light. At this point a tragedy occurs, and the girl is found dead in the fountain by the sundial in her employer's garden. Appearances point to suicide or accident. Nobody guesses that the poor woman is the victim of foul play, and I don't suppose they ever would if, perchance, I had not come here in my yacht for a little change and the thing happened to come to my ears. Rightly or wrongly, I concluded there was something wrong and sent for my friend Mr. Grey. To make a long story short, we discovered that I was absolutely right, and in a few hours we shall be able to prove that your sister was deliberately murdered. Whether Mrs. Charlock met with the same fate or not, we are not able at present to say. And now, Bark, are you going to deny your conviction, or stick to the fable that your sister's death was an accident? Didn't you come here with the intention of seeking out the hiding-place of those jewels? Take time to reply. You will gain nothing by lying. We happen to know where the jewels are, and we can put our hands upon them at any moment. We are not in the least afraid of being anticipated by you, because, even if we gave you a plan of the hiding-place, you couldn't touch them. If you attempted to do so, a third victim would be added to those who have already lost their lives in connexion with those ill-fated gems. You can please yourself whether you speak or not; if you like, I will unlock the door and send you ashore at once."

But Bark did not appear anxious to accept this offer. He sat writhing uneasily in his chair, his face turned eagerly to Tanza, as if waiting for the latter to continue. But the Italian said no more. He had given Bark his lesson and waited patiently for its effect.

"You are too many for me," Bark said presently. "You know too much. I might just as well tell the truth. My sister did write to me and tell me all about Arnold Rent, and I came here hot-foot to help her in the matter of those jewels. It was a shock to me to hear of her death, but I didn't suspect anything at the time. She was always a hot-headed, impulsive girl, and I naturally thought she had committed suicide. But when I came to inquire into the matter I formed another conclusion altogether. I asked myself a question or two, but I couldn't answer them. It occurred to me that perhaps Arnold Rent could. I had known him for some years. He is all right as men go, but put him in a tight place and he would stick at nothing. I thought the matter out, and at last I began to see my way. Hortense had been murdered. There was no doubt about that. But how had it been done? There were no marks of violence. There was nothing to show that she had met with a violent end, except that she was lying in the fountain. I couldn't get rid of the notion that Rent was in some way connected with this business, and I was confirmed in my opinion by his keeping out of my way. It is a pity he isn't able to tell us the truth. He knows all about it."

"You should have thought about that before you assaulted him," Grey put in quietly. "Don't forget that you are responsible for Rent's present mental condition."

A queer sort of laugh broke from Bark's lips.

"Oh, so you know about that, too?" he exclaimed. "It does not appear to be much good trying to keep anything from you gentlemen. Mind you, I didn't mean to do him any harm, but he refused to pay me money he owed me, and I lost my temper. If I had waited a bit longer I could have told him a thing or two which would have compelled him to listen to me. I could have forced him to give me all the money I needed. But there it is, and the thing can't be helped. And I don't think I could tell you any more if you kept me talking till daybreak. I'll help you all I can. I'll do anything you want me to do. I think I have sense enough to know when I am in a tight corner."

Tanza rose and unlocked the door.

"That is all at present. I should like to see the letter your sister wrote you—I mean the letter about the hidden jewels, which gave you the clue to the hiding-place. We can put you up for the night on the yacht, if you like; indeed, you will be well advised to stay here. I don't think, after what has happened, you are likely to play us false. You have had too severe a lesson."

Bark asserted, with many oaths, that he had no intention of doing anything of the kind. He evinced a not unnatural anxiety to be alone. He was thoroughly cowed and as wax in the hands of his captors. Grey gave a sigh of relief as Bark vanished from the cabin.

"His room is preferable to his company," he said. "What a pestiferous little rascal it is! I don't think he is likely to give us any trouble in the future. And how well you handled him. Your cross-examination was masterly."

Tanza shrugged his shoulders modestly.

"Could I have failed," he asked, "with all the cards in my hand? Why, the fellow hadn't the ghost of a chance. But he has been useful to us, and the only thing that remains to be done is to get this matter over as soon as possible. I am correct in assuming, I suppose, that Mrs. Charlock met the same fate as her maid?"

"You mean that she was murdered?" Grey asked.

"Well, I didn't want to put it so brutally."

"I think you are wrong," Grey went on. "Mind, I am only theorising. I believe that Hortense was murdered in cold blood. But as regards Mrs. Charlock, I treat that more or less as an accident. The man who laid the trap forgot to take the bait out of it, and thus unwittingly brought about the second catastrophe. But that we shall be able to clear up later. It is a ghastly business altogether, and, for my part, I am sorry I was ever brought into it. Not that I have the least sympathy with the guilty parties. But I am grieved for the innocent people who are bound to suffer. It will be hard upon Mrs. Rent."

Tanza nodded gravely. He was about to reply, when he was interrupted by the sound of footsteps on deck overhead and the entrance of a sailor with the information that Mr. John Charlock had just come on board and desired to see Mr. Grey on important business. At the same moment Charlock thrust a haggard face into the cabin and the seaman vanished.

"What is it?" Tanza demanded.

"A terrible thing has happened," Charlock said hoarsely. "Arnold Rent has thrown himself out of his bedroom window. He is not dead, but I am told he cannot last many hours. And, strange to say, he has been asking for you, Mr. Grey."

CHAPTER XLV
THE HIDING-PLACE

"How did you come to know?" Grey demanded.

"Miss Hargrave told me. I suppose she couldn't think of anybody else, and she could not bear to break the news herself to Mrs. Rent. It was just before daylight."

"Daylight!" Tanza echoed. "Daylight, when?"

"Why, this morning," Charlock went on. "Don't you know that it is morning? I suppose you have been sitting here with the blinds drawn over the portholes, oblivious of the flight of time. At any rate, it is nearly five o'clock. But please allow me to go on with my story. As far as I could gather from Miss Hargrave, she went into Rent's room yesterday afternoon and found him fast asleep. He had apparently been reading a bundle of letters, for they had fallen from his knee and lay in a mass on the carpet. Quite mechanically the poor girl picked the letters up, and a word in one of them caught her eye and she began to read. She was so shocked and upset by what she saw that she came to me at once and told me about it. But you shall read for yourself, for the letters are in my possession."

"I don't think you need worry about that," Grey said. "Unless I am greatly mistaken, I know pretty well what those letters contain. They had been written by Rent to the French maid, Hortense; in fact, they are the very letters which Rent obtained from your house on the night that Miss Hargrave came inquiring for Rent. But, of course, I have forgotten that you know nothing about that, because you left me to see Miss Hargrave home. But don't let me interrupt you. I only want you to know that we are not quite so ignorant as you think us. I suppose I am right as to the gist of those letters?"

"Absolutely," Charlock went on. "You can imagine Miss Hargrave's state of mind. I was touched to see how she confided in me and promised to do all I could to help her. There were passages in those letters which throw a lurid light upon many things that have happened lately, and that was why I implored Miss Hargrave to do nothing rash. You see, I wanted to save Mrs. Rent and herself from as much trouble and scandal as possible. I implored the girl to go back home and say nothing whatever about her discovery. She promised that she would do so, and when she had regained control of herself I allowed her to go. But I might have known that one so ingenuous and innocent would find it impossible to carry about so dreadful a secret. For some time she managed to master herself, but an hour or so ago Rent had a lucid interval and guessed something was wrong. Perhaps his seared conscience pricked him. Perhaps he surmised that the trouble had something to do with himself, for he insisted upon the girl telling him everything. She did so, with the result that you already know. So far as I could gather, when Miss Hargrave came to me just now in a state of mind bordering on distraction, Rent affected to take the matter quite calmly. He rose from his seat and talked on indifferent topics for several minutes. Then he lighted a cigarette and stood by the open window of his bedroom admiring the beauty of the morning. A minute or two later he flung himself over the balcony on to the stones below, and was picked up by a labourer in a dying condition. They carried him into his room and sent for the doctor. I am told the poor fellow suffers only occasionally, but they say that he cannot recover from the shock and that death is not far off. He has fits of insensibility, followed by periods of lucidity, during which time his mind is clear. Strange to say, the blank in his memory has been filled up, and, from what he told Miss Hargrave, he knows everything that has taken place during the past fortnight. As yet, his mother has not been told; indeed, she was asleep when I came from the house."

There was a long pause when Charlock had finished. Tanza and Grey regarded one another significantly.

"It is a shocking thing," the latter said presently. "But it has all happened for the best. Of course, I will see Rent if he wants me. I shall be here all day and you have only to send a messenger over."

"That is very good of you," Charlock murmured. "If you don't mind, I will go back at once. There are many ways in which I can be useful. Directly Rent gains consciousness again I will not fail to send."

Charlock went on his way back to the darkened household. It was not too late to snatch an hour or two in bed, and, despite the startling events of the evening before, Grey slept soundly directly he reached his cabin. When he woke the sun was shining brightly and Tanza was standing by his side. Grey sat up in bed and rubbed his eyes.

"Anything fresh?" he asked. "I suppose you have had no messages yet from Charlock?"

"Not a word," Tanza said. "I have allowed Bark to go away under a promise that he will remain at hand and come here whenever he is wanted. I have not the least fear that he will play us false after what has happened. Meanwhile, for the last hour or so I have been bestowing my attention upon Swift."

"I hope he is better," Grey murmured.

"Well, he is clear and sensible, if that is what you mean. He is in a terribly shaken state and hasn't the smallest idea what took place last night. I have been reminding him about one or two things and you will find him ready to answer questions. I have given him a soothing draught, and I don't think he is likely to trouble us for some time, at any rate. After breakfast you can interview him."

Grey found Swift a white and pitiable object, propped up by pillows, doing his best to coax down a little food. There was a half-pleading, half-defiant look in his eyes as Grey seated himself on the bed.

"You needn't be afraid of me," Grey said. "I only want you to give me a little information. My dear fellow, if you only knew it, Tanza and myself are the best friends you have. Tanza has announced his intention of devoting himself to your case, and if you only play the man, he will set you on your feet again. I cannot understand how one of your ability should sink so low. Surely, if we hold out a helping hand——"

"That is all I want," Swift interposed eagerly. "I am a double-dyed fool, Grey, and no one knows it better than myself. When I started to go down hill my friends began to turn their backs upon me, and I went on drinking out of sheer bravado. For the last two years I have been alone in the world; but, low as I have fallen, I would make a big effort to pull myself together if I could find a congenial friend. If Tanza would take me in his employ it would be a godsend to me. I could make a struggle under a man like that. But, there, you did not come here to talk about myself. What have you discovered? And what can I do for you?"

"Practically, we have discovered everything," Grey said gravely. "We have made certain of what we have hitherto regarded only as suspicion. You are weak and ill, and I don't want to bother you unnecessarily. Tell me in a word, has Arnold Rent discovered intermittent electricity or not?"

Swift nodded his head vigorously.

"That will do," Grey went on. "You need not say any more. There will be plenty of time to go in for explanations when you are well enough. All I want to know now is the exact position of the underground dynamo which was established some time ago within a few hundred yards of Rent's offices. I don't suppose he told you about it, but I am sure you know where the thing is to be found."

By way of reply, Swift reached for his coat, which was lying across the back of his bunk, and took from the breast-pocket a sheet of tracing-paper, which he handed over to Grey. The latter glanced at it and smiled. When he turned to Swift again the patient was lying with closed eyes as if on the verge of sleep. Grey stole from the cabin to the deck where Tanza was seated.

"Come along," he said. "I have it at my fingers' ends. I'll just get a pair of india-rubber gloves and shoes and a mat and we can set out at once."

They came at length to a spot some little way from the workshop, where Grey proceeded to make a close examination of the turf. He lifted a sheet of sod presently and disclosed a small grating underneath. Kneeling on the india-rubber mat and carefully shielding his hands with gloves of the same material, he proceeded to pull out a switch or two and cut through a cable which led into the tiny manhole. Then, without a further word to Tanza, he strode right on until he came to the lawn of Charlock's house, pausing at length in front of the fountain which surrounded the sundial. With the gloves still upon his hands, and the long rubber boots upon his feet, he waded through the water until he stood by the side of the sundial. He raised the cap and threw it aside. Then from the cavity below he produced a small box.

"There!" he said, with an air of subdued triumph. "Will you please examine the contents? I will forfeit my reputation if Mrs. Charlock's jewels are not inside."

CHAPTER XLVI
THE PRICE OF A CRIME

Tanza unfastened the box and removed a sheet of cotton wool which lay on the top. The sun gleamed on a heap of stones of various sizes, diamonds for the most part, which streamed and twinkled as if they had been running water. Then he laid out the rings and necklaces and the various odds and ends, which went to make up a collection of stones worth a considerable amount. The Italian knew something about jewels, and in his estimation at least ten thousand pounds' worth of jewels lay on their bed of cotton wool.

"Mrs. Charlock appeared to have a pretty taste in this respect," Tanza remarked. "These things might have belonged to the wife of a millionaire. So this is the end of our search. Well, those stones have done mischief, goodness knows. I suppose you can tell me how they managed to get there?"

"All in good time," Grey replied. "We had better return to the yacht and talk the matter over. Besides, Rent may send for me at any moment, and I should not like to be out of the way when his message comes. It has been an exciting venture on the whole, and, to a certain extent, I have enjoyed it. But I would give half of what I possess not to have to face Mrs. Rent, as I shall be compelled to do presently."

Tanza nodded sympathetically. He understood what Grey was alluding to. The latter replaced the capstone on the sundial and proceeded to strip off his rubber boots and gloves. Tanza touched these articles lightly with his finger-tips.

"Did you really need these?" he asked. "Was there actual danger? I saw you were taking no risks."

"It was a necessary precaution," Grey explained. "Of course, you know that in handling high-volted coils and cables there is always danger. Anything beyond five hundred volts needs great caution. You are well aware, also, that a voltage which is almost harmless when one is dry or standing on dry ground becomes dangerous in the presence of moisture. The perfect safeguard is in using india-rubber gloves and boots. With these one can handle cables carrying practically any power."

Tanza nodded his approval.

"I know all that," he said. "But what first put the idea of electricity into your head? As you know, from the very first I suspected foul play. I felt certain the Frenchwoman met her death by some new and ingenious method of manslaughter. In thinking the matter over, electricity suggested itself to my mind, but I could not for the life of me see how it was worked. That is why I called you in. You seem to have known from the start what to do and what to look for. Isn't that a fact?"

"Well, I had luck on my side," Grey admitted. "You remember bringing me to have a look round the place and giving me a minute account of the way in which Hortense met her death. You will recollect telling me that her dress was more or less singed, which seemed remarkable, seeing that she had apparently met her death by water. There were no marks of violence on the body, either, which was another thing that aroused one's suspicions. I was still asking myself a few questions in this direction when I had the good luck to pick up a thumb torn from an india-rubber glove. Now, you know india-rubber gloves are worn almost entirely by electrical engineers; indeed I know no other use for them. I am aware that burglars have adopted the same precaution to prevent any identification of finger-marks. But, then your average burglar does not give as much as two guineas a pair for india-rubber gloves, which is somewhere about the price of those from which the thumb was torn. As soon as that evidence came into my hands I knew that somebody connected with electricity had been near the sundial. But the mere presence of a fountain disposed of the suggestion that anything like the usual electrical business had been contemplated by the owner of the property. I dropped a hint to Charlock, and he knew nothing about it. Now why had this mysterious individual been here? And what was he doing in the neighbourhood of the fountain? A little farther up the lawn I discovered a small piece of cable properly insulated, and then I became more or less certain of my facts. Somebody had laid a wire from the sundial to a power station in the neighbourhood. It puzzled me why this had been done till I began to put things together, and I suddenly recollected what you told me about Hortense's clothing being scorched. It seemed fair to assume that the sundial and the fountain were charged for some reason with a dangerous load of electricity, and that directly the woman came into contact with the water she was killed instantly. Doubtless she fell forward into the fountain, which would account for the scar upon her forehead. You see, the current might have been powerful enough to cause instant death without unduly injuring the body. Before I left these premises that day I knew beyond the shadow of a doubt how the French maid had met her death. You follow me?"

"Absolutely," Tanza said. "It is quite logical."

"Of course it is," Grey went on. "There is no other way of accounting for it. Then I began to ask myself what the woman was doing near the fountain. Until I could get to the bottom of that I was more or less groping in the dark. But, then, as you know now, I had an opportunity of examining Hortense's bedroom, where, in the fireplace, I found a torn photograph of two men, one of whom was Rent. Who the other man is probably we shall never know, and, in any case, it doesn't matter. At any rate, we have the fact that Hortense was in the possession of Rent's photograph, which she had torn across the middle, no doubt in a moment of petulance and passion. I may be wrong, but that is the interpretation I put upon it. It was more or less natural to conclude that tender passages had passed between Hortense and himself. I could not guess why for the moment, but it became clear later. But this is not all the evidence I discovered. In the grate were fragments of a letter which pointed to the fact that some secret was on foot connected with the sundial. It was not till after I heard that Mrs. Charlock had lost her jewels that I began to wonder if the gems had been hidden in the sundial. I had to speculate upon this for a day or two, until I caught Bark loafing about the lawn, and then I felt sure my supposition was correct. When I saw that Bark had severely burnt his fingers in the waters of the fountain I became certain of my ground. It was lucky for him that the night was fine and the grass dry, or he would have shared the fate of his sister. By this time my suspicions were growing pretty strong. I could not come to any other conclusion but that Rent was at the bottom of the whole business. Where else could the power station which supplied the electricity be except in Rent's own workshop? And who besides himself was interested in getting Hortense out of the way? Beyond a doubt she had found out how she had been fooled and had threatened revenge. Therefore he determined to get rid of her by this diabolically ingenious means, which it would be impossible to trace. He had only to let the girl know where the jewels were hidden, and she was certain to try to steal them. To a man who has discovered the secret of intermittent electricity the thing was easy. You know in how small a compass an electrical plant goes and how easy it is to manipulate. Suppose a hole is cut in the ground by the fountain and a wire inserted into the water. Then, a quarter of a mile away, another apparatus is hidden underground, the current turned on from the works, and without intermediate wires a contact is made between one pole and another. Of course, I know it sounds very extraordinary, but if you can telegraph and telephone without wires, why shouldn't you transmit an ordinary electrical current? At any rate, Rent succeeded in doing so, as Swift more or less intimated to me; in fact, he found out what was going on and gave me a plan of the direction in which the apparatus ran. I shouldn't be surprised if Swift knows as much as we do, and no doubt his guilty knowledge has driven him to drink. I have proved how this thing was done and how the French girl was sent to her death."

"You think she was murdered?" Tanza asked.

"Most emphatically I do. Otherwise, why should Rent go to the trouble of all these elaborate preparations? He was afraid that Hortense would betray him to her mistress. He was so infatuated with Mrs. Charlock that he was prepared to run any risk to retain her good opinion. I feel convinced that Hortense was sent deliberately to her death, and if you and I had not happened to be in the neighbourhood the thing would have been forgotten and nobody been any the wiser. Why, apart from such proofs as I have given you just now, there are other people who could support my assertions. Don't you suppose that that blackguard Bark knows all about it? And he was prepared to keep his mouth shut and leave his sister's death unpunished if only he could get possession of the jewels. It is a ghastly business altogether. And now you understand why I am not anxious to face Mrs. Rent. And you will see that the matter cannot be allowed to rest here. What a sensation there will be when it all comes out!"

CHAPTER XLVII
ABSOLUTION

Tanza shook his head slowly and sorrowfully. "Terrible!" he murmured. "I wish we could find some way of keeping Mrs. Rent and Miss Hargrave out of this matter. But after what has taken place the thing is impossible. Mrs. Rent will have to give evidence, and so will Miss Hargrave. One is naturally loth to interfere with the course of justice. But if ever there was a case where a policy of silence would be pardonable, this assuredly is that case. Only in one contingency the world need know nothing of this miserable affair."

"And what may that be?" Grey asked.

"Why, the death of Arnold Rent, of course. If he would considerately die, we should be perfectly justified in keeping our own counsel. Why should the thing be dragged to light? Why should the whole painful story be made public when the culprit is beyond the reach of the law? I think you will agree with me."

"Oh, I do," Grey confessed. "But please don't imagine that Arnold is worse than he appears to be. You don't suppose that he is responsible for the death of Mrs. Charlock as well? That would be too dreadful."

"Is there any other conclusion?" Tanza asked.

"Well, yes, in common justice to Rent, there is. I believe that Mrs. Charlock's death was a sheer accident. Let me retrace the ground, and I will show you what I mean. We will admit, if you like, that Rent is a man without heart and without principle. We will make one exception, and that was his pure and disinterested affection for Mrs. Charlock. He was prepared to sacrifice his future for her sake. Oh, yes, I know that he stole her diamonds. But no doubt that was in the early stage of his infatuation. Afterwards he must be credited with good intentions. You see, he had removed the French maid, and the ground appeared to be clear. So deeply in love is he that he takes Mrs. Charlock to stay with his mother. Mind you, in taking that step he knew what he was risking. He knew how strict and rigid his mother was, and how little versed she was in the ways of the world. These upright and honourable people are apt to be narrow-minded. And religion and charity are not always the same thing. I say that when Rent took Mrs. Charlock into Devonshire he was running the risk of losing every penny of his expectations. Of course, there was the hope of conciliating his mother, but that was what one might call a sporting chance. As you know, the scheme was a failure, and Mrs. Charlock went away, posing as a martyr, prepared to accept any sacrifice rather than injure the prospects of the man who had befriended her. Anyway, there was an end of her so far as the home in Devonshire was concerned. Now, if my theory is correct, there was a subsequent interview between Mrs. Charlock and Rent, in which the situation was reviewed from a worldly point of view. You see, they were bound to face the situation sooner or later; in sporting parlance, the thing wasn't good enough for Mrs. Charlock, and she probably let Rent know it in her sweet, unsophisticated way. No doubt he had time to think the matter over and began to grasp what he was sacrificing. Whether they parted in friendly fashion or not doesn't matter. They *did* part, and Mrs. Charlock came back to her husband. Before she started, Rent doubtless did the fair thing and told her where her jewels were hidden. But there was one thing he forgot—he neglected to turn off those switches, and left the fountain in the same dangerous condition as when Hortense met with her dreadful death. Either that or Swift had been experimenting with the apparatus. But the fact remains that the charge had not been drawn from the mine, and when Mrs. Charlock went to regain possession of her jewels she went to certain death. That is my rendering of the matter, though I may be wrong."

"I should think it exceedingly probable you are right," Tanza said. "You have given me a sensible and logical account of what has happened, and I fail to see any flaw in your argument. We had better return to the yacht now, and later I will hand these stones to Charlock. There ought to be enough here to free him from all his difficulties and enable him to come back to his own house. Unless I am mistaken, he will be glad to resume possession once more."

"Why should he be?" Grey asked.

"Because he is in love with Ethel Hargrave," Tanza said. "One can see that with half an eye. And what is more, the girl is in love with him. But these things are in the air at present. So far as I am concerned, I should be disposed to keep our discovery a profound secret. That rascal Bark will not dare to say anything, and I flatter myself I can find a way to keep Swift's mouth closed. Unfortunately, Miss Hargrave has made some discoveries, but we may be able to convince her that she has made a mistake. If Arnold Rent dies, which seems more than probable, we may save the scandal altogether. Charlock we can trust."

They were back at the yacht again presently, still discussing the tragedy in which they were both profoundly interested. There was no sign of Bark, and Swift seemed to be decidedly better. After luncheon Tanza had a long talk with him, and left him in appreciably higher spirits. Just as the Italian arrived on deck again an urgent message came for Grey, saying that Mr. Rent desired to see him immediately.

Grey found Rent sitting in bed, propped up with pillows. It needed no practised eye to see that the end was near. Mrs. Rent and Ethel were with the sufferer, and at a sign from him they left him and Grey together. Rent was very weak and low, yet there was a resolute look in his eyes, and he lost no time in coming directly to the point.

"You know why I sent for you?" he demanded.

"I can give a fair guess," Grey murmured.

"Ah, I am glad of that, because it will save me a deal of talking, and time is precious. Tell me in a few words what you have discovered. It would be a kindness to speak frankly and openly to me."

"Perhaps it would," Grey said. "Then I may say I have discovered everything. Nothing is hidden from me."

"This is what I expected," the dying man murmured. "I have felt that ever since you have been in the neighbourhood. Oh, I know what Tanza was after. I have not been altogether blind. But I swear to you that so far as Mrs. Charlock was concerned I am absolutely and entirely innocent. It was a cruel misfortune—but go on, please. Let me hear your story first."

"There is not much to tell," Grey said, picking up the thread. "To begin with, I know all about your entanglement with the French maid. An accident put me on the track, but it is a waste of time to go into that. I know what happened between your workshop and the fountain. I know how you laid the trap which led Hortense to her death. But perhaps I had better tell it to you just as I told it to Tanza a little while ago."

Grey proceeded over the familiar ground, the dying man following with rapt attention. At the end of the recital he nodded more or less approvingly.

"So far," he said, "you have not made a mistake. You have the thing as clear and plain as if you had been in my place. But you are wrong as far as Mrs. Charlock was concerned. I had disconnected the electrical apparatus which communicated with the fountain; indeed, I was going to destroy everything but for an accident which prevented me. I call it an accident for want of a better term. But now I see the hand of Fate in it. I was playing with the apparatus one night when Hortense's brother, Bark, came into my office. He asked me for money, which I was not able to give him, and one word leading to another, the whole thing culminated in a serious quarrel. I was knocked down and sustained an injury to my head which, as you know, affected my brain. In most ways I was sane enough, but memory of the events of the past few days had been wholly blotted out. I was haunted by the feeling that I had left something undone, but I could not for the life of me recall what it was. You can imagine a murderer who has gone off and left a clue behind. That was the sensation that maddened me and spoilt all my rest till Ethel Hargrave found me poring over certain letters. It was only when she began to speak that remembrance came back to me swiftly and unexpectedly. Ethel knew too much. I knew that I could not hope to silence her tongue. Besides, she had already confessed all she had discovered to John Charlock. Then it was that a feeling of abject despair came over me, and in the madness of the moment I threw myself out of the window. When sense and reason returned once more everything was wonderfully clear again. I recalled the whole train of circumstances. And the more I pondered it the more hopeless my position seemed. I tell you, I was glad to know that I must die, that I was going to leave all this shame and misery behind me. And it is simply because I am dying that I sent for you to-day. I want you, if you can, to prevent a scandal. I want these dreadful things kept from my mother."

CHAPTER XLVIII
SEALED IN THE GRAVE

"It can be done," Grey murmured.

The pupils of Rent's eyes dilated strangely.

"Man, it must be concealed," he said hoarsely. "Try to conceive the cruelty of making all these matters public when the one human being who ought to suffer is beyond the reach of justice! What you know and what Tanza knows I can regard as safe. I could die comfortably in the knowledge that you would never speak, and I am certain that John Charlock would remain silent for the sake of my mother and that innocent girl who has come to think so ill of me. Surely you need not undeceive her! Surely you can think of some plausible fiction! If ever there was a case where a lie is justified, this is the occasion. Now promise."

"I will do all I can," Grey said freely and heartily. "And I know that I can speak for Tanza, too; indeed, I may go further and say that he advocated the very course you are suggesting. He assumed that if the worst happened—I beg your pardon, I should not have put it as bluntly as that."

"But that is just the way I want you to put it," Rent insisted. "You don't know what a load you have taken off my mind. And now I will ask you to leave me. I should like to have my mother with me for the little time that remains——"

The speaker broke off suddenly. Something seemed to choke his utterance. He dropped back on his pillow, breathing faintly. His eyes closed. Very gently Grey crept from the room downstairs to where the others were waiting. The expression of his face was quite enough for Mrs. Rent, who hurried away, followed by Ethel. A little while later the girl came downstairs, her manner soft and subdued. Grey raised his eyebrows interrogatively.

"Yes," Ethel whispered. "He went off peacefully. The nurse and doctor were in the room at the time. I don't know whether you will mind my bringing up the subject just now, but Mr. Charlock has mentioned the matter to you. There were certain letters which my relative had in his possession——"

"I hope they are destroyed," Grey said. "I know what you are alluding to. But it would be as well if those letters were burnt, because it is probable they may lead you to a wrong conclusion. I know you have had a rough time lately, but that mustn't make you suspect crime. I think Mr. Charlock is of the same opinion as myself and deprecates your arriving at a hasty inference. Try to recollect that, however black a case may look against a person, the whole complexion of the thing may lie changed when his defence is disclosed."

A look of relief crossed the girl's face.

"I suppose that is so," she suggested timidly.

"Indeed it is," Grey said emphatically. "But, whatever you do, don't allude to anything in Mrs. Rent's presence. She has enough sorrow and misery to contend with as it is. Now, if you will excuse me, I had better go. This is no place for a stranger."

Grey was glad to find himself outside the house, glad to know that his unpleasant errand had ended without more disastrous consequences. He went at once in search of John Charlock, whom he found disconsolately wandering about his garden. He looked somewhat guilty as Grey came up.

"I don't know what you must think of me," he said, "but I find it difficult to tear myself away from this place. You see, all my hopes and ambitions were centered here. It was here that I looked forward to a happy life. I have just begun to see the fruition of my ambitions, to see my reputation established. I am a free man now and the grave contains my one mistake. I don't say that I feel any regret at what has taken place, beyond the horror that such tragedies bring. But I don't want to talk about myself. What can I do for you?"

"You can come aboard the yacht and talk matters over with Tanza," Grey suggested. "We have several things to discuss with you and one or two confessions to make. I may be a false prophet, but I am sure that the best part of your life's happiness is still to come. But let us eschew platitudes. Come with me and let us have the matter out."

Charlock expressed himself willing, and a little later the two men were on their way to the yacht. For the best part of an hour or more Charlock listened to all that Tanza and his companion had to say. Finally he took the case of jewels which the Italian handed to him and slipped it in his pocket.

"I am infinitely obliged to you gentlemen," he said. "As to these jewels, they rightly belong to me. They have been paid for, too, and their sale will enable me to take possession of my old house again. I daresay I shall be reasonably happy. No doubt I can find some worthy woman who will act as housekeeper and look after my servants. But I am afraid that my dream of a perfect home must remain a dream, for it is never likely to be realised. I am forced to the conclusion that I am not the sort of man to make a woman— —"

"Pardon me," Grey interrupted. "That is just where I think you are wrong. You have as much generous feeling and emotion as most decent men, but you are afraid to show your real nature. At the risk of being considered impertinent I was going to suggest that the lady calculated to make your home happy is not very far off. I was thinking of Miss Ethel Hargrave."

A deep frown knitted Charlock's brows. Then, in spite of himself, something like a smile came over his face.

"Do you really think so?" he asked almost eagerly. "But I am talking like a fool. She is a girl in a million, mind you. A man like me, rough and reserved— —"

"Why belittle yourself?" Tanza said. "You are famous. You are on the road to wealth. Hundreds of women would be proud to call you their husband. But I won't flatter you. I am a pretty good judge of human nature, and if ever I saw a girl in love with a man, that girl is Ethel Hargrave and the man is John Charlock. You are a lucky fellow, my dear sir, if you have sense enough to see it. But, after this exhibition of gratuitous impertinence on my part, I am afraid to say more. Let us change the subject, and perhaps Grey will ask the steward to bring us cigarettes and coffee."

John Charlock said nothing. There was no outbreak of anger or impatience on his part; on the contrary, he smiled with the air of a man who is well pleased with himself. There was something like a gleam of happiness in his eyes.

The white wings of the yacht were folded. She came to an anchor again after a year's absence on a voyage round the world. As the boat put off from the side for the shore, Swift, bronzed and happy-looking, shook his head with a smile as he declined to accompany Tanza and Grey.

"I should be in the way," he said. "Besides, they don't want me. I read in the papers this morning that John Charlock and his wife had only just come back from their honeymoon, in which case they are not likely to require either of you."

"Oh, yes, they will," Tanza exclaimed. "I flatter myself that they will be agreeably surprised to see us."

The boat reached the shore, and after a few minutes' walk Tanza and his companion stopped in front of the house. The windows frowned at them no longer. The casements were flung open. Silk and muslin curtains fluttered on the breeze. The paths were trim and neat. The lawns were ablaze with a wild riot of colour. On all sides were signs of prosperity, peace and happiness. Grey pointed to the long lawn gleaming in the sunshine like a broad ribbon of green velvet.

"There is only one change I see," he murmured. "The old sundial has gone. But that is no matter for surprise."

Before Tanza could reply there came the sound of voices from behind a belt of shrubs. It was almost impossible to recognise the tones of John Charlock, so full and hearty and generous with the flow of life were they. They could hear also the quiet ripple of laughter on the part of his companion, and a moment later husband and wife came in sight. There was no doubt as to their welcome. They came forward with delighted surprise and hands extended. Not much was said for a little while, until they divided into pairs, and Charlock walked down the drive, with Grey, somewhat silent and speculative, by his side.

"What a paradise you have made here!" the latter exclaimed.

"I haven't done it," Charlock said joyously. "It is my wife. Everything she touches she adorns, and I owe you and Tanza a deep debt of gratitude for what you said to me that day on board the yacht. It seemed impossible that she— —"

"The impossible has become the real," Grey said.

Charlock paused a moment and threw back his head.

"Indeed it has," he said in a voice just above a whisper. "I have found what I was looking for at last. I have been paid for all my suffering. But I can't talk about such matters. They are a bit too sacred. Now let us go inside I want to show you my ideal of an English home and an English life."